TH
IN THE

John Pendleton

Chapter One
The Bomb

It's October 12th, 1984, and a young man is quietly descending the narrow carpeted stairs of a guest house in the English south coast resort of Brighton. His plan is to put his suitcase in his car parked on the street outside the house and then return inside to have breakfast.

But, as he reaches the bottom stair, the dining room door opens and he is greeted by one of the two landlords of the premises, a burly man wearing a tight teeshirt and displaying brawny, heavily tattooed arms.

The landlord looks at him quizzically – suspiciously almost.

"Are you going?" he asks.

"No, just putting my suitcase in the car to save time later," replies the young man.

"Have you heard what's happened?" says the landlord.

He opens the dining room door widely. This reveals a clutch of guests gathered closely around a television set. Some of them turn round to stare at the young man.

He looks at the television where he observes a scene of devastation and a newsreader talking about a bomb going off. The name of Mrs Thatcher, the Prime Minister, is mentioned, then the Cabinet and the Grand Hotel. The young man quickly ascertains that some terrorist attack has occurred at Brighton's premier hotel. He leaves his suitcase in the hallway and stands at the back of the dining room watching the drama unfold.

He has a slightly uneasy feeling that his innocently-intentioned attempt to quietly leave the guest house and put his suitcase in the car has led the landlord to surmise that he might be the bomber making his getaway.

For the next half hour the guests and the landlords watch in stunned silence as the horror of the notorious Brighton Bombing unfolds on the TV screen.

It is a curiously mixed gathering: two elderly couples enjoying a few days' holiday at the seaside; a young commercial traveller with slicked-back hair and teddy boy-style sideburns; two besuited middle-aged delegates to the Conservative Party Conference; a poorly dressed young couple enjoying a cut-price honeymoon; and the two male atypical landlords, noticeably hairy and of rough countenance and yet quite obviously a gay couple. And yet on this far from typical morning all those assembled are displaying a remarkable bond of humanity. Both physically and mentally they are huddling together to try to offset the chill of what they are witnessing.

The landlords offer all of their guests extra cups of strong tea to alleviate their sense of shock. If there are any political differences amongst those in the room these are suppressed by the deeper affiliations of membership of the human race.

****

The bomb, planted about a month earlier by Provisional IRA member Patrick Magee, had exploded at 2.54 that morning in an attempt to assassinate Margaret Thatcher and as many as possible of her Cabinet. Five people died as a result of the blast and 31 were injured, including Margaret Tebbit, who was left paralysed and permanently disabled, and her husband Trade Secretary Norman Tebbit, who was less seriously harmed but who looked ghastly white, like a victim in a horror movie, as he was stretchered out of the hotel. When asked at the time whether he was allergic to anything, he famously answered "bombs".

The Grand Hotel was hosting the Conservative Party's top brass who were gathered in the town for the Annual Party Conference and the young man staying at the guest house, Graham Robinson, was one of the delegates. The highly successful young businessman was based in Nottingham and he had been assiduously cultivated by the area's Conservatives. He had quickly become a branch treasurer and when one of the old stalwarts was taken ill close to the date of the conference, Graham took the man's place as one of the delegates to represent the local Association.

He was still a Johnny-come-lately to the Party and he found that the only delegates from the East Midlands area with whom he was acquainted had booked their accommodation months ahead of the event. Many hotels and guest houses were already fully booked when Graham started looking for somewhere to stay but he eventually found the reasonably priced guest house in a back street adjacent to the promenade.

On the first morning of the conference he was greeted warmly by his two hosts at the guest house, gruff-sounding men with broad Yorkshire accents. They told him that they had met on the road as heavy lorry drivers and had only recently become involved in hospitality. One of the men – the burly individual mentioned earlier – had his hair dyed jet black, was wearing a piratical red bandana and was sporting a large gold earring. The other was even stouter than his friend, and, although the younger of the two, had a deeply lined face which smacked of a life too well lived. They several times referred to each other as partners and Graham correctly

3

assumed that their partnership extended beyond the realm of business.

During his first couple of days in Brighton, Graham spent his time at the Conference Centre following the speeches and debates in the main hall. At night he walked along the promenade back to the guest house to have relatively early nights in bed. As he sauntered along he became aware that the resort had a strange, almost sinister, atmosphere, quite different from what he had been used to at the happy-go-lucky sea front at Sanderholme, the English east coast holiday resort where he had been born and spent his formative years.

He passed several pockets of badly dressed and unkempt young men and women who eyed him in an unfriendly way. He wondered if they were members of a Brighton under-class, perhaps drug addicts. Or perhaps they had travelled to the town to stage some kind of protest against Maggie Thatcher and her Conservative Government. Whatever might have been the case, they were clearly not there for a fun family holiday.

Graham was snappily dressed in his best dark suit and so stood out a mile as being a Conservative Party delegate. He felt it was unsurprising that he was getting some dirty looks.

However, one particular passer-by would remain in his memory for the rest of his life. The man walking towards him on the narrow pavement was probably aged around 40. He was scrawny, of moderate height and unshaven. He was wearing black from head to toe – dirty black shoes, black teeshirt, scruffy black jeans, and a black baseball cap. Graham saw that the man was staring at him – staring with a look of absolute hatred; a vicious look, which sent a frisson racing through Graham's body. He found himself speeding up to put as much distance as he could between himself and this unprepossessing individual. Graham's immediate thought was that the man *looked* like a terrorist. He chillingly felt he had looked into the face of pure evil. He had never had that thought about anyone before, and in the rest of his life to come would only have similar feelings about one other individual.

Graham sensed an atmosphere of menace in the town that week. And in the days that followed he would question whether he had had some kind of premonition of the tragic event which was to rock the country. Or might he actually have encountered the Brighton bomber during his promenade walk? When it turned out later that the bomb had been planted in the Grand Hotel some weeks previously that idea was knocked on the head. But he would always believe that there were some people with ill intent abroad in Brighton in that Conference Week.

On the eve of the last day of the conference Graham had plans to finish up in the Grand Hotel bar. Several of his acquaintances in the Party had told him that they would be meeting there at around midnight with other delegates who would have been attending the traditional Party Ball at the resort's Top Rank Entertainment complex.

Graham would have liked to have attended the ball himself, but being a newcomer to Party conferences he had not had the foresight to buy a ticket. Instead, he decided to explore some of the sea front pubs that Brighton had to offer.

He settled in one very busy pub not far from the Grand Hotel. The bar was clearly a popular haunt for the Bright

Young Things of the area. However, when he noticed a number of men in dark suits among the drinkers, he guessed it had also attracted a smattering of other conference delegates. Wearing a conventional, sharp, dark suit himself, with a light blue shirt and matching bright blue tie, Graham therefore had no feelings of being a fish out of water.

He managed to find an empty table and sat down contentedly with a pint of bitter, surveying the bustling scene. At the next table was another single drinker, a tall, good-looking, gangly man who looked to be in his early twenties – a few years younger than Graham. His long fair hair contrasted starkly with Graham's short, perfectly groomed, jet black hair. And his tight, faded skinny jeans and his black teeshirt emblazoned with a fiery red dragon motif were a far cry from the other man's conventional suit.

Normally this was not the type of stranger that Graham would be likely to engage in conversation. He had quite traditional views about dress and would tend to be suspicious of someone who would choose to display a large dragon on his chest.

However, noticing that the man was looking at him in a friendly and slightly inquisitive way, as if he wished to make contact, Graham nodded politely.

"Hi, there. Are you here for the Conference?" asked the younger man.

"Yes, that's right," said Graham.

"Have you come far?" said the man in a refined Home Counties accent, with the hint of a stammer.

"From a village between Nottingham and Mansfield. But I'm originally from Sanderholme. It's a holiday resort on the Lincolnshire coast. Are you local?"

"No, I'm here for a few days. I come from Margate, another holiday resort."

The man offered his hand to Graham, saying: "I'm Sebastian."

Graham revealed his name and gave a firm handshake.

"Are you enjoying the conference?" asked Sebastian.

"Yeah, it's been really interesting. I've not been to one before."

"I'm really into politics," said Sebastian. "But I'm not a Tory, I'm afraid."

"Fair enough. It's a free country."

"What makes you a Tory?" asked Sebastian in an amicable, non-threatening way.

Graham paused in order to give considered thought to a question he had never been asked before and then replied: "I believe in freedom of the individual and free markets, but alongside traditional family values and strong defence and law and order. A few other things, but they're the basics."

"But Margaret Thatcher. She's a dictator really, isn't she?"

"No, not at all. She wants to see a small State, but she needs to be strong and assertive to achieve that."

"I want to see a Small State too. I'm an Anarcho-Syndicalist."

"Tell me more. I've heard of Anarcho-Syndicalism. I know it's got something to do with trade unions, but I don't know much more than that."

"We don't believe in either capitalism or Big State socialism," said Sebastian. "We favour direct action and direct democracy, starting, yes, through the trade union movement. My man's Proudhon. He said that if workers sell a product of their labour they ought to receive money, goods or services in exchange that are equal in economic value. The product of a worker's labour should take account of the amount of physical labour put into the price of their product."

(Pierre Joseph Proudhon was a 19th century French libertarian socialist, politician and economist, an exponent of mutualism and considered to be the "father" of anarchism.)

"So this isn't the type of Communism which Karl Marx had in mind," said Graham. "I know that Marx envisaged the eventual withering away of the State. But in the meantime there was always going to be a long period of Big State Communism, such as what we have seen in Soviet Russia."

"You're dead right."

For the next two hours the men chattered affably about their respective political beliefs, buying each other pints of beer in the process.

They enjoyed each other's company and tended to concentrate on areas of agreement rather than being confrontational.

Sebastian argued forcefully for the legalisation of all drugs, and was evidently an habitual user of several varieties of them. Graham had never touched a drug in his life. He thought of drug users with a high degree of disdain and not a little disapproval but nevertheless accepted the principle of individual freedom of choice.

They concluded their discussions by raising a glass to "The Small State", glossing over their very different concepts of what this meant.

Sebastian even conceded that some Tories might be well-meaning and interesting and that Graham was a much more reasonable person than he had ever expected a Tory to be.

Graham, though, found their conversation strangely unsettling. His new acquaintance had been almost too keen to find common ground between themselves. He might be a very nice Anarcho-Syndicalist. He might be just taking the mickey out of a greenhorn Tory. Or could he just be trying to learn more about the capitalist enemy he felt he was destined to overthrow?

Although both men had gone out of their way to find some common ground, Graham did not admire his companion. Sebastian had disclosed that he came from a rich family, had been educated at a public school and then gone on to gain a degree in economics at university. There was nothing for Graham to object to in any of that. But what grated on him was that Sebastian had apparently never had a job and was wasting his life engaging in extreme political activism and drug-fuelled hedonism. Graham's dislike of illegal drugs was partly because of their very illegality, but mainly because he hated the idea of people not being in control of their own minds. He liked the odd beer and a glass of wine, but he fought against anything which might hamper his rational judgement.

"I'll have to go now," said Graham, ending their freewheeling episode of frenetic conversation. "I want to see if any of my colleagues have arrived at the Grand Hotel bar."

"Could I come with you?" asked Sebastian. "I would find it very interesting to meet some more of your Party members."

Graham hesitated. He wasn't at all sure that he ought to take an Anarcho-Syndicalist into the midst of a group of diehard Conservatives. He thought this might lead to some embarrassment and even to some hostility towards himself.

"As far as I'm concerned you would be quite welcome to come along. But I'm not sure what the security arrangements would be for non-delegates."

Sebastian sensed his unease and didn't push the point.

The two men walked along the sea front together. As they approached the Grand Hotel there was no obvious security barrier to anyone entering the building. Graham and Sebastian cordially shook hands and said their goodnights, Graham then making his way to the busy Victoria Bar, leaving his new acquaintance at the door.

He made a beeline for a group of five or six Nottinghamshire Conservatives whom he knew quite well and who were keen to welcome their go-ahead young member. As he looked around the crowded room he recognised several Government ministers and a few Members of Parliament. The one "celebrity" he saw was Richard Whiteley, the ITV Calendar News presenter and popular host of the Countdown TV show.

People were there to be *seen*. The room was a hotbed of naked ambition cloaked by bonhomie. Young wannabe Parliamentary candidates rubbed shoulders with crusty old aldermen and the odd middle ranking Government minister. Middle-aged ladies with big lacquered hair and wearing smart cocktail dresses added glamour to the noisy and amiable scene. And go-getting journalists hovered on the periphery hoping to foster useful new contacts or to smell out a scoop.

The chatter and the drinking carried on in the bar for several hours. At around 2am Graham looked around the room and was surprised, and just a little alarmed, to see

Sebastian happily conversing with a huddle of Party delegates. It crossed his mind that the rather pushy young man might be there in a vain attempt to disseminate his political ideas. However, on further consideration he decided that the most likely explanation was that Sebastian, with his smooth southern manners and accent, actually felt quite at home with the people he was talking to – a case of social class outweighing political affiliation.

Just after 2.35am Graham's acquaintances decided it was time to turn in for the night and ordered a taxi. They were told it would take at least 20 minutes to arrive. Graham had been offered a place in the taxi, but as the guest house where he was staying was only five minutes' walk away he decided to return on foot. He took leave of his companions and made his way along the sea front back to his accommodation, missing the cataclysmic main event at 2.54am.

****

Entering the conference hall later that morning felt something akin to an out of body experience for Graham. The sea front and the conference centre were teeming with police, including a number of severe looking armed officers.

The main auditorium was filling up with people but there was an unnatural and unsettling hush.

Before he took his seat in time for Mrs Thatcher's 9.30am speech, Graham found himself craning his neck looking for familiar faces, especially the people who had been in the bar earlier that morning. He had learnt from the television that the ceiling had collapsed on to the bar and that a number of people had been taken to hospital injured.

Then one of his Nottinghamshire colleagues, a middle-aged local councillor called Warwick Sparling, walked past and Graham caught his eye.

"Are you okay?" he asked. "Were you still in the bar when the bomb went off?"

"Yes," replied the councillor. "We all threw ourselves on to the floor – or were blown on to the floor. It was difficult to say which. Chunks of the ceiling fell on to us and the dust was choking us. I'm all right and so are most of the others we were with, but Beatrice Andrews was taken to the Royal Sussex Hospital suffering from shock and with a leg injury. Some others from the bar were taken to hospital too. I haven't seen John or Sheila yet, so I don't know what's happened to them. I'm going to the hospital later to see Beatrice, after Mrs Thatcher's speech.

"I've been told that some people who were staying at the hotel had to evacuate still wearing their pyjamas and nightdresses. They've been taken to Marks and Spencers, which has opened early specially, and fitted them out with suits, dresses and shoes."

"Dreadful business," said Graham. "I left the bar about a quarter of an hour before the bomb went off. I can't believe I didn't hear anything of the explosion. Oh, look, there's John over there."

"Thank goodness for that," said Warwick. "I'll go over and talk to him."

"Yes, thanks for the information. Please give my best wishes to Beatrice."

"Of course. Will do."

Graham listened with emotion to the Prime Minister's

speech, full of admiration for her bravery.

As he left the hall to make his way to his car a thought came to him which troubled him. He had taken Sebastian to the threshold of the Grand Hotel the previous evening and had then seen the self-proclaimed Anarcho-Syndicalist hobnobbing with delegates in the bar several hours later. Could he have introduced the bomber to the conference hotel? Was Sebastian as smooth and amiable as he had appeared, or was he hanging around the Grand Hotel with a sinister motive?

Graham gave some minutes' thought to the idea that he should perhaps inform the police about Sebastian's presence the night before. Was he part of some secret cell plotting to overthrow the Government? But he soon satisfied himself with the conclusion that the young man was just a politically naive character, who was probably easily led and might even end up as a Tory! However, it was only months later, when Patrick Magee was convicted of murder for detonating the bomb, that his scintilla of doubt about Sebastian was finally put to bed.

It is a fact that Magee had accomplices, but the bomb had been planted in a cavity beneath the bath of his hotel room, number 629, precisely 24 days, six hours and 36 minutes before it exploded, and those involved would have been long gone by the time of the conference.

Magee was released from prison in 1999 under the Good Friday Agreement, having served only 14 years of his 35-year jail sentence.

Chapter Two
Schooldays

Graham was never one to dwell on past events, especially the bad things that happen. The present and the future were always more important to him.

But thoughts of those horrific events in 1984 would often return to him in the ensuing years – sometimes during the waking hours and sometimes in recurring dreams.

Before the bombing he had given little thought to questions of good and evil, reaching manhood at a time in Western history when moral relativism was predominant in contemporary philosophy.

There had been little in his upbringing to push him into having an absolute moral code. His parents were typical of many people in Middle England during the 20th century. They were nominally Christian and nominally adherents to the Church of England, only attending church for weddings and funerals and the occasional carol service at Christmas. They did have strong values, including beliefs in respectability, good manners and kindness, and a gut instinct of what was right and wrong. They didn't thrust any particular ideology on their son, opting instead to lead him by example and trusting that he would find the right paths in life for himself.

Graham would often chew over the moral dilemmas which arose from issues in the news with his long-standing best friend, Jim Nott. As an immature youngster Graham had come to the conclusion that the sole human motivation amounted to nothing more than selfishness. His observation was that all human actions were guided by what people saw as being in their own interests and self-survival.

Jim was unconvinced by this and challenged him to explain those actions which appeared to be altruistic. For example, why did some people risk their own lives by jumping into water to save others from drowning? Why did men volunteer to go to war at the risk of their own lives when their self-interest would point to staying safe at home and furthering their own ambitions?

Graham's answer was that people behaved in those ways to gain the approbation of others, thus leading them to feel good about themselves. He was not an overtly selfish person in his interactions with other people and even he secretly suspected that his argument might be fallacious and contrived, but it suited his professed outlook on life at the time. Good and bad, right and wrong were irrelevant according to his world view. What mattered was doing what was beneficial for oneself. This, then, was his over-riding philosophy as a teenager and he largely clung to this view into his twenties. But gradually, over the years, it dawned upon him that some people's actions could not be explained merely by self-interest. There was an element beyond this which he could only describe as *humanity*.

German philosopher Friedrich Nietzsche said: "My humanity is a constant self-overcoming."

****

It was in their first year at Sanderholme's Havenmarsh Secondary Modern School that Graham Robinson met Jim Nott.

Superficially, two characters more unlike each other would have been difficult to imagine. Graham was a confident, smart, good looking boy, who shone in maths and practical subjects and was popular amongst his peers. He was ambitious and relatively streetwise. By contrast, Jim was shy, podgy, nerdy and dishevelled, and quickly became the butt of a great deal of teasing. He was always the last boy to be chosen for any team game.

In many respects theirs was an uneven friendship. Graham was certainly the dominant half of their partnership but he was always quick to stand up for Jim whenever he was bullied by other pupils. The relationship could be described as symbiotic: Jim was dependant on Graham for friendship and defence against the bullies; Graham needed Jim in order to explore the kinder side of his otherwise rather hard and uncompromising outlook on life.

Jim observed the world with a crinkly smile and a wry, intelligent, sense of humour. Graham appreciated his friend's quirky character, which contrasted with his own straightforward, some would say, abrupt attitude to life.

There were some similarities in the two boys' backgrounds, both being the "only child" of local traders. Graham's parents, Ray and Daphne, ran two Spar corner shops which were famous for being "open all hours" and into which they put a great deal of hard work.

Jim's parents, Jim Senior and Martha, were similarly dedicated to their newsagents' business, which also sold sweets and tobacco, and which they had inherited from Jim Senior's own parents, Cecil and Margaret.

But there the similarities ended. Ray and Daphne, though not in any sense "flashy", were not afraid to display the rewards of their successful businesses, owning a stylish four-bedroomed house in the smartest end of town, driving expensive cars and going on occasional exotic holidays. Very soon into his adulthood it became clear that Graham had inherited much of their drive and entrepreneurial spirit.

By contrast, Jim Nott Senior and wife Martha, somewhat older than Graham's parents, brought up Jim Junior in the small flat above the newsagents'. They had a humdrum and modest lifestyle, drove an old van and gave themselves no time for family holidays.

Whereas Graham was encouraged to play out in the streets and go to the local youth club, Jim, who was an asthmatic, was never allowed to wander far from home and led a quiet, over-protected and almost reclusive existence.

Aside from his aptitude for maths, Graham Robinson was not naturally academically gifted. However, in the latter years of his schooling he developed an unquenchable thirst for knowledge on a wide range of subjects. His parents dearly wished to see him spread his wings, see the world beyond Sanderholme and eventually become a successful businessman.

His father, Ray, was a well read man and once quoted to his son a passage from Anthony Trollope's novel "Is He Popinjay?" in which the Dean offers his thoughts on ambition and enterprise: "It is a good thing to rise in the world. The ambition to do so is the very salt of the earth. It is the parent of all enterprise, and the cause of all improvement. They who know no such ambition are savages and remain savage."

Jim's parents' ambitions for their no less deeply-loved son were for him to learn the family business and become the third generation of Notts to run it.

The two boys remained close friends throughout their time at secondary school, leaving aged 16 having gained good O' level and CSE results.

Most people in the United Kingdom's academic world now consider Secondary Modern Schools to be well-consigned to what they would think of as being the "Dark Ages" of pre-Comprehensive education. And it has to be admitted that the parents of both boys would have been happier if their sons had passed the 11-plus exam and gone to the much acclaimed Sanderholme Grammar School. Havenmarsh Secondary Modern, though, was one of the very best examples of its genre and turned out many pupils who went to achieve notable successes in their careers, both in the academic and practical spheres.

Graham went on to take a Business Studies course at the nearby Holland College of Further Education while Jim took his place behind the counter of Notts' Newsagents on Sanderholme High Street.

In this role Jim Junior finally emerged from the cocoon of his boyhood bedroom, meeting hundreds of customers each week when they collected their newspapers, cigarettes and other goodies. He was a patient listener and as the years went by came to know a tremendous amount about the lives of the shop's customers. As he grew in self-confidence he used all the information he had accrued to become a voracious and good-humoured gossip. In fact he became notorious locally for being the "go-to" source for any juicy stories that might be circulating in the town.

Unusually, even as a small child Graham already had a clear idea of what he wished to achieve as an adult. He was profoundly interested in his parents' shops. He knew the name and price of every item on every shelf and would sit engrossed at his mother's side as often as possible as she "did the books" at the end of each day's trading. As soon as he was old enough, at around eight or nine, he made himself useful in the shops, stacking the shelves, and often helping his mother do her sums when she cashed up.

In his spare time he would design his own shops on pieces of scrap paper, not corner shops but giant department stores, staffed with a full panoply of departmental managers, floor walkers, window dressers and even cleaners. Each store had its own cafeteria and Graham would draw up menus so inviting that he salivated with anticipation of actually consuming the fare on offer. Sunday lunch with roast beef and all the trimmings was to be the crowning glory of his offerings.

As he reached his teenage years, going into business and becoming an entrepreneur was his obsession, and almost all his thoughts and actions were directed towards achieving his goal. Almost. For, as might he expected, he also had a little time and inclination for the normal carnal instincts of a red-blooded male.

It was while he was studying at Holland College, some 30 miles along the coast from Sanderholme, that Graham first met Anita Albright.

Anita, at 17 the same age as Graham, was a stunning leggy brunette who was training to be a beautician. She had recently moved to Sanderholme from London with her parents, both doctors in general practice, and two younger sisters.

Her good looks meant she had a busy social life and she was often found on the dance floor until the early hours of the morning at Sanderholme's busy sea front night clubs.

The Albright family had moved into a large detached

house overlooking the sea and just four doors away from where Graham lived with his parents. Anita had passed her driving test first time and her parents had bought her a Mini to get to and from college. So when she and Graham got to know each other it was only natural that she should offer him a daily lift.

It was not long before Graham became infatuated with his new-found friend. As she drove along he found it impossible to avoid admiring her long slender legs, as she habitually wore very short miniskirts and figure-hugging tops. Her long, deep brown, lustrous hair cascaded down to her slender waist. Her makeup was immaculate and her skin radiant and soft.

Anita was a free spirit, potty-mouthed, a heavy drinker and the occasional user of cannabis. She had a string of male admirers and a reputation for being generous with her favours towards them. She oozed carefree sexuality and was entirely at one with the hedonism of Britain in the Seventies.

Graham was a tall, healthy and athletic young man, with a fresh, open face and thick, neat, jet black hair. So it was unsurprising that Anita soon started to fancy him, not letting his gauche lack of experience with the opposite sex deter her.

One day as they neared home on the way back from college she took the initiative. It was a stiflingly warm summer's evening as the pair arrived back in Sanderholme. Knowing that her parents were both away for the day on a doctors' course, Anita invited Graham to join her for a drink on the patio which adjoined the extensive and perfectly manicured lawn at the rear of her house. Graham jumped at the opportunity.

They sat at a bench overlooking the lawn, both sipping

at cool beers straight from the fridge. Anita looked stunning in a blue denim miniskirt and white short-sleeved blouse, tantalisingly unbuttoned to show off her well-proportioned cleavage. Graham was in tight-fitting jeans and a white teeshirt.

They indulged in aimless small talk and drank several more beers before Anita suddenly took hold of Graham's hand and smiled playfully. He immediately recognised these actions as a sign that their relationship was entering an exciting new phase. He gently pulled her towards him and kissed her on the lips. This kiss quickly turned into a long, deep and passionate one.

Anita stroked Graham's leg above the knee and he responded by sliding his hand along her bare leg, finding no resistance.

"Let's go on to the grass," she said, rising from the bench and leading him by the hand on to the immaculate green turf.

Very soon they found themselves naked and enjoying passionate sex on the greensward.

The evening's excitements did not end there. Anita invited Graham to her bedroom and they spent two hours in intense lovemaking.

At last she said it was time for Graham to leave as her parents were expected home at any time.

"That's fine," he said. "My parents will wonder where I've been. It's nine o'clock and I was expected home for tea at six!"

"Tell them you met a mad, wild girl who propositioned you for sex," she laughed.

"No, I couldn't possibly tell the truth. I will have to make something up. Like your car got a puncture, or something."

"How boring is that?" she asked. "My story is much better."

"Yes, but they'll never believe it," he replied. "The puncture it has to be."

She slapped his shoulder and pointed for him to go.

"We must do this again some time," he said.

"Why not?" she replied coquettishly.

The next morning was a Saturday and so no college to go to. Graham decided to walk along to Notts' newsagents to see his mate Jim. He couldn't wait to tell his friend about his conquest of the previous evening.

The shop was busy and Jim was alone that morning, so Graham had to wait for him to serve a small queue of customers before they had a chance to talk.

"How are you?" asked Jim politely.

"I'm never been better, mate," chirped Graham, beaming effusively,

"Actually, you look like the cat that's got the cream," said Jim, grinning.

"That's exactly right," said Graham, who then went quiet to tease his friend by repeatedly refusing to provide an explanation for his elated mood.

"So, come on then. What's all this about?" said Jim, becoming impatient.

"No, I'm not telling you anything. You wouldn't believe it anyway."

"Try me," said Jim.

"Oh go on then. If you must. I shagged Anita last night. You know, the girl who gives me a lift to college."

Jim chortled in a husky asthmatic kind of way.

"You bugger. I've seen her about. She's gorgeous."

"Too right," said Graham.

"You're punching above your weight there, mate," said Jim.

"Cheeky bugger. But you're right. I wasn't expecting it, that's for sure."

"Well, well. Did you come in here just to tell me about your disgusting love life?"

"No, I only told you because you made me."

His friend replied sarcastically: "Of course you did."

Jim was secretly a little jealous of Graham for his "achievement", but was far too good-natured to let it show. It was the achievement he envied rather than the fact that the deed had been done with an extremely attractive girl. He had never got so far as kissing a girl himself. He was intelligent and self-aware enough to know that girls didn't find him desirable and it didn't bother him overmuch. He had recently grown a substantial beard and side whiskers, his mode of dress was slovenly and, even though he was a non-smoker, he had a faint tobacco smell, which came from working all day long in a tobacconists'. So not much of a catch then!

The two lads agreed to meet up for a pint in town that night with Graham affirming: "I'll promise not to gloat about Anita."

He lied.

Chapter Three
First Loves

Photography was Trevor Bincroft's life.

His interest began when his father, a keen amateur photographer himself, made him a pinhole camera – and it worked. After that, when Trevor was aged ten, his dad presented him with an ancient box brownie, in a classy, but slightly weather-beaten leather case. Trevor loved it and his obsession with taking photographs started from that date.

By the time he moved from primary school to Sanderholme's Havenmarsh Secondary Modern he was an accomplished snapper, often bothering schoolmates by insisting on taking pictures of all their activities. He should have been Japanese!

Some fellow pupils considered Trevor to be an irritating nerd. He was the tallest boy in school but also the fattest with a large bulbous nose, further reasons for him to suffer bullying. One day an older boy grabbed his beloved box brownie and hurled on to the floor, damaging it irretrievably.

Trevor burst into tears, which made him even more vulnerable to the bullies, who now dubbed him a cry baby.

His father was determined that his son should not be deterred from his interest in photography so that Christmas he arranged for Santa Claus to deliver a brand new 35mm Canon Demi camera. Trevor, who at eleven still believed in the bearded old fake, was very excited and rushed out on Christmas morning to take photos of anything interesting he could find around the council estate where his family lived. Neighbours, flowers, birds, trees all got snapped.

Trevor found it difficult to make friends at school. In modern times he may have been identified as being autistic. But two of his peers at Havenmarsh did show him friendship and compassion – Jim Nott and Graham Robinson.

As has been noted previously, Jim himself was subjected to bullying and therefore had empathy with Trevor's plight. Graham, Jim's faithful protector, was willing to put Trevor under his wing too. Graham hated bullies. As a confident and secure person himself he suspected that most bullies were hiding their own weakness and insecurity. He pitied them for it but at the same time was often in the front line when it came to confronting them.

He liked single-minded people and Trevor certainly fell into that category. To Graham, he would never have been as close a friend as Jim Nott, who was a much more subtle and intelligent individual, with a warmth which underlay his sarcastic and slightly cynical exterior. Trevor, though, had a vulnerability which meant he needed to be treated with kindness and understanding.

The three boys spent a good deal of time together until they reached the upper reaches of the school when Jim and Graham were in the "A" stream and Trevor was in "B". But they were never to completely lose touch. One of the chief benefits of school is learning how to make friendships which will endure.

When Trevor left school he predictably fulfilled his childhood dreams and started a career in photography. He worked as a cameraman for a local firm, Farndales, taking "walking pictures" of passers-by in the main tourist areas of Sanderholme. People would collect the photos from a kiosk a few hours later.

The photographers wore brightly coloured striped blazers and sometimes had a pony or a large fluffy dog with them to add to the appeal of the photos.

Trevor readily took to this work, overcoming his natural awkwardness and developing a friendly banter with his clients which made him a popular figure on the Sanderholme promenade. He was soon the company's most successful cameraman, producing nearly double the number of rolls of film per day than most of his fellow workers.

After he had been in this job for three years, his boss, Robert Farndale, asked him to take a rookie photographer under his wing for a few days to show her the ropes. This was Shirley Meade, a 16-year-old Sanderholme Grammar School girl, who was working for the firm during the school summer holidays.

Shirley was a pretty, petite lass with a shock of blonde curls, a ready smile and a tremendous sense of fun. Trevor's cheery manner with his customers belied his absolute seriousness about his trade and an obsession to get the best possible results from his camera. At first he found it difficult to gel with a workmate who struck him as being little more than a giggly flibbertigibbet.

His banter with people was merely a means to an end, to take brilliant pictures of them and to persuade them that they needed to buy them. Once that had been achieved he passed quickly on to his next "victims". Shirley, on the other hand, liked to chatter to people for what Trevor considered to be an inordinate and wasteful length of time.

Sometimes he found it necessary to offer a mild rebuke to his charge to focus her attention on the job in hand. She always took this in good part and was an attentive listener when he explained the tricks of the trade to her.

By the time they had been working together for a couple of weeks they had established a good rapport. Shirley had come to have a great respect for her mentor and started to take her work more seriously. For his part, Trevor had been quietly pleased with her progress, and, more significantly, for the first time in his life, had begun to have feelings of an amatory nature.

At the end of their second week working together Mr Farndale announced that he was satisfied that Shirley was now competent enough to have her own pitch further along the sea front. Both she and Trevor felt a twinge of disappointment that their time together had come to an end. The more Trevor thought about this prospect the more that "twinge" turned into a desperate desire to keep in contact with Shirley. So he "screwed his courage to the sticking place" and, on their last day of working side by side, said to her: "I wondered if you would like to come for a drink with me one evening?"

Shirley was initially taken aback by this question, Trevor having given no hints of his growing feelings towards her, and having given no indication that he had any kind of social life.

However, true to her outward going and uncomplicated attitude to life, she said: "Yes, that would be nice. Where shall we go?"

Trevor, who had been thinking about this for several days, replied: "Well, we could go to one of the night clubs on the sea front, or perhaps we could push the boat out and go to the Buckthorn Arms and have chicken in a basket."

"Wow. Chicken in a basket sounds good to me," she said.

"Tomorrow night perhaps?" said Trevor.

"Yep."

Trevor was totally surprised when Shirley agreed to go out with him. He had never had a date before. In fact he had never asked anyone for a date before. He had never considered himself even remotely attractive to girls.

Even though Shirley was an inexperienced schoolgirl, she had a well developed and infectious personality and was a firm favourite among the boys at school. Trevor knew that he was an unlikely suitor and was apprehensive about the likely outcome of their fledgling relationship.

He was keen to make an impression on their first outing, so he secretly borrowed his mother's hair dryer to blow his dark brown unruly locks into a more acceptable shape. He also put on his charcoal grey suit, which had previously only seen service at his sister's wedding, his grandfather's funeral and his job interview with Mr Farndale,

Not having his own transport, Trevor walked to Shirley's home, a pleasant semi-detached house built in the 1930s in one of the many tree-lined avenues in the central part of Sanderholme and only half a mile away from the Bincroft residence.

He entered by a wrought iron gate and made his way along a path towards the front door. To his horror he soon realised that the concrete he was walking on had only just been laid and had not yet set. When he looked behind him he saw his footprints which had made deep impressions in the path.

Trevor was panic-stricken by what he had done. He

sheepishly knocked on the door and was soon greeted by a wiry middle-aged man.

"I'm terribly sorry. I didn't realise the concrete was still wet and I'm afraid I've made a mess of it," said Trevor.

The man stared at the damage and sighed, but soon put Trevor at his ease by smiling and telling him not to worry.

Trevor's black shoes, which he had spent much time polishing earlier that day, were covered in wet, grey concrete, which had also bespattered his suit trousers, specially pressed by his mother for the occasion.

"I'll get you a cloth for your shoes," said Mr Meade. "By the way, you are?"

"Trevor Bincroft. I've come to see Shirley."

"Oh, okay. I'll tell her you're here."

Mr Meade called out to his daughter and then disappeared into the house to fetch the cloth.

A few seconds later she appeared in the hallway – a vision of vivacity and prettiness in a bright yellow floral minidress and with bubbly hair like Shirley Temple's.

"I'm afraid I've had an accident," said a shamefaced Trevor.

Shirley, who quickly understood what had happened, burst into a fit of giggles, so infectious that the normally deadpan Trevor couldn't help raising a smile himself.

Mr Meade returned with a damp cloth and passed it to Trevor who proceeded to do the best he could to remove the grey matter from his shoes and trousers.

"You'll not want to be seen with me in the Buckthorn," he said, feeling excruciatingly embarrassed.

"Don't be silly," replied Shirley. "No one's going to be looking at you. They'll all be looking at me, naturally."

Trevor looked at her quizzically. He had never thought of Shirley as being vain but her last comment made him wonder. Shirley could see that doubt rising into his mind and went into another giggling episode.

"Don't take any notice of her," said her father who was still hovering on the doorstep. Surprisingly he started to sing, albeit quietly and out of tune.

"She's so vain she thinks this song is about her."

Trevor now looked askance at Mr Meade. He was unused to such fun emanating from a member of his parents' generation.

"Now get you gone," Mr Meade continued. "You look fine now. The way you're going you'll still be wiping away with that cloth when it's closing time!"

"What shall I do with this?" asked Trevor, pointing to the sodden concrete-filled cloth.

"Just pop it in the dustbin over there," replied the father.

The couple set off towards the pub. Trevor was still feeling that the date had got off to a disastrous start, but the good humour shown by Shirley and her father had considerably lightened his mood.

The evening went swimmingly. The chicken and chips in baskets were delicious, Shirley was loquacious and even at times flirtatious, and Trevor joined in with the conversation freely, although mainly to hold forth about photography. This didn't deter Shirley in any way as she was becoming utterly fascinated by the art herself.

This infatuation with photography slowly but surely led to an unshakeable bond between the young couple. Over the next year they became inseparable and very much in love. Shirley's outwardly girlish and giggly demeanour belied a depth of character which enabled her to see beyond Trevor's unappealing physical appearance and to appreciate the basic decency of the man.

Their relationship quickly blossomed to the extent that some of the lads who had bullied and mocked Trevor at school were to become intensely jealous of his relationship with this very attractive young woman. His true friends, Graham and Jim, were as surprised as anyone at his success, and really happy for him.

As Shirley embarked on her final year at Grammar School, the couple were already starting to make plans for a future together. She was studying Art, English and History at A' level. She had a precocious talent for art, producing some audacious abstract pictures and always the first port of call when scenery needed painting for the school's dramatic productions.

She was the driving force behind the plan that she and her boyfriend hatched up. She would go on to study graphic design at an art college and then go into business with Trevor. They would be able to offer a complete package to clients, producing brochures and other advertising material as well as providing all of the photographs required for these. Wedding and portrait photography and some freelance Press work would be other sources of income.

And so it came to pass. Shirley achieved an "A" grade in A' level Art and went on to study at Lincoln Art College, just over 40 miles from Sanderholme. She was able to commute each day by bus and still work for Farndale Photographers during holiday times.

It was during her second year at college that she and Trevor became engaged to be married, sealing their future both domestically and in business.

At the end of the third year she passed her graphic design course with flying colours. Trevor left Farndales as together the couple had saved enough money to rent a shop unit just beyond the town centre.

Business was exceedingly good in the first few months and they were confident enough in their financial security to plan their marriage for the forthcoming year.

Mr and Mrs Bincroft had well and truly arrived.

****

After their first passionate encounter, Graham's alliance with Anita lasted for a few more weeks and he was entirely smitten with her.

As "a pretty regular sort of guy", he happily admitted to one eccentricity, which was to remain with him for the whole of his life. Like many other people, he often had music, usually a song, in his head. But he went further than this, constantly singing under his breath, sometimes hissing a tune, sometimes humming. He could use his fingers to produce a tune on his teeth or on his cheeks, or use his knuckles to pound out a melody on top of his head. Often he would change the words of a song to suit whatever emotion he was feeling at the time. When, later, at the age of 18, he passed his driving test and was alone in his Ford Anglia car, he would sing out loud – very loud.

At this particular time, though, the song most often in his head was the Barry Manilow favourite "Copacabana". However, he had changed the opening words from "Her name was Lola, she was a showgirl" to "I love Anita, I could just eat her", a line he repeated to himself hundreds of times. It was an indication of a growing obsession.

Anita, on the other hand, already being a woman of experience, soon tired of Graham's novice fumblings. Although still ostensibly his "girlfriend" she had secretly already gone on to pastures new – actually two much older men at the same time.

Jim, the best gossip in town, somehow got wind of her new associations and loyally told his friend about them. Graham had already sensed that Anita was cooling towards him and he felt it was time to tackle her about it.

It was with an air of relief that she confessed to her treachery and she suggested to Graham that it was time for them to go their separate ways. She had correctly sensed that he was taking their relationship more seriously than she was. It was not so much what he had said but the way he gazed at her in the manner of someone admiring a painting by an Old Master. She was flattered by this attention but slightly scared when she realised that he was experiencing the desperate pangs of a first love.

"You're a very nice boy," she said. "But you're the sort who would want to settle down and get married and I'm not ready for that yet – not for a long time."

He protested, none too convincingly, that he was far too young to be thinking of marriage. But his pleas were to no avail. He reluctantly accepted the situation but it hit him hard as the loss of a first love always does.

However, he was 17 and reasonably handsome and so told himself that other girls would come along in no time. He licked his wounds over Anita and headed back into the fray.

Chapter four
Tying the knot

When he left college with his Business Studies qualification Graham applied for a job as a store assistant with the Asda supermarket chain in Nottingham. Over the next two years his rise was meteoric and, at the precocious age of 20, he was appointed as a store manager. He worked like a Trojan, used his "spare" time acquiring new skills and knowledge and planned his next career moves.

The next step came at the age of 22 when, with a helping hand from his parents, he bought his own corner shop in a Nottingham suburb. His flair for organisation and salesmanship guaranteed him success and, within the next four years, he had opened 20 more shops throughout the East Midlands and had also begun building a substantial property rental portfolio.

He even found time to design and project-manage the building of a ten-bedroom mansion in the pretty village of Papplewick, on the edge of Nottinghamshire's Sherwood Forest, complete with indoor swimming pool, games room, a large garden with a pagoda and a trout fishing lake. There he entertained business and political contacts and several eligible young ladies.

The fact that he had not so far contemplated any new long-lasting relationship was more down to the unsuitability of the women he chose, or who chose him, than to any great failings on his part. He tended to fall head over heels in love with women very quickly but also to choose the "wrong type". His obvious wealth attracted pleasure-seeking money chasers who soon tired of having to fit around his punishing work ethic.

So, at the age of 26, he was unattached.

Throughout these years he paid regular visits to Sanderholme to see his parents and to catch up with old friends, especially Jim Nott, who filled him in with all the latest local chit-chat.

During these trips he always paid a call to the Buckthorn Arms, a local pub which was a magnet for the better off young people around the area. It was there one night that he unexpectedly came across Anita Albright, looking as radiant as ever, although rather overdone in the makeup and fake tan departments.

When Graham entered the bar she was standing in the middle of the room on her own. She greeted him warmly with a kiss on the cheek and a hug. Old memories came flooding back to Graham all too quickly. She remained the sexiest and most desirable woman he had ever met.

"Hello, Anita. It's been a long time."

"Too long," she replied.

"You're looking great, as usual. I hear you're running your own beauty salon."

"Yes, it's all going well, thanks."

"I'm just going to get a drink," said Graham. "Would you like one?"

"No, it's okay, thanks. A friend is buying me one."

At that point they were joined by a swarthy looking man in his late twenties with thinning brown hair and a trim figure. He was wearing a sharp blue suit and was bedecked with various chains and other jewellery. Graham recognised him as Henry Fulford, who owned two bargain shopping outlets in the Sanderholme area. His demeanour and appearance marked him out as what was in those days described as a spiv. He had attended the same secondary school as Graham, although Henry had been a few years older. They had clashed a couple of times at school as Henry and some of his friends had often found some pleasure in teasing and bullying Jim Nott.

Graham was not one to bear grudges and so greeted Henry in a friendly way, saying "hello" brightly and offering to shake hands. Henry returned this overture with a cursory nod and a half smile, returning the handshake half-heartedly and quickly withdrawing his paw. He knew that Graham was a highly successful businessman and that he had been "an item" with Anita in the past. And he was jealous.

Graham felt the bad vibes and quickly excused himself by saying he had to get to the bar while there was a gap in the queue for service. Anita smiled and furtively winked at him. He was left feeling unsure as to whether the wink was a recognition of the uncomfortable atmosphere with Henry or perhaps a hint of seduction. Winking is an action used sparingly by women, but when it is employed it usually has some significance. And so it proved to be in this instance.

After spending an hour chatting to a couple of old school friends in the crowded bar, Graham left the pub and walked across to his Porsche in the car park. As he got into the driving seat he noticed that a note had been placed under a windscreen wiper. He got out of the car and read it:

RING ME 870076 ANITA X.

Anita had still been in the bar as he left the pub so he wondered how she had managed to slip out and place the message. Then he remembered he had seen her walking in the direction of the Ladies, so he deduced that she had taken the opportunity to nip outside then.

Graham was in no doubt that Anita was seeking some new liaison with him. She was that sort of girl. Was it sex she wanted, or money? Decidedly both. His first thoughts were that she was welcome to both sex and money, but not money for sex.

He was staying with his parents, now in their early fifties and still running their shops. They were always pleased to welcome their son on his brief visits. They were immensely proud of him as he had succeeded in business way beyond what they had dreamed of.

Mid-morning the next day Graham phoned Anita who was manning the reception at her beauty salon.

"Hi Graham," she said. "I hoped you would ring when you saw my cheeky note. It was great seeing you again. It's been an age."

"Yes, it has. But I've been over to Sanderholme quite a lot over the years. I can't believe we haven't bumped into each other before now. I did hear at one time that you were living in Spain."

"That's right. I was there for a couple of years – with a guy. A Spanish guy called Pedro. He owned some bars and I used to work for him as his manager. But, you know, it all went stale and I came back here and opened my salon."

"How long have you been seeing Henry?"

"About six months now. To be honest I'm getting tired of him. He's so insanely jealous. He even kicked off last night because I spoke to you for a few seconds. It was the last straw. I'm ditching the cocky sod."

"How will he take that, do you think?"

"Badly, I would imagine. But tough shit. He's had his

chance. The thing is, I wondered if you fancied meeting up – nothing heavy, just a drink or something?"

"I'd like that. What would you fancy doing?"

"Why not come round to mine tonight? 14 Burbidge Road. About 8ish? We could open a bottle of wine or something. Chat about old times!"

"Old times? You make us sound like two old aged pensioners," Graham joked. "Seriously though, I'd love to do that. 8ish it is then."

"It's a date, love."

Graham, always a dapper dresser and well groomed, made a special effort to look good for the impending date. He knew what Anita was like and was under no illusions that their "date" would begin and end with a glass or two of wine. She would inevitably seduce him and he would gladly succumb.

And, sure enough, he was not to be disappointed. It was a hot summer's evening and as soon as Anita opened the door to him it was obvious what she had in mind. She was wearing a white blouse tied with a bow above her navel and unbuttoned far enough to display a tantalising amount of her ample bosom. Her brief and tight-fitting shorts showed off her bottom and long tanned legs to great effect.

"Come in," she said, grinning broadly, like a spider enticing a hapless insect into her web. But Graham was no helpless insect. He was fully prepared to be trapped and, if necessary, eaten by his predator.

Anita led him along the broad hallway and into a spacious, modern lounge, furnished in a minimal way but redolent of a comfortable and affluent lifestyle.

"Come and sit down," she said, pointing to a plush

leather sofa. "I've got the wine open."

She sat beside him and leant over to a coffee table where there was an opened bottle of Bourgogne Rouge and two glasses. She poured a glass each and handed one to Graham. Lifting her own glass, she clinked it against his.

"Cheers, darling!"

"Good health!"

They drank a mouthful of wine each and Anita put her glass back on the table.

Looking at him closely and flashing her eyelashes she declared: "Put your glass down".

Graham obeyed her and, as he anticipated, she snuggled up to him and kissed him on the lips.

"God, I've missed you," she said. "I must have been mad to treat you the way I did. I've been with some right tossers since I was with you. But no one like you."

"I'm flattered," said Graham, and he leant over and kissed her on the lips too.

They kissed deeply now and as they did so he felt her hand squeezing the top of his leg.

Aroused, he moved closer to her and pushed her backwards so that she was laying outstretched on the sofa. He started to unbutton her blouse.

"Hang on a minute," she said. "Let's go upstairs."

They stood up and he took her hand and led her quickly to the staircase at the end of the lounge.

Their love-making proved to be far more satisfying than their earlier attempts when Graham had been an unschooled teenager.

Eventually, when their passion had died down, they returned to the sofa and finished the wine.

"I have really missed you, you know," said Anita.

"Thank you for that," said Graham. "I've missed you too."

"Any time, love. And I mean that. Any time."

"What about Henry?" asked Graham.

"He's ex-Henry," she replied. "I'll chuck him tomorrow."

"Will he be angry?"

"Of course he will. He's angry about everything. But he'll have to get over it. He treats me like dirt sometimes. I've had enough."

"Will you mention me?" said Graham.

"No. Are you worried about him?"

"Not much worries me. I take life as it comes. But maybe it would be best if he didn't know you had been with me before you told him you were chucking him?"

"Yes. Good point. I'll keep stum."

In his love life, as in the business world, Graham exercised bravery and caution in equal measures.

Graham was a workaholic but he was enjoying himself so much with Anita that he decided to lengthen his stay at Sanderholme for a few more days, keeping in touch with his office through phone calls and faxes.

She had, as promised, "chucked" Henry, in a phone call of her own. He had been incandescent with anger and dashed round to the salon where he unleashed a tirade of abuse at her in front of a handful of embarrassed customers and staff members. So aggressive was he that the women clients were fearful for their own safety. However, he stopped short of physical violence, letting off a head of steam by accusing Anita of being every swear word his limited vocabulary would allow. When he eventually left, slamming the front door of the salon, the customers had to be profusely apologised to by staff and by Anita herself, who quickly recovered her composure and ordered mugs of calming tea and coffee all round.

Later that week business compelled Graham to return to Nottinghamshire but he promised Anita he would be back in Sanderholme the following weekend. He had been utterly captivated by her all over again. There was a directness and basic honesty about her which had rekindled his former infatuation. Sexually, he was under no illusion that he could trust her to be completely faithful. This had ruined their relationship previously. Now he told himself that he would expunge all feelings of jealousy and accept her for what she was – a sex-mad money-grubber, but otherwise loyal and a great deal of fun.

Anita was under no illusions either. She really liked Graham and fancied him enormously. She also liked the trappings of wealth which he could offer her. But she knew too that she could never stop lusting after other men. She was essentially a sexual being and it was not in her nature to be the proverbial "one man woman".

Therefore they were able to rekindle their relationship with eyes wide open, promising to each other nothing deeper than great sex and enjoyable company.

Both accepted the flaws in the other. She was incapable of being sexually continent. He was so wrapped up in work that he was unable to give a woman the undivided attention that most craved. So in many ways they were the perfect match. They just hadn't come to terms with that the first time around.

Both had had conventional upbringings, but Anita had thrown off the yolk of her relatively old parents as soon as she reached puberty. From that age they had been quite appalled at the provocative way she dressed, her promiscuous behaviour and her bad language. They were both respectable doctors with squeaky clean morals. Her mother put the blame on her own mother who had always had a somewhat rakish lifestyle. The genes must have skipped a generation! In the end they gave up trying to reform their wayward daughter, trusting that they would have better luck with her two younger sisters. In the main, they did.

Over the coming weeks Graham found time to travel to Sanderholme more often than usual so that he and Anita could continue their relationship. He spent many nights with her at her smart semi-detached house in one of the town's grid-patterned tree-lined avenues.

It was on one damp and miserable Sunday afternoon that he took the plunge: "Will you marry me?"

Without hesitation Anita responded: "Oh course I will, you daft bugger."

Anita was sitting in an armchair and Graham, who was standing in front of her, produced a sparkling white gold diamond engagement ring from his jacket pocket and slipped it on to her finger.

She beamed her pleasure, jumped up from her chair and kissed him tenderly on the lips.

They immediately began to lay their plans for a short engagement and a lavish wedding the following June at Sanderholme's St Crispin's Parish Church followed by a reception at the best hotel in town. Anita would be given away by her father and her two sisters would be bridesmaids. Jim Nott, referred to by Anita as "Smelly Jim", would, of course, be best man. Following a honeymoon in The Maldives, Anita would move into

Graham's Papplewick mansion. In the meantime she would take steps to sell her business and her house.

Graham had never felt happier as he kissed Anita goodbye that afternoon to return to Nottinghamshire. But his mood quickly changed as he left by the garden gate. He looked in horror at his blue Porsche parked in the road in front of the house. It had three deep scratches in the passenger side door.

He turned white with anger. Considered rationally, the insurance would pay for the damage, and he could well afford any higher premium. But Graham's reaction was much the same as any other human being's would be – he felt as if *he* had been violated.

His first thoughts were that the car had been attacked by vandals, either kids or someone with a chip on their shoulder about wealth. He returned to the house, banged on the front door and led Anita out to survey the damage.

"Some bloody kids or someone with a grudge against anyone with money," he declared.

Anita went quiet.

"Maybe," she said after a while.

She paused again and then said: "There's something I should tell you. I came across Henry in the street earlier and he was still ranting and raving about you. Eventually I had to run off down the road to get rid of him. He was bloody vile. I think he could have done this."

"I'll go to the police," said Graham.

"Are you sure? If it is Henry and he gets arrested or something he could turn really nasty. He could turn on you, or me."

"I'll risk it. No one should get away with this. You can come and stay with me straightaway if you would feel safer getting away from here."

"Thanks", she replied, giving Graham a peck on the cheek. "You must go ahead and do what you've got to do. I'm totally pissed off with Henry anyway."

Graham drove to Sanderholme police station and reported his suspicions. Officers eventually questioned Henry who fervently denied knowing anything about the damage to the car and nothing was ever discovered to link him to the crime.

****

In the coming months there were no further incidents, with Henry apparently keeping his distance.

June came and the wedding went well. Graham's parents were underwhelmed by their son's choice of bride, her reputation of being something of a wild child having gone before her. But they kept their own counsel. As typical Middle Englanders they would do anything to avoid unpleasantness on their child's big day.

Life was sweet for Graham and Anita in the first year of their marriage. As usual Graham was working very long hours, managing his substantial business and making acquisitions of both new retail outlets and property developments. His frequent absences caused no concern to his wife, who settled quickly to the life of the lady of "the big house".

She had little work to do in the large mansion as Graham employed a daily cleaner, a cook and a gardener. She was able to indulge her interests in acquiring a permatan, attending to her hair and nails and generally pampering herself. She also enjoyed entertaining Graham's business contacts and their spouses and partners and his newly acquired political contacts within the local Conservative Party. She found herself quite capable of being on her best behaviour, even moderating her normally salty language.

Unsurprisingly, she was popular among Graham's male acquaintances, who found her sexy and flirtatious. Some of them always secretly fancied that they might be "in with a chance" of being seduced by her, and she was well aware of her own particular charms. Womenfolk were, again unsurprisingly, less than enamoured with her, but put up with that to enjoy the lavishness of the hospitality that Graham and Anita offered and the social kudos of mixing in their generally well-heeled and influential circle of friends.

As for Graham, he was dedicated to expanding his business empire and was keen to cultivate any connections which would further his over-arching ambition. He encouraged Anita in her activities as a hostess, but although quite sociable was certainly no party animal himself. He welcomed his guests warmly and did all the necessary mingling and glad-handing, but for him the parties were merely a means to an end, the "end" being enhancing his business prospects. He always felt a sense of relief when the parties were over.

Two of the regular guests were John and Polly Hampden. John was a chartered accountant and financial adviser who was also chairman of the local Conservative branch. Poppy owned and ran a floristry business, with three thriving shops in the area.

John, a tall, portly man with a ruddy complexion, double chin and thick shoulder-length dark brown hair, was in his late forties, 20 years older than his wife. He had the air of a patrician, his large frame and loud voice giving him, quite unintentionally, a somewhat demanding presence. He was also sensible, kind and good-humoured.

Poppy was short, blonde and effervescent, with entrancing piercing blue eyes and a slender figure.

On social occasions Graham and John would often stand on the periphery and discuss business and politics while Poppy circulated widely in the assembled company, chatting happily to both men and women. Anita, who had never previously sought to have many female friends, found that in Poppy she had a soul-mate. The two of them became "ladies who lunch" together on a weekly basis. Later they began to explore the nightlife of Nottingham, regularly visiting restaurants, bars and night clubs on Friday or Saturday nights. Graham and John, neither of whom were especially jealous people, were content to give them free rein.

Meanwhile John had persuaded Graham to become involved in the Conservative Party. Graham had never previously shown any great interest in politics but he had recently become excited by the free market policies being pursued by the Thatcher government. He believed a thriving economy powered by a strong business sector was in the best interests of everyone in the country.

He was especially drawn to the idea that a market economy was the way to spread wealth and power among the population rather than this being concentrated in the hands of the State, the nationalised industries and over-powerful trade unions.

He had an idealistic streak and his motivation in his business career had never been primarily about enriching himself. He liked a big house and a nice car, but creating new businesses and the extra jobs which resulted from these was the mainspring of his ambition.

Graham's particular passion was for nurturing popular capitalism, especially through wider share ownership. Every employee in his companies, from top executives to cleaning staff, was given shares in the business. His aim was to have a loyal and contented workforce and to set an example to other employers.

Chapter Five
Infidelity

It was his new interest in politics which led him to attend the fateful Tory Party Conference of 1984.

On the day of the bombing of the Grand Hotel, Brighton, he tried several times to speak to Anita on the telephone to assure her that he was safe. But there was no reply from home. His intention had been to drive into London for a business meeting after Margaret Thatcher's conference speech, spend the night at a hotel in the capital and return to Nottinghamshire the next day. Now, though, he felt it was important to get home as soon as possible to see his wife and reassure her, so he cancelled the meeting and the hotel booking.

As he drove home Graham thought a great deal about the traumatic events he had been at the periphery of. At first he felt a strange numbness, which he didn't much like. He thought that he should be overwhelmed with horror at what had happened on that tragic night. He of course utterly deplored what had occurred at the Grand Hotel but he was not filled with the anger and desolate sadness which he believed would have been appropriate to those circumstances. In fact his primary feeling was one of relief that he had avoided direct involvement in the tragedy. Mrs Thatcher had shown that "the show must go on" and that was his attitude too.

But later in the journey his mood changed. He still had a nagging feeling of guilt about being idiotic enough to lead an Anarcho-Syndicalist to the precincts of the Conservative Party Conference hotel.

Rationally he knew it was highly unlikely that the

young man he had met was a bomber. He had appeared to be a pleasant, unthreatening individual, extremely naive rather than dangerous. Nevertheless he felt ashamed of his own naivety in being so trusting of this total stranger.

He made a determined effort to snap himself out of these dark thoughts. He reverted to singing out loud such optimistic songs as "Driving Home for Christmas" and "Don't Worry Be Happy". This more positive mood, though, was soon to change abruptly.

As he motored along the long driveway to his house he noticed a Ford Anglia car parked at the front of the property. It was not a vehicle he recognised. He entered the unlocked front door, walked through the grand hallway and into the lounge. Finding there was no one there, he looked in the kitchen, which was also empty. He decided to go upstairs with the intention of taking off his suit and hanging it in the bedroom wardrobe.

When he opened the door he was assailed by the sight of a man's bare buttocks on his marital bed. There was a woman's screech of "Oh" and the man turned round sharply to see a shocked Graham standing at the door. When he turned he exposed Anita who was laying naked underneath him.

"What the hell's going on?" shouted Graham.

"Not much I can say, mate," said the young man, who looked to be little more than a teenager. "Sorry to surprise you like this. I'd better go."

"Yes, get out," said Graham, extremely agitated.

The man scrambled to find his clothes and quickly left the room clutching them.

Anita looked mortified.

"I'm so sorry, Graham. I thought you weren't coming home until tomorrow."

"I'll bet you're sorry," said Graham. "How could you do this to me? I trusted you, you know."

"I know," said Anita, red-faced and shaking slightly. "I promise nothing like this will ever happen again."

Graham had no reply. He stalked out of the room, slamming the door hard behind him.

Having largely overcome any bad vibes about the Brighton bombing, to come home to find his wife in bed with another man metaphorically brought him to his knees.

He was slumped in an armchair in the lounge when Anita finally came downstairs after dressing.

"Will you forgive me?" she said.

"No, why should I? Who is this bloke? Is he still at school?"

"No, of course not."

"He doesn't look much older than a school kid. Who is he anyway?"

"Does it matter? You'll never see him again."

"Of course it bloody matters. Who is he? What's his name? And how long has this been going on?"

"He's called George. I met him at a night club in Nottingham last night. I was drunk. It hasn't been 'going on'. It was a one-off."

"So you were drunk last night. But what about this afternoon? You aren't still drunk now, are you?"

"Well no. It just sort of carried on."

"Get out of my sight. You disgust me."

"Please, Graham. I'm disgusted with myself too."

He rose from his chair and snapped: "I'm going out to get some fresh air."

A frost descended over the Robinson household and remained there for the following week, with Graham and Anita doing their best avoid each other's presence and shunning eye contact.

Then one morning she sat down next to him as he ate his breakfast at the kitchen table.

"Graham".

"Yes," he snarled.

"I've something to tell you. I'm pregnant."

"Pregnant! Whose is it?"

"It's yours, of course."

"Are you sure?"

"Yes, of course. I've not been with anyone else. That time with George was just a stupid act of madness on my part. And even then we hadn't actually done the deed when you disturbed us."

"Are you telling me the truth?" asked Graham.

"Yes, I swear I am."

Graham fell silent for a few moments and then asked: "Are you pleased about this pregnancy?"

"Yes, really pleased. And you?"

The frost suddenly thawed.

Graham smiled. His first genuine smile since his homecoming from Brighton.

"Yes, I'm pleased. A new start for us?"

"A new start, love."

She kissed him.

****

Graham somehow found time in his hectic business schedule to immerse himself in the local Conservative Party. Encouraged by John Hampden, who was chairman of the Nottingham Forest Branch, he had been co-opted on to the branch committee and at the annual general meeting was voted in as treasurer. The other members expected that with his strong business connections he would be able to extract some sizeable donations to boost branch funds. And he very swiftly succeeded in doing just that.

The branch committee already contained some doughty campaigners, not least the vice-chairman, Miss Norma Whitehouse, and the secretary, Captain Anthony Goodwin.

Miss Whitehouse was a malodorous retired hospital matron, used to getting her own way among her underlings at work and so inclined to expect similar deference from those she engaged with in the voluntary sector.

This attitude inevitably ruffled a few feathers in the branch. In particular, she was at almost permanent war with Captain Goodwin, a salty retired naval officer, who was also used to having his orders obeyed with precision and without question.

John Hampden, a good-natured man despite his rather lofty patrician persona, spent much of his time as chairman trying to keep this prickly pair of septuagenarians from tearing at each others' throats.

As an ambitious newcomer Graham was courted both by Miss Whitehouse and Captain Goodwin who wished to claim him as their protege and who both hoped he would take their side in their interminable battles.

Miss Whitehouse began her campaign by inviting Graham to her house for a cup of tea one early evening to discuss her ideas for a membership recruitment campaign.

Her secluded home, inherited from her parents, was a substantial detached old house at the edge of Sherwood Forest, hemmed in by large sycamore trees which allowed very little light to penetrate the building's interior.

When Graham arrived for his visit he had to get out of his car to open a big wooden gate at the end of the long driveway. Both sides of the gate had become warped by age and damp and had to be lifted with great difficulty and then scraped along the ground in a most undignified fashion. Graham undertook this exercise with the greatest of care, fearing that any amount of rough treatment would lead to the rotting wood disintegrating in his hands.

The feat of opening the gate was followed by slow progress along the weed-choked drive where little remained visibly of the tarmacked surface underneath.

Having parked in a rough gravelled area at the side of the house, Graham made his way to the front door. This was ill-painted, in company with the rest of the property, and he was immediately struck by the overwhelming atmosphere of decay which enveloped him. There was also a strong smell of cooked food apparently emanating from inside the building.

There was no bell to assist entry to the property so Graham lifted the huge metal door knocker in the shape of a monkey's head and pounded it against the woodwork. This made an ear-splitting clang which could have wakened the souls in Hades.

Soon he heard a woman's voice coming from the inside of the house.

"Bugger. Bloody thing. I'll be there in a minute. Can't get this bloody key to turn."

Eventually, after further cursing and loud rattling, the

door was prised open and there stood Miss Whitehouse. She was wearing a dingy brown gilet over a grey shirt and faded blue denim jeans, her mop of unbrushed grey hair making her look a fright.

"Oh, it's you, Graham," she declared in a loud voice. "Do come in. It's a bit of a mess, I'm afraid. I never seem to get the time to tidy up."

What immediately struck Graham was a vile, rancid stench, as if someone had been cooking fried breakfasts for a hundred years without ever opening a window. As he entered the long hallway he found himself catching his breath and his eyes began to smart and run with tears owing to the acrid fumes.

He recalled John Hampden joking that when he visited Miss Whitehouse he had managed to hold his breath for an inordinate length of time – for so long in fact that he declared he was thinking of applying to the Guinness Book of Records claiming a world record for breath-holding!

A mangy brown dog of middle size and indeterminate breed waddled towards Graham demanding to be stroked. Graham leant down to pat the animal before he realised that the dog had a revolting smell all of its own, redolent of a badly managed pig sty. Graham quickly regretted touching the dog as the stench had transferred itself to his hand, causing him to retch.

"Don't mind Marmaduke," said Miss Whitehouse. "He's getting on a bit. But he's very friendly, isn't he?"

"He does seem like a friendly fellow," replied Graham, privately thinking that he would rather have met Cerberus, the dog from Hades, on a bad day.

He had in fact come across this dog previously, when Miss Whitehouse took the hell hound along to a branch meeting in the Conservative Club committee room.

John Hampden, who, as usual, was chairing the meeting, was sitting behind a card table where he had placed his papers and a pint of beer. Suddenly Marmaduke came from nowhere and disappeared under the table. His nose shot up like a torpedo from a submarine between Hampden's legs, taking the chairman by complete surprise. Hampden fell head first on to the card table, which collapsed and propelled him full length on to the floor. His beer glass followed him down, spilling its contents all over the back of his suit jacket.

Miss Whitehouse sprung up from her chair to help the chairman to his feet and used her handkerchief in an effort to wipe away the beer.

"Don't worry about it, John. Marmaduke was just trying to be friendly," she said.

Hampden, red with embarrassment, had smiled ruefully. Most of the other committee members, including Graham and the chairman's wife, Poppy, were by this time doubled up with laughter.

They had so enjoyed this incident that when, at the next branch meeting, secretary Captain Goodwin proposed that dogs be banned from future meetings, he could not even find a seconder.

After this new meeting with Marmaduke, Graham was contemplating whether Miss Whitehouse and her house had picked up the smell of the dog, or whether it was vice versa. However, before he reached a conclusion on that point, he had another inmate of the house to be introduced to. Standing at the end of the hall was a stumpy bewhiskered woman of greater age than Miss Whitehouse, even more dishevelled and, if possible, even smellier than Marmaduke..

"This is my sister, Ethel. She has recently come to live with me after she lost her husband."

Graham pondered on what an unfortunate chap her spouse must have been to have lived with such a creature, but then admonished himself for having such uncharitable thoughts.

"Hello," he said. "I think I may have met you once before – at the Christmas Fayre."

"Oh, yes," she replied, her happy smile revealing a mouth full of rotting teeth. She offered her hand for him to shake. Realising that his right hand stunk after his encounter with Marmaduke, Graham offered his left, which Ethel shook with some vigour. He now found that both his hands smelt badly. It was a toss-up as to which hand was the more unpleasant.

Having completed these charming introductions he was shepherded into the living room, a cold cheerless room with dark brown wallpaper and books and papers piled up seemingly indiscriminately across the floor and on all items of furniture.

Miss Whitehouse cleared half a dozen copies of The Times from the sofa and indicated that Graham should sit down.

"Would you like some tea?" she asked in a demanding tone which brooked no refusal.

Graham acquiesced graciously and was joined on the sofa by Marmaduke, who was keen on the idea of licking his face.

"You've made a friend there," said Miss Whitehouse, as she signalled to Ethel to set about making the tea.

"It seems so," replied Graham meekly, as he held up both arms in defence against the dog's onslaught.

When the tea arrived it was served in delicate china

cups from a blue Royal Worcester porcelain tea set. As Graham looked around the room he noticed that it was a treasure trove of antique furniture, glassware and china, much of it hidden by everyday items which no one had bothered to clear away. The surroundings reeked of distressed gentlefolk, he recounted later.

The customary pleasantries having now been completed, it was down to business.

At election times, Miss Whitehouse was noted for her organisational skills. She ran the committee room in the local Conservative office with an almost military precision. Those who doubted her abilities for administration on account of her unprepossessing appearance and odour were soon disobliged of such notions. She had an encyclopaedic knowledge of the likely voting intentions of people in the area and in her time had delivered leaflets to almost every house in the Constituency.

Some of her methods raised a few eyebrows amongst her fellow committee members, but went unchallenged owing to the force majeure of her personality. Her most repeated boast was that she could go to every local care home and procure the postal votes of the majority of residents by "helping" them to put their crosses in the right places on the ballot papers. Unsteady hands were guided purposefully towards the Conservative candidates.

Such was the confidence of the members in her that she had been charged with overseeing a major membership drive, with the ambitious aim of doubling the number of members within the local branch catchment area. She had duplicated a typewritten list of all of her proposals and passed a copy to Graham.

He was impressed by some of her imaginative and

original ideas and added some of his own. Now he began to understand why Miss Whitehouse was such a respected member of the Party.

He stopped trying to hold his breath and engaged in stimulating and positive conversation with this strange but talented lady.

When they had finished their discussions Miss Whitehouse declared: "I think we have had a very useful afternoon. Of course Goodwin won't like any of our ideas."

Graham smirked and remained steadfastly non-committal.

"Maybe you're right."

As he got into his car to leave he realised that he was taking the smell into the vehicle with him. So he opened all the windows and tried to waft the odour away by flapping his hands. Miss Whitehouse and her sister thought he was waving goodbye to them and so waved back at him enthusiastically.

"I think that young man likes us," said Miss Whitehouse. "Could be a very useful ally against Goodwin."

****

Seven months on and baby Austin arrived. A big, bouncy boy.

Graham doted on him. Anita was not the most maternal woman in the world but she coped with the child with the help of Erica, a young live-in nanny from Nottingham.

John and Poppy continued to visit the Robinsons regularly over the next few months. Graham gradually overcame some misgivings he had about Poppy whom he suspected of leading Anita astray. Not that she needed much leading!

It wasn't long before the two young women reverted their previous pattern of long lunches and night-time visits to the local night spots. Graham didn't approve of this but knew Anita well enough to accept that she was a bird that would never be caged, so he kept his own counsel.

The weekend routine was that Anita and Poppy, who lived only a couple of miles apart, would take a taxi into town, have a main course at a restaurant, spend a couple of hours in a variety of city centre pubs and then go on to a night club. They would return home by taxi in the early hours of the morning, by which time their stay-at-home husbands would have been tucked up in bed for several hours.

One weekday evening Graham and John attended a Conservative Party meeting at a local hotel and had a drink together afterwards. After a while the subject of the girls' nights out came up.

"We give them a long leash, don't we?" said John. "But I suppose it's a nice break for them, isn't it?"

"Yes, they're good friends aren't they?"

"There's one thing I don't quite get though," said John. "This business of the taxis."

"What's that?"

"I can't understand why they go into the city in one taxi and then come home in two separate ones. It always seems like a waste of money to me. Poppy says that she prefers to use the taxi firm that we always have but Anita has taken a dislike to the late night driver, so she gets her own."

"It seems a bit daft," said Graham. "Our houses are basically on the same route, aren't they?"

"Exactly. I'm not mean, but at that time of night – or I should say morning – it would be much cheaper for them to share a taxi, wouldn't it?"

"You're not mean. You're a chartered accountant," joked Graham. "But I agree with you that it doesn't make sense. I'll have a word with Anita about it."

"As I said, I'm don't think I'm being mean but taxis at two o'clock in the morning are pretty dear. Well anything after midnight is."

"Two o'clock in the morning! More like half past four," said Graham.

"No, I don't think Poppy's ever been later than two."

Graham looked surprised. He had noticed that Anita had not returned home until around 4.30am over the previous few weeks. He decided not to say anything more to John on the matter. But suspicions about his wife's behaviour were resurrected.

When Graham returned home that night he found Anita was still up watching a film on television and polishing off a bottle of white wine which she had enjoyed all by herself.

After exchanging some routine pleasantries he asked her about her taxi-riding habits.

"Why do you and Poppy use separate taxis to come home in at the weekends?"

Anita looked slightly annoyed by the question and then replied: "Oh, I hate the taxi driver she uses. He's a rude sod and never opens the doors for us."

"That seems a fairly minor thing to worry about," said Graham. "It adds to the expense for both of you not to be sharing a taxi."

"Oh, I am sorry if I'm wasting your money," said Anita, sarcastically.

"Anyway why does Poppy manage to get home by two o'clock when it always seems to take you until 4.30. You must use a very slow taxi."

"Ah, well. You know what I'm like. I get talking to people at the club and time just seems to fly."

"Would these *people* happen to be men?"

"Oh, so this is an interrogation, is it? Some of them are probably men, yes. Just talking."

"I believe you."

"Good. So how did your meeting go?"

"Interesting, thank you. I'm going to bed."

"I'll just finish watching this film, which you so kindly interrupted."

"Goodnight."

Graham still loved Anita. She had a captivating beauty and a fascinatingly forthright personality which never seemed to pall. But now he realised he still could not trust her. He knew that she would never be constant sexually but would often pretend, even to himself, that this was not the case. Now he was almost certain that she was being unfaithful to him again.

He began to question why John had really brought up the subject of the taxis. Was it a very subtle hint to a friend? Did John know more than he was letting on? Perhaps he didn't. Perhaps he did.

Graham was unsure whether to bury his head in the sand and say nothing, to undertake some sort of surreptitious surveillance, or to confront Anita head on with his fears.

He was ashamed to admit to any feelings of jealousy. He believed to be jealous was the ultimate sign of lack of confidence. It was for lesser mortals than he.

However, in business he had an image of being uncompromising and nobody's fool and he felt he was being weak not to apply the same characteristics to his personal life. He would not countenance being made an idiot of by his wife.

Now there was not only himself and Anita to consider. He didn't wish to do anything precipitate which would put Austin's future in jeopardy. So he resolved to bide his time and be watchful.

****

One sunny Sunday afternoon in May Graham was sitting at a table on the patio at the rear of his house, drinking a glass of wine while reading his Financial Times. Bees were buzzing around the buddleia plants which were growing up a nearby pergola. A pied wagtail wagged across the beautifully mown lawn and moorhens were scuttling in and out of the reeds at the edges of the trout lake.

An E-type Jaguar drew up on the gravel drive and out stepped John Hampden. Graham beckoned him over and pointed to a chair opposite his.

John had a serious demeanour, his permanently florid face looking more flushed than usual.

"I hope you don't mind me bothering you on a Sunday afternoon, old boy," he said.

"Not at all, John. I'll shout Anita and get her to bring you a glass."

"No, not yet. I have some news to give you first. The

thing is – Poppy's left me. Got another fella."

"Oh, no, John. That's awful. I'm so sad to hear that."

"Thank you. It's come as a big shock, I can tell you."

"So, what's happened?"

"Well, she told me after dinner last night. She's found this young chap, a bloody doctor at the Queen's Medical Centre – married – but only in his early thirties and she's left home today to go and live with him in a flat in the city. He's left his wife and two kids. It's a rum do. It's left me devastated. I suppose I shouldn't be surprised, given the age gap between us. And, of course, we've never had children. Wanted them but it's just never happened. But it's knocked me for six nevertheless."

"Oh dear, oh dear. How long has it been going on, with this doctor?"

"About four or five months, she says. It all comes about through these late nights out at weekends. She met him at some club in town. Anita must have known what was going on, but I don't blame her, of course. Apparently this business we spoke about regarding the taxis – it was all a sham. Her and Anita would go for a meal and a drink at a pub. Then they would go to a club and the guy would meet up with Poppy and leave Anita to fend for herself for the rest of the night."

Graham was nonplussed. All this time he had thought that it was Anita who might be having an affair. He remained suspicious, though, as to why she got home so much later than her friend.

"So I wonder what Anita got up to after Poppy left her? She must have been *on her own* for hours."

"I'll be truthful. I wondered that myself, old boy. In fact I had suspected that this separate taxis business might be to cover up Anita playing away. But apparently not. At least that what's Poppy's told me. She said: 'You know what Anita's like. Very gregarious. She could always find someone to talk to.' "

"Hmm."

"Hey, Graham. Don't for a moment think that I've come here trying to cast any aspersions in your wife's direction. She's the innocent party in this as far as I'm concerned – just covering up for her friend. Please don't go jumping to any conclusions. We've become good friends, the four of us, and I just wanted to let you know that things had changed – for good."

"I appreciate that, John, and hope that the three of us can still be good friends."

"Of course. But it might be a little time before I'll feel like socialising. I'm sure you'll understand that. I'm feeling pretty damned low at present."

"You will be. Time's a great healer you know, but that will be little comfort for you now."

At that moment Anita came out through the patio doors. She ran up to John and threw her arms around him, kissing him on the cheek.

"John, I'm so sorry. Poppy's just rung me and told me the news. What a bugger, eh?"

John gave a half smile, shook his head and then said: "You must have known about all this carry-on."

"I'll admit I did know that Poppy had met Dr Brian. But I didn't realise things had gone so far."

"But you've been covering up for her for months. You can't tell me it wasn't obvious what was happening."

"I'm sorry. We girls stick together you know. It's not fair on you men, but it's a fact of life."

"Well lying and deceit are not usually part of my life," John retorted.

"You've banged me to rights. I can only say sorry again, love. But these things happen. You'll get over it."

"You're not being very sympathetic, Anita," said Graham.

"Don't worry. I'm not here to stir anything. Just wanted to let you know how the land lies," said John. "I'll be on my way."

"You'll not stay to help me finish this bottle of wine?" asked Graham.

"No, thanks. I'm driving. Another time, friend."

"Don't make it too long", said Graham, getting up to shake John's hand.

"See you soon, John," added Anita, looking somewhat shamefaced.

John trudged across the gravel and drove off slowly along the drive.

Graham couldn't decide whether to be annoyed with his wife for her subterfuge. Or annoyed with her for staying out all night in clubs with who knows what disreputable company. Or mightily relieved that it had turned out to be Poppy who was having the affair. So he merely picked up his glass and carried on reading his Financial Times. Anita shrugged her shoulders, smiled at him and went indoors.

****

The Conservative Association held regular fundraising events throughout the year and one of the highlights was a summer garden fete. Prominent members of the Association who had large enough gardens would take it in turn to host this auspicious occasion, which invariably attended by the Member of Parliament.

This particular year the hosts were Graham and Anita Robinson.

Their extensive lawns were ideal for siting a refreshments marquee and for the setting up of various games, such as skee-ball, pin the tail on the donkey, hoopla, skittles and steady hand. There were tombola stalls and competitions such as guess the number of sweets in a jar and guess the name of the doll.

The adjoining meadow was ideal for clay pigeon shooting and the next door neighbour's grazing field was useful for that ever-popular game in rural parts of the country – cowpat bingo.

The event was well patronised by Association members and neighbours and friends from throughout the area. The ladies had the chance to show off their best summer dresses, while the more outgoing of the menfolk displayed their loudest blazers and nattiest straw boaters.

Anita was the perfect hostess, nipping in and out of the house with a variety of enticing crudites and fancy cakes, all home made by her cook who was being generously paid for her overtime.

Neither Graham nor John Hampden were great party-goers, both preferring more intimate get-togethers. Therefore at the first polite opportunity they managed to sneak away from the main huddle of guests. Each with their glass of red wine in one hand and a folding chair in the other, they ventured to a quiet part of the garden and found an ideal spot to sit under the shade of a large, ancient oak tree.

Since taking an active part in the Conservative Association Graham had become somewhat frustrated by the fact that when the members met they rarely discussed pure politics.

Most of the discussions at branch meetings centred either around fund-raising or the mechanics of getting the Member of Parliament or local councillors elected. There was very little talk of the policies which a Conservative Government should pursue and nothing at all about political theory.

John Hampden, as chair, occasionally tried to introduce some controversial political topic, but this hardly ever resulted in any meaningful dialogue or course of action.

Therefore when Graham and John found themselves alone there was nothing they liked better than to have a serious and in depth political discussion.

Going through Parliament at the time was the 1986 Public Order Bill, partly triggered by the most disturbing episode of the UK miners' strike – the notorious Battle of Orgreave, at the Orgreave Coking Plant, near Rotherham, where 51 picketers and 72 policemen were injured.

The Bill sparked off the conversation between Graham and John that afternoon. Both agreed the new law was needed to prevent disruptive strike action. But Graham believed that the long-term solution to strikes lay in his own approach to employee relations.

He explained at length to John how he had established a "partnership" with the staff in his retail business.

"Everyone has a stake in our business, from myself as owner down to the cleaning staff. We all have shares in the company and we all also receive annual bonuses depending on how much profit the business has made in a particular year. Everyone is given a decent wage. We all have a meaningful interest in the success of the company.

"Because of the way we do things no one has a good reason to go on strike. If our system was replicated throughout the whole of the country there would be no need for anyone to strike, would there?"

John said that what Graham was doing in his company was admirable. But how likely was it to be simulated widely enough to bring about a radical transformation of the economy and the labour market?

"A lot of employers won't be as generous as you clearly are. For most companies it's only the bottom line that counts. Sharing profits will not appeal to many business owners. So how would you persuade others to adopt your ideas?" asked John.

"It's not easy, is it? I would hope to sell my system to as many people in the business community as possible. But I accept that won't be enough. I believe I would have to convince government that it's the answer to many of the nation's problems.

"We are seeing an upsurge in strikes at present. It would surely appeal to the Government that there might be a way of reducing the number and effectiveness of those strikes. I ought to be kicking at an open door. After all, this is entirely consistent with the present Government's housing policies – sale of council houses in particular. Those policies are designed with the precise aim of giving people a stake in the country. If people have that they are more likely to be content with their lot, to be law-abiding, to be patriotic and not to go on strike. Also, the fact that they may have mortgages to pay off will make it unlikely they will wish to take the risk of losing money through striking.

"Increased home ownership is a win, win for them – and a win, win for the country.

"Much of the same would apply if more people were given a stake in the businesses that employ them. They would derive more pleasure from their work, have more pride in what they were achieving and have greater loyalty to their employers. Evidence from my own company and from throughout the business world shows that productivity levels increase because employees have a vested interest in seeing that the company succeeds. You get less absenteeism and better staff retention.

"For some time I've been interested in a cross-party body called the Wider Share Ownership Council. In one of its reports it talks about the importance of employees beginning to 'develop the owner's eye'. That's what I'm aiming at.

"I honestly believe that many politicians, mainly Conservatives and Liberals, share my vision that by diffusing economic power in this country – spreading wealth – we can reduce the 'us and them' attitudes which cause so much damage in our society."

"I agree with all you have said," said John. "But what can Government do to encourage more share ownership and profit-sharing in businesses? You're surely not thinking of compulsion are you?"

"No, of course not," replied Graham. "We need to educate employers in the benefits of these schemes. Perhaps tax breaks would provide some encouragement."

John continued: "You mentioned Liberals. The Liberals appear to believe that companies should have workers on the boards – more participation in management. You don't believe in all that sort of thing, do you? Surely workers are not necessarily the best managers. Each to his own, as they say."

"No, I don't believe in that sort of thing at all," said Graham. "I am talking about giving workers a stake in the business, not a change in control."

"I'm glad to hear it," said John. "You are really talking about the private sector here, though. I do agree that your proposals would to some extent lead to fewer strikes in that sector. But you can't really apply your ideas to the public sector, can you?"

"That's a question I have been asking myself and I am, shall I say, only at base camp in finding an answer.

"I wondered whether the solution might lie in cooperatives or some sort of mutual business model like that of the John Lewis Partnership. Why do public services have to be run by the State? Wouldn't workers be more motivated if they felt they were running the show themselves rather than by remote control from Whitehall?"

"You make a very good point, Graham. You should prepare a paper for the Conservative Political Centre. Then perhaps they would circulate it to all the CPC groups in the country."

"I might just do that," said Graham.

At that point the conversation was cut short by the arrival of branch secretary Captain Anthony Goodwin, who looked agitated as he asked John to excuse his interruption.

"It's that bloody woman again!"

John instantly knew he was referring to vice-chairman Miss Norma Whitehouse.

"Okay, what's the problem, Anthony?"

"She's just had a blazing row with Alma Fortescue in front of the MP and everyone else. I have never been so embarrassed."

"What on earth were they rowing about?" asked John.

"It was all about whether the sandwiches should have had butter or margarine on them. I thought they were going to come to blows. The Member had to intervene to calm things down."

"Who started the row?" asked John.

"I didn't see the beginning of the argument. But I'm certain it would have been Whitehouse. Most trouble seems to start with her."

Graham saw the funny side of the situation and could not help grinning as he asked the question: "Who was on the side of butter and who wanted to have margarine?"

The Captain looked indignant.

"Why does that bloody matter? If it's important to you, Alma had already spread margarine and Whitehouse said she should have put butter on."

"I must say I rather support Miss Whitehouse on this matter," Graham chortled.

"I despair," said the Captain. "I can see you're not taking this seriously. It's brought the branch into disrepute. John, you should demand that Whitehouse should resign."

John replied: "I will speak to both ladies and find out exactly what happened."

Graham chipped in: "Yes, we can't just assume that Miss Whitehouse was the one to blame."

The Captain threw back his head and tutted loudly.

"Well, it's getting to the point that either that woman goes or I do."

"Oh, come on, Anthony. Calm down."

"Calm down?" snapped the Captain. "I can assure you that I am perfectly calm. I didn't captain a destroyer in World War Two without the ability to stay calm in every type of emergency. I am merely stating a fact that I cannot continue as secretary of this branch unless some disciplinary action is taken against Miss Bloody

Whitehouse.

"And another thing… if I were you John I would be going over straightaway and apologising to the Member that he had to become involved in this horrible incident."

"I will do – now," said John. "Excuse me, Graham. It appears I have to see active service in the Great Sandwich Spread War."

The Captain strode off shaking his head and quietly mouthing a string of unmentionable swear words.

John went over to the refreshment tent where he found the Member of Parliament surrounded by a gaggle of admiring middle-aged ladies.

Sir Dennis Selby-Applewhite MP was an imposing figure in his late forties, six foot five inches tall, with a full mane of dark brown hair and smooth facial features. An Old Etonian, he had served with distinction as a Colonel in the Life Guards and had gone on to pursue a career as a barrister before being elected to Parliament for a marginal constituency in the North West. He had been knighted following a successful spell as a Defence Minister but had lost his seat to Labour before moving to this safe Conservative constituency in rural Nottinghamshire. He had a deep cultured voice, a broad smile and an easy charm which made him popular with women and men alike.

As he noticed John approaching he turned from his huddle of admirers to greet him.

"Ah, John. There you are."

"May I have a quiet word?" said the chairman.

"Of course."

The two men walked a few paces away from the gathering of guests and John quietly addressed the MP.

"I believe I have to offer the apologies of the branch

for the disgraceful conduct of two of our lady members."

Sir Dennis replied: "Oh, do you mean the spat over the butter? If you do, then I must say I rather enjoyed it. Quite livened up the afternoon."

"According to Anthony you had to calm things down."

"I suppose I did. I don't think the ladies would have come to blows. But I thought it best to make sure that didn't happen."

"Oh, my God." said John. "So it really was that bad. I'm so sorry."

"Don't worry about it, John. I really enjoyed the sandwiches – with the margarine."

"Thank you for being so tolerant, Sir Dennis."

The garden party went off without further incident, and a princely sum of £600 was raised for Association funds. Norma Whitehouse and Alma Fortescue had continued to attend to the refreshments without ever having to speak to each other again that afternoon. Captain Goodwin swore to drive Miss Whitehouse out of the branch.

It was as Graham was saying his goodbyes to the garden party guests that Norma took him on one side for a discreet conversation.

"Graham," she said. "I'm sorry about that contretemps earlier. But that Fortescue woman really does take the biscuit."

"Never mind," said Graham. "It's all over now. I'm sure it will soon be forgotten."

"I don't think so, dear," she replied. "I know that Goodwin's already on the warpath. But nothing new there.

"There's something else I want to talk to you about," she said, conspiratorially.

"Fire away."

"I wondered if you would be one of my executors when I kick the bucket. I need someone I can trust. My only close relative's Ethel and she's even older than me, and as dim as a Toc H lamp. I need people with a bit of oomph about them."

"I would be honoured," said Graham. "It's not something I've done before, but I'm sure I would soon be able to learn the ropes."

"Capital," said Norma. "By the way I've already asked John Hampden to be the other executor. I hope that's okay with you."

"That's great," said Graham, "I get on so well with John that there would be no qualms about that whatsoever."

Chapter Six
Troubled times

It was two years later that Anita left Graham to live with George. Their affair had been continuous since Graham found them on the bed together. Her departure came as no surprise to her husband.

By mutual consent, Austin stayed with his father, assisted by nanny Erica, with Anita having unlimited access whenever she could find time to see her son.

Graham had been deeply saddened by this turn of events and admitted to himself that he would be weak enough to take Anita back if she ever showed any wish to return. But he would never have dreamt of admitting this weakness to any other person. To family, personal friends and neighbours he was kindly and empathetic but never one to reveal his innermost thoughts. In his business world he was rational and hard-nosed, an image he would sometimes go to great lengths to foster. He paid good wages to those who worked in his shops and kept his numerous rental properties in excellent condition with fair rents charged. But he showed no compunction in firing employees if they were not up to scratch. And tenants would be evicted with little hesitation if they fell behind with their rent without a reasonable explanation or transgressed in any other serious way. He remained true to himself, but an enigma to many who knew him.

The hard line which Graham tended to take with tenants who failed to meet their obligations led him into a situation which he afterwards thought of as one of the darkest periods of his life. A handful of his disaffected tenants who lived in a new-build Nottingham housing estate had been given notice of eviction for non-payment of rent. Spearheaded by one or two hotheads, they organised themselves into a protest group and took their stories to the national press, claiming cruel treatment by their landlord.

This led to a tabloid headline one day which read "Is This The Worst Landlord In Britain?", illustrated by a head and shoulders photo of Graham and another of some forlorn looking banner-waving tenants. Some newspapers highlighted his Conservative Party membership, which led to his resigning from the Party to spare it any further embarrassment.

There were stories of families with very young children being pitched into homelessness after only missing a few months' rent. One newspaper also reproduced some of the stock letters sent out to people who fell behind with their payments which were dubbed as "cold, callous and unsympathetic".

Graham defended himself in the accompanying article by pointing out that he was actually a very caring landlord, who kept all his properties in good repair and was open to any reasonable requests from his tenants.

However, he claimed that those tenants who repeatedly got behind with their rents without good reason were being unfair to those who paid on time. He said that his company listened carefully to any representations made to it by people who might be struggling temporarily. And he also maintained that most of those evicted had issues other than non-payment, such as anti-social, or even criminal, behaviour, or neglect of their contracted responsibilities for the upkeep of their homes.

This national shaming of Graham as a bad landlord had a profound effect upon him. It was completely out of kilter with the image he wished to cultivate to the outside world, and, more importantly by far, contrary to the self-image he portrayed to himself.

Ever since he had started out in retail sector management he believed he had striven to combine ambition and efficiency with compassion for staff when he deemed that they deserved this and care for customers. When he ventured into the property rental business he had tried to uphold those same values. He had an expensive car and a lovely big house but beyond that he had very little interest in material possessions or lavish spending on luxury items. He wished to build highly successful businesses, of course for a personal sense of achievement, but also for the good of the communities they served and for the enrichment of all those who worked for him.

A further body blow was a barely concealed rebuke from his father. He warned Graham with a quotation he had picked up while studying Shakespeare's Macbeth at school of "vaulting ambition which o'erleaps itself. And falls on th'other".

Graham's parents had recoiled in horror when they saw the bad Press publicity he had received. They rarely attended church, but as declared Christians they had brought him up to temper his laudable aspirations with modesty and consideration for others.

The paternal rebuke and criticisms which found their way into the local Press too brought Graham as close as he had ever been to a state of depression.

He felt a deep sense of injustice about the way he had been treated by the newspapers. He had always been a strong advocate of a free Press, believing it to be a vital bulwark against over-mighty governments and all those who used power corruptly and oppressively. But on this occasion he felt that more weight had been given to what he thought to be the wrong-headed complaints of his tenants and not enough to his own rational and reasonable points of contradiction.

Graham was a passionate believer in the rights of property and felt that these were being eroded by legislation which unfairly favoured the interests of tenants over those of landlords. He thought that if landlords were emasculated by rules and regulations, however well-intentioned these might be, then the result would be that rental properties would be taken out of the market. He asked to whose benefit that would be? Obviously it would deprive landlords of potential income, but it would also lead to a dearth of properties to rent with the inevitable result that many people would become homeless.

In an effort to understand their concerns, he had held several meetings with a handful of the leaders of the "tenants' revolt". But he had been disappointed to discover that the motives of these leaders were largely political rather than being concerned with the plight of those they claimed to be representing. They were people who wished to overthrow the entire capitalist system and who appeared to hate him as a landlord on principle. They had nothing constructive to suggest as to how his company could deal better with people who fell behind with their rents, or who indulged in behaviour which led to a deterioration in the state of their homes. They also failed to take seriously examples of anti-social behaviour.

These meetings left Graham with a dilemma. On the one hand he felt that most of the complaints levelled against him were spurious and ill-intentioned. On the other hand he was keen to restore his own and his company's reputation for fairness. He told himself that in future he needed to temper efficiency and profitability with greater kindness.

Graham had always looked up to his parents. They were successful in their business and nobody's fools but they were essentially kind people. They were kind to him and kind to others and he hoped he had inherited their values.

In the case of some tenants Graham had to exercise his kinder approach through gritted teeth. He would have appreciated French essayist Joseph Joubert's observation: "A part of kindness consists in loving people more than they deserve."

****

Although keeping a judicious distance from the local Conservatives, Graham retained his close friendship with John Hampden, who had handled his resignation from the Party with tact and understanding.

One day Graham was in his Nottingham office when he received a phone call from John.

"I'm sorry to tell you that I have some bad news. Norma Whitehouse passed away a couple of days ago."

"Oh dear. I'm sorry to hear that. I liked Norma."

"Yes, she could be a curmudgeonly old stick, but her heart was always in the right place. I will miss her."

"What did she die of?"

"A heart attack, I believe. She was 86 so I suppose she had 'a good innings' as they say."

"So I guess that means we have to swing into action as executors," said Graham.

"Yes, I think we should perhaps go to see her sister, Ethel. She went into the Springwood Care Home a couple of months ago. Are you agreeable to that?"

"Yes, of course."

"I'll phone the care home and see how the land lies with regards to visiting her – and I'll get back to you."

"Just one more thing," said Graham. "What's happening to the abominable Marmaduke?"

"Fortunately, I think, the animal died not long before Norma. She rang me to tell me about it a couple of weeks ago. Her wish was that the dog's ashes should be buried with her when she died."

Two days later the two men arrived at the care home and were escorted to a private sitting room for their meeting with Ethel. They were pleased to find her quite bright, cheerful and compos mentis. Her habitual odour had been diluted to just a gentle whiff of old age and her moustache and beard had been neatly trimmed.

She delved into her colossal handbag and gave the men the keys to the house.

"You just get rid of everything as best you can," she said. "There's a few antiques which might fetch some money at a sale. But other than that, take whatever you want and give the rest to charity, if there's anything that would be of any use to anybody."

John enquired whether there were any relatives or friends who needed to be told of Norma's death.

"She had a few old friends that would like to know," said Ethel. "There's an address book in the bureau in the study. That might be some help. I already asked the matron here to let some cousins know, but they won't be very interested, especially as she hasn't left them anything."

This interview having gone very smoothly in the circumstances, John and Graham took their leave and decided their next move should be to contact Norma's solicitor to find out what was in her will.

Their interview with the solicitor revealed that she had left the lion's share of her estate to her sister. There were also some large bequests to a number of 'doggy' charities and a small sum to the local Conservative Association.

Two hundred mourners packed the village church when Norma's funeral service was held two weeks later. The traditional service was followed by burial in the churchyard. One notable absentee was Captain Anthony Goodwin, who had himself died two days before Norma, a fact which would have caused her inestimable pleasure.

Two months later, when probate had been settled, John and Graham set about the task of examining Norma's rambling house.

John had already visited the house once to find the address book. He warned Graham about the vile stench which still emanated from every corner of the dwelling, and so the two men had agreed that it would be sensible to "mask up" for the next visit.

As soon as they entered by the front door it was clear that their caution was entirely justified. The overwhelming odour had not dissipated by one jot. They took a series of deep breaths and plunged into the spacious hallway.

The task they faced was to be a daunting one. The first room they tackled, the living room, was full of a wide variety of clutter, with half-read newspapers and piles of this, that and the other filling every available floor space and also commandeering every item of furniture.

When they opened the first drawer of an oak bureau they found it was stacked full of plastic supermarket bags. The second drawer was overflowing with sundry photographs which had never found their way into any album. Another drawer contained thousands of old postcards, representing a lifetime of holidays and excursions undertaken by Norma, and probably many memories of trips made by her parents, grandparents and great-grandparents.

It soon dawned on the two executors that Norma had plainly been a hoarder on a heroic scale.

A cupboard in the bureau was the home for thousands of newspaper cuttings, many of them relating to events involving the Royal Family, including The Times report on the funeral of Queen Victoria. The two men spent a few hours sifting through the cuttings, many of which gave a fascinating insight into the events of the 20th century.

Three particular newspaper articles stopped the pair in their tracks. They told of a 28-year-old Nottinghamshire farmer from Edlingley, near Newark, who had been gored to death by one of his bulls as he tried to load it into a trailer.

Wrapped up in one of the cuttings was a photograph of the farmer with an attractive young woman standing at his side.

Graham read the cuttings carefully and it had been reported that the farmer, Gordon Strawson, had recently become engaged to a woman from a well known local family called Miss Norma Whitehouse.

"This is sad, isn't it?" said Graham.

"It is indeed," said John. "Very sad. She was quite a looker in her day, wasn't she?"

"Quite stunning," said Graham "I understand she came from a very well-to-do family. Strange how she turned out in the end. This must have been a life-changing event for her. Poor Norma."

"Perhaps it explains why she developed what seemed to be a very thick hide in her later years," said John, brushing away a single tear which he had been unable to prevent from falling on to his cheek.

Their next visit to the house led them into the kitchen, which had as its crowning glory a rusting Victorian coal-fired range. A fridge-freezer and a washing machine were the only modern appliances in evidence.

Off the kitchen was an old-style pantry, burgeoning with tins of food, many of which looked scarily ancient. There was still room for more massive piles of empty bags, both of the plastic and brown paper variety.

There were signs of Marmaduke everywhere, including numerous food and water bowls, chewed-up doggy beds and mangled fluffy animals and squeaky toys from which the dog had long since removed the squeaks. All these still bore the instantly recognisable stink of their erstwhile playmate.

The treat of exploring the upper floor of the house was in store, involving several days of further work for the executors.

After a week's break so that they could catch up with their business affairs, John and Graham returned to their duties. First they examined what had obviously been Norma's bedroom. There were clothes strewn all over the bed and much of the floor but many more to be found in the large wardrobe.

There were hundreds of dresses which Norma had saved every year since her childhood. These included dozens of 1920s-style flapper dresses which were a very far cry from the staid outfits she wore in later life.

"She obviously liked having a good time," said Graham.

"I wonder if the good times stopped when she lost her fiance?" asked John.

The second bedroom was the next to be examined. That was where Ethel had been sleeping in recent years. But that too was dominated by Norma's clothes' collection, including a drawer stuffed with undergarments which the executors declined to examine in any detail.

On to the third bedroom – and there the men were in for a shock.

Graham turned the doorknob but found it impossible to open the door. There appeared to be a considerable weight bearing against it from inside the room. He tried pushing with his knee but that was to no avail. Then both men attempted a big heave-ho, which succeeded in opening the door by a couple of inches. They gave a mighty push and heard something big crashing to the ground along with a sound of shattering glass.

Eventually they managed to squeeze themselves into the edge of the bedroom. The scene confronting them was something they never could have imagined. There were items of furniture sitting askew on top of other pieces of furniture. What appeared to be a bed was covered with miscellaneous objects, including hundreds of books, ranging from "penny dreadfuls" to a 3000-page translation of Marcel Proust's "In Search of Lost Time", a heavy version of Dostoyevsky's "Crime and Punishment" and a beautiful illustrated but badly damaged copy of

John Bunyan's "The Pilgrim's Progress". The book "collection" was interspersed with random glass photographic slides and numerous old newspapers and magazines.

Various pieces of detritus were stacked up against the window, so much so that only a small chink of light was able to permeate the room. These objects included scores of old planters, some of these still containing soil and others spilling over with withered and cracked dead plants.

It took the men nine hours over three separate days to create a narrow passage from the door to a wardrobe which stood at the far side of the bedroom. When they eventually managed to force open the door of that wardrobe they found it was full of mackintoshes and overcoats. They were careful to go through the pockets of all of these garments as in other rooms of the house they had found oddments of money, including notes and coins.

John was rifling through the pockets of one mackintosh when he pulled out a small fragment of paper.

"Hey, Graham. Look at this," he called out, as he fumbled in his own pocket to find his spectacles.

"What is it?" asked his colleague.

"It's a bus ticket and it's dated just a week before Norma died."

"What?" shouted Graham as the implication of what they had found dawned on him.

John continued: "How could she possibly have got to the wardrobe to put this coat inside?"

"Are you sure you're right about the date?"

"Yes, I'm sure. It's for a trip into Nottingham. This is unbelievable."

The men were dumbstruck.

"Could it be that all this stuff was put into the bedroom after the bus trip?" asked Graham.

"Not a chance," replied John. "No one's had a key to the house except us – and Ethel for a few days after Norma died. "I can't imagine her coming from her care home and filling the room with all this stuff, can you?"

Graham laughed.

"No I can't imagine that."

"I think this will always remain as one of life's mysteries," said John.

****

The regular contact he had with Anita over childcare was good for the child but no good at all for Graham. He still got a thrill every time he saw her and even each time he spoke to her over the phone. He clung to a desperate hope that she would return to him. She might not be a one man woman but the sad fact was that he was a one woman man.

He had always known she was fickle and psychologically incapable of being totally faithful. She had extremely strong sexual urges, so much so that she could never be entirely trusted to restrict these to one partner – or two, three or four, ad infinitum. Having grudgingly accepted this fact Graham now discounted it. If Anita would come back to live with him he told himself he would have been willing to turn a blind eye to her transgressions. He was not entirely without a jealous streak, despite hating to admit that to himself, but was convinced that he would be able to suppress that side of his personality to keep his one love.

When he had time to think about it, Graham cleaved

86

strongly to the opinion that jealousy was corrosive of any healthy relationship. As the poet John Dryden had it, "Jealousy is the jaundice of the soul". George Eliot also hit the nail on the head with her declaration: "Jealousy is never satisfied with anything short of the omniscience that would detect the subtlest fold of the heart."

However, on other occasions he chided himself for thinking he could be so naive as to believe that he could entirely erase any feelings of jealousy from his character.

In truth he was suffering from an unreconcilable dichotomy. He loved Anita with every fibre of his being and had done so since the first time he met her in his college days. She was an angel incarnate whose every word and action he hung upon like a silly puppy. But simultaneously he knew that she was a worthless, quite crude individual, almost entirely selfish and capable of being cruelly cold. Throughout their relationship he had heard other people describe her as a "tart", an attractive "tart", but a "tart" nevertheless. And he knew they were right. But it didn't make any difference.

Graham's love for Anita became an obsession. When she came to collect Austin – something that happened less than he would have wished for – he made sure he was at home to see her, even though the nanny, Erica, was at hand to oversee the changeover. He would telephone her on the flimsiest of pretexts and even change his route to and from work so that he could drive past the Nottingham city centre flat she shared with George on the half-chance of catching a glimpse of her.

There were times when his behaviour would have been seen by some women as stalking. But Anita never did see it that way. In fact she did nothing to discourage him in his attentions. She saw him on occasions driving past her home, but she didn't mention it to anyone.

This reaction on her part was a manifestation of an important part of her character. She had no desire to let go of anyone. She was always flattered by the attention of men, even ones she had put on to her discard pile – perhaps only for the time being. To Anita, nothing in relationships was final. She never ruled out a change of direction in her love life, which meant that all her ex-lovers sensed that there might be a way back. They may have thought her behaviour towards them was cold and heartless but she was never openly nasty to them and rarely disparaging of them to new lovers. Her only disloyalty was sexual.

Of course, this only made things worse for Graham. He was unable to move on to any meaningful new relationship, even after their divorce was finalised. Anita was always the elephant in the room.

The saving grace of all this was that he did have the ability to compartmentalise his life. Even when he was married to Anita most of his waking hours were entirely concentrated on his business and his vision of a better future for capitalism.

****

Although Graham observed that capitalism was the best way of creating wealth and promoting and preserving free, happy and democratic societies, he also feared that it had within it the seeds of its own destruction. And this was because capitalist countries almost invariably tolerated wide divisions between rich and poor. Benjamin Disraeli famously highlighted the dilemma of the "two nations" in his novel "Sybil". Graham had read that and it was a description that frequently came into his mind.

He noted that the efforts by communist states to eradicate such divisions had totally failed, often resulting in even greater discrepancies in wealth and power. But he knew that there would always be those who would claim that "proper communism" had never yet been tried and would be willing to experiment with its theories again.

Both in terms of countering the threat of authoritarianism and in bringing about greater social justice, Graham had come to believe that capitalism needed to radically reform itself. Wealth needed to be shared more equitably, not through the dead hand of the State but through wider share ownership, property ownership and co-operative working.

He often thought back to that bar-room discussion he had had in Brighton with the young Anarcho-Syndicalist, Sebastian. Graham thought the man was extremely naive in believing that any form of anarchism was compatible with a civilised society, or in fact with man's flawed nature itself. However, there were some germs of ideas that Sebastian had put forward which were worth further consideration.

Mutuality was the word the young man had used a number of times and this concept had some appeal for Graham. If only owners, managers and other employees would work together towards a common goal then there might be no need for trade unions and strikes, or for the payment of low wages. Everyone should feel they had a stake in whatever business or other enterprise they were involved in.

As has been noted earlier, Graham was enough of an elitist to oppose the idea of putting, say, manual workers or retail counter staff on the boards of his companies. He did, though, wish to see everyone who worked for those companies getting a share in the profits and feeling their labour was properly valued.

He read widely on the subject of worker participation and wider share ownership. Putting his ideas into practice in his own business was one of the main motivations for his intense workload.

Chapter seven
Forging ahead

It is almost three decades later. Graham's career has gone strength to strength and he is seriously rich. His retail company now comprises 50 corner shops, including the two in Sanderholme previously run by his parents, and his property company owns around 500 rental dwellings throughout the East Midlands. He is chairman of the two companies and his son Austin, who has inherited his father's drive and work ethic, is their chief executive.

Graham's personal life, though, has not progressed at the same rate. He still owns the Nottinghamshire mansion, where Austin, his American wife, Phoebe, and family of a boy and a girl are in residence, as well as two dogs and a cat. Following his expensive divorce from Anita – now on her fourth marriage, to Darren, a some time musician and DJ 30 years her junior – Graham has never remarried. He has had a handful of casual relationships but has fought shy of anything approaching long-term commitment.

His parents, both in their mid-eighties and very healthy, are enjoying their retirement, spending half their year in Sanderholme and half at their villa in Valencia.

Jim Nott still runs the newsagents and has never married. His parents have passed away and for company he has acquired an adorable partner in the form of a beautiful chocolate labrador he has named as Benjy.

Graham himself, a fit and quite handsome 61-year-old with a lean figure and a good head of hair, has recently purchased a large house in a residential area called Marshsea, overlooking Sanderholme Golf Club and just a stone's throw from the beach. But this is in no way a holiday or retirement home. Graham has ambitious and exciting plans for his home town.

Over the years he has been an important benefactor to the town, supporting many local charities. However, the achievement which has given him most satisfaction has been spearheading and paying for the establishment of a multi-million pound high tech business studies suite at his old school, now renamed as Havenmarsh Academy.

Now, in 2018, a much more ambitious multi-million pound development he has planned is coming close to fruition – a retail, leisure and hotel complex centring on a section of the resort's boating lake. One end of the lake and the surrounding area has been been modernised and provides excellent leisure activities and a variety of eateries. But the other end has looked tired and has been only partially used for years.

The idea came to Graham while he was taking a stroll one day along the Sanderholme foreshore. Memories of his childhood came flooding back to him as he reached the boating lake. In an old book on the history of the town he had seen photographs of the extensive lake crammed with rowing boats. Gents in suits or blazers and flannels were showing off their rowing skills to their wives and girlfriends as they negotiated the packed lake. Some precocious fellows were even standing up in the boats and propelling them like canoes with single oars. There were signs of some "lake rage" as crafts bumped into each other or became held up in the traffic jam. There were several islands in the lake where some courting couples would surreptitiously tie up their boats to indulge in whatever such couples got up to on the grassy mounds between the trees.

When he was a toddler Graham's parents would often

take him for walks around the perimeter of the lake. This included a memorable walk undertaken one sunny summer's afternoon. This was the infamous day when Graham pooed his pants! His father removed the pants and decided to wring them out in the water at the edge of the lake. Unfortunately he bent over a little too far and fell headlong into the water. There was much hilarity among the holidaymakers who witnessed this embarrassing incident, and even Mrs Robinson had to strain herself to control her mirth as her husband shamefacedly scrambled up the concrete bank, dripping wet from head to toe.

This was a tale which remained in the Robinson family folklore forever and a day, much to the chagrin of Mr Robinson Snr.

When Graham was a little older the family were regular attendees at a weekly fireworks display held at the lake. The fireworks were let off from one of the islands while the audience sat on a tiered bank of concrete steps, rugs wrapped around their knees on what were usually chilly evenings.

As the years went by the boating lake was split into two, with the southern end now home to petrol-driven motor boats. It was here that Graham got his first job in the school summer holidays, helping customers in and out of the boats and showing them how to drive them.

Taking his stroll all these years later he was shocked and saddened by what he saw. The motor boats had gone and instead the southern end of the lake had become a kind of poor man's nature reserve.

There were some ducks to feed and hundreds of Canada geese which defecated liberally on the paths around the lake. A dead muntjac deer was floating in the water.

Something had to be done! And Graham's entrepreneurial spirit and imagination went into overdrive. In spite of the air of neglect which currently pervaded the area, he saw the potential attractiveness of the lake and its surroundings.

Over the next few years Graham became obsessed with the notion of developing the site commercially. So far he had built his successful business empire cautiously with the bottom line being the main consideration. Now he was dreaming of creating an enterprise which would not only be profitable but would also be an asset to the community he loved. But it would also be a risk. Sanderholme teemed with many thousands of visitors during the summer months but was a quieter place for the rest of the year. To make his proposed development viable Graham would need it to attract footfall all the year round. To achieve this he felt the project would have to be so impressive that people would willingly travel for miles to Sanderholme just to visit it.

The landscaped and waterscaped complex, called Beachworld, will comprise 50 retail outlet units, a conference centre, hotel, bars and restaurants, a garden centre, an outdoor craft market, children's adventure playground and large car park.

The development site borders the beach and the North Sea, which can be unpredictable, particularly during the winter months. Over-topping by high tides has caused flooding problems several times during Graham's lifetime and, before that, during the tragic East Coast Floods of 1953, when lives were lost in the area and extensive damage was caused to property. To guard against repetition of such incidents and to enable insurance cover to be obtained for the scheme, Graham has agreed to make huge financial contributions to additional sea defence works being carried out by the Environment Agency, including "beach nourishment" work and the raising of the existing sea wall.

To further Graham's dream he has put together a package backed by banks and big corporate investors. He has acquired the land from the local council on a 99-year lease and, despite strong and often angry opposition, has won planning permission for the scheme.

The opposition has come from a number of vociferous individuals and groups, who see the development as a threat to existing shops and markets, and from local nature conservation bodies, which are concerned about the effect on the nearby nature reserve.

However, there have been plenty of supporters too, who see the development as an opportunity to bring more people into the resort, especially during the winter and other off-peak times of the year.

Unfortunately, during the construction period there have been some serious setbacks, including two fires which destroyed retail units nearing completion, requiring them to be completely rebuilt. Arson is suspected in both cases but no culprits have ever been found.

****

One advantage of Graham's move back to Sanderholme is that he can be closer to his parents in their later years. Another is that he is able to see more of his old pal Jim Nott.

Jim has not aged as well as his friend. He is looking fatter and more dishevelled, with long grey ungroomed hair, growing not only on top of his head but also in alarming volumes in his ears and nose. He has a frightening grey pallor and smells even more strongly of tobacco than he has always done.

However, he has not declined mentally and has a dry and mischievous sense of humour which still greatly appeals to Graham. He also remains the biggest gossip in Sanderholme. He has collected a tremendous range of knowledge about local people and their embarrassing stories. When he tells his tales he always knows more than he will first admit to and will offer his hearers tasty morsels knowing they will come back for more. In fact it is rumoured that he increases his trade at the shop by stringing out his stories so customers have to return to find out the extra details.

His gossip-mongering could have led Jim to attract a number of enemies. But, strangely, this is not the case. Even those who have been the butt of his mischief have appreciated that there is no malice in him. Some have even been quite proud of the notoriety he has given them. People know that he is at heart a kindly and reliable man, with an indefinable charm and a smile always playing around his lips and eyes.

Jim always has a menu of juicy tittle-tattle to share with Graham when they meet and he unfailingly makes his friend laugh.

But one October afternoon he has some news which is no laughing matter: he has to go into hospital for a heart bypass. Disarmingly, he has no complaints to make about his condition, which he ascribes to a totally unhealthy diet. In fact he has his mother to thank for this, as she was always of the "old school" view that babies should be "as fat as butter" and that children needed plenty of stodge to give them energy. She continued to follow this food philosophy throughout Jim's adulthood. And when she died Jim stuck to the regime which she had instilled in him.

He tells Graham that his loyal staff at the shop have agreed to cover for him while he is away in hospital and during his recuperation. But he needs someone to look after his ageing and much-loved labrador, Benjy.

Graham is devastated by Jim's news. For the first time in his life thoughts of mortality strike him. "Look no further, mate," says Graham. "Benjy can come to my place and I will look after him for as long as you need me to."

"I would be ever so grateful," says Jim. "I know I can trust you and it's a load off my mind."

****

When construction work on Beachworld got under way Graham was keen to have every stage of the work recorded for promotional purposes and for the benefit of posterity.

He needed someone to visit the site regularly to take photographs and film videos. His thoughts immediately turned to his old school friend Trevor Bincroft, who over many years had established a reputation as the outstanding man in his trade throughout the county.

When Graham contacted him, Trevor immediately agreed to take on the work and also suggested that his wife, Shirley, could be useful for designing any promotional literature required for Beachworld.

The result was that Trevor and Shirley were both invited to Graham's office to discuss what exactly he needed to be done.

Graham had heard that Trevor had suffered a serious heart attack but was nevertheless shocked by the physical change in his old school friend. He had lost a great deal of weight, his face looked pinched and deeply lined and he was walking with a slight limp.

Shirley on the other hand had aged remarkably well and could have been taken for half her age.

The meeting began cordially and promised to be financially very rewarding for the couple.

A few months previously at one of the consultation meetings when planning permission was being sought for the development, Graham had noticed Trevor sitting quietly at the back of the room, but had no opportunity to speak to him.

"I saw you at one of the consultation sessions," said Graham, when they had completed their business meeting. "It was quite a noisy affair, wasn't it?"

Trevor replied: "Yes, it was certainly a bit stormy."

"There was a lot of unreasonable opposition, I thought," said Graham.

Trevor nodded but then said: "Some people got too heated. But I have to admit that I was one of those who was against your plans."

Shirley gave her husband a disapproving glance and Graham looked surprised.

"Oh, I see," he said. "I'm disappointed to hear that. What do you think now?"

"To be honest with you I haven't changed my mind. I think Beachworld could have a devastating effect on some of the long-standing traders in the town. And I don't like what's happening to the wildlife that used to congregate on the boating lake."

Shirley chipped in: "Trevor's a bit of the twitcher, I'm afraid."

Graham was somewhat crestfallen to be told that someone to whom he had just given lucrative work was actually opposed to his plans. Had Trevor not been a friend he would undoubtedly have shown him the door at that point.

He always relished a challenge, though, and he decided to make it his mission to change Trevor's mind.

"Have you not noticed that Sanderholme High Street has lost many of its better shops over recent years? For example, there are hardly any national chains represented now and there's a large number of charity shops and non-retail premises.

"My contention is that, far from harming existing businesses, Beachworld will actually benefit them because of the thousands of additional people it will attract to the town. Much as I might like them to stay all day at Beachworld and spend all their money with us, I am certain that's not what will happen. Most people will venture out to see what else the area has to offer. It will be a great opportunity for existing businesses to step up to the mark and improve their offer."

"You've got to be joking," said Trevor. "People only have a limited amount of money to spend. By the time they have spent their money at your place they won't have enough left to spend anywhere else."

"I couldn't disagree more," said Graham. "What we will be providing is healthy competition. Those who don't step up to the mark and improve their offer may well go to the wall. So be it.

"Just think of what the alternative would have been if your attitude had prevailed over the last century. If competition had been stifled as some backwoodsmen would wish, Sanderholme would only have one grocer's shop, one butcher's, one baker's, one candlestick maker's – one hotel. And would still have a deprived population of perhaps only one thousand, instead of the 20,000 it has today.

"And another thing – think of the hundreds of extra jobs which Beachworld will provide directly, and the hundreds more indirectly. Believe me, it will be a big boost to the town. In fact to the whole of Lincolnshire."

"Well, I can't accept for a minute what you say about jobs," said Trevor, warming to the argument. "There's loads of businesses now that can't recruit staff. If your development pinches hundreds of workers then the situation will get worse for everyone else."

"But I'm talking about growth," said Graham. "We will expand the town's trade, increase its population and make everyone better off."

"With due respect to you – and I really do respect you, Graham – that's just poppycock. You're looking at everything through rose-tinted spectacles.

"And – I've got my birdwatcher's hat on now – what about all the wildlife that is being chased out of the boating lake?"

"What wildlife did you have in mind?" asked Graham.

Trevor replied: "Lots of bird species have made that their home here for years now – several species of ducks such as shelduck, wigeon and teal. And there's the Canada geese and Brent geese. It's not just the birds who use the boating lake that are at risk though. Your site is next to the nature reserve, which is so important for migratory birds and all kinds of waders. They're bound to be affected by the noise and other disruption from your place, particularly that huge car park you're planning to have.

"And it's not just that. This end of the town has been a nice quiet area for people to enjoy, away from the hustle and bustle of the central area. Now it's going to be crowded out with noisy shoppers or the stag and hen parties your new hotel is bound to attract."

Graham replied: "I'll have to take you on a tour round our site. We are keeping the lake and spending a great deal of money on landscaping the whole area. I am sure that lots of birds will choose to stay with us, even the very messy geese with their foul, smelly droppings. If some do decide to move on then the nature reserve is huge. I'm sure they will find plenty of places to go. We have already planted hundreds of trees to provide a buffer between the car park and the salt marsh. So we'll be keeping disruption to a minimum.

"As for stag and hen parties, we will definitely be doing all we can to discourage that kind of trade. We will be turning a rundown area of the town into a vibrant but tasteful haven for our visitors. And, of course, locals will be able to use it as well. I think they will love it. I think people from throughout Lincolnshire will love it too, Many more of them will decide that Sanderholme is a great place for a day out. The town's still thriving, but to keep its position as one of the country's top tourist destinations it needs a new magnet for visitors – and this will be it.

"A lot of the people who are opposed to Beachworld are quite frankly living in the past. They would like Sanderholme to go back to being some imaginary sedate resort which they believe may have existed in the 1950s. It's largely a myth – and we can't go backwards. We have to cater for today's tourists and all the statistics show that a good retail experience is one of their very favourite leisure pursuits.

"Sanderholme is a wonderful resort. It's got some of the best sandy beaches in the country, it's climate is dry and sunny and there's been some exciting developments here over the last few years. If we stand still we will die. Have you seen all the rundown holiday resorts round the British coast? Some of them are desolate because they haven't kept up with the trends. They have social problems that are as bad, if not worse, than those in some of the inner cities.

"We can provide a massive boost to the local economy – more money, more jobs and higher wages for local people. It's a win, win for everyone."

"I wish I could share your optimism," said Trevor. "But I'm afraid I can't."

Graham was becoming increasingly dismayed by the turn the conversation had taken.

"You've got a successful business, Trevor. I can't believe that you're so deadbeat about my business. Are you sure you want to work for Beachworld? If your heart isn't in it then perhaps we need to rethink our arrangement."

Trevor replied: "I'm a professional. If you give me a job I will do it and do it properly. I wouldn't have wasted my time coming here today if that wasn't the case. I can put my personal views to one side. Do you remember when I used to work for Farndales, taking the walking pictures? Did you know I hated that job? I hated making small talk with the grockles. But I did it – and I did it really well. I made loads of money for that firm.

"I am quite capable of turning out some bloody good pictures which will make your place look fabulous. And Shirley will produce some really great brochures and advertising material for you. I can absolutely promise that. I can put my own views on the back burner."

While this conversation was progressing Shirley was shuffling uncomfortably in her seat, looking discontented and longing to have her own say. Now she found the opportunity.

"I just want to say that I totally disagree with my husband."

She turned towards Trevor, whom she seldom contradicted, and said: "Sorry, dear."

"I think Beachworld will be marvellous for the town – just the tonic we need to breathe some extra life into it. I'm looking forward very much to designing some great promotional stuff for you. Just looking around the site my brain's already brimming over with ideas.

"Don't take too much notice of Trevor. Once he gets a camera in his hand he turns into a true artist. He will never let you down."

Trevor had seemed rather put out when his wife suggested that Graham shouldn't take too much notice of him, but then looked as pleased as Punch to be have been described as an artist.

Graham was partially convinced by what he had just heard but nevertheless felt he needed to lay down the law.

"I'm disappointed, Trevor, that you are not fully on board with my project. I believe you when you say you will perform professionally. But if you want this job I need you to give me an assurance that you will keep your negative views to yourself for the duration of your work here. Also I want you to promise me that you won't attend any meetings or make any public statements critical of what I am doing here. If you step out of line, you'll be out on your ear."

Trevor bridled at that last remark.

"There's no need for that sort of threat, but of course I'll behave myself. You have my word."

Graham smiled and stood up and shook Trevor's hand.

"I'm sure that over the next few months I will be able to change your mind about Beachworld," he said.

"By the way, have I ever told you about my business methods as regards treatment of my workforce? Every single person who works for me gets a share in the profits, whether it's through shares in my companies, or performance bonuses. And this will be the case at Beachworld. It will be a great place to work. I intend to provide jobs for the kids who have studied at the Business Suite at Havenmarsh Academy. I will be offering lots of apprenticeships in the hospitality sector. Some of those apprentices will become my managers. Good jobs for local people. That's my vision here."

Shirley, who ran a graphic design course at the Academy, expressed her enthusiasm for these aspirations. Trevor stayed mum.

Chapter eight
Good friends

Walking Jim's dog Benjy gave Graham the opportunity to soak up the atmosphere of the salt marsh which extends for many miles south of the built-up area of Sanderholme, skirting past the Marshsea golf course and residential area. The tracks through the marsh run behind the dunes parallel to the sandy beach and the North Sea.

On one particular fine, sunny afternoon a thin haze hovered over the shimmering sea, obscuring the usual view of the multiplicity of wind turbines a few miles out and of the Norfolk coastline further away. A bracing easterly wind had enough bite to redden the faces of a handful of afternoon strollers, who were otherwise well covered up against any unfavourable elements. In the distance two or three souls were venturing on to the flat golden sand which stretched southwards as far as the eye could see. They looked like figures plucked out of a Lowry painting and plonked onto a new beachy canvas well away from their industrial home.

Benjy was the ideal walking companion, trotting along perfectly in step with Graham for mile after mile and only stopping very occasionally for a pee or to sniff at an especially juicy piece of grass. Sometimes he would look longingly at the numerous tiny paths which were threaded through the undergrowth on the side of the marsh which bordered the town. But he was too well behaved and good-natured to deviate from the main track unless Graham relented and let him do some exploring.

The dog's perfect behaviour allowed Graham to become lost in his own thoughts and imaginings. He cast his mind back to his childhood when he would visit the marshes with his mother, father and paternal grandmother. These visits would usually take place on Sunday afternoons, with the family's Daimler car parked up on the esplanade which overlooked a large lagoon produced by a breach in the sandhills which helped to keep the North Sea at bay. This lagoon sometimes froze over in the winter, providing a tempting skating rink for local families. Graham's father was an accomplished skater, who had his own ancient set of skates inherited from his own father. These would be dragged out of retirement once a year for a session on the lagoon. Graham was allowed his own turn with the skates, but he always lost interest quite quickly after falling over a couple of times.

The main object of the Sunday afternoon walks would be to forage for food. In the late summer there was a plenitude of blackberries to be picked and Graham enjoyed eating them straight from the bushes, invariably ending up with purple hands and lips. He loved blackberry pies and crumbles but was always a little disappointed when his grandmother turned most of the berries into a tart blackberry vinegar to put on to cereals. They also used to harvest samphire, which would be pickled, making it, in Graham's view, quite inedible. It was only later in his adult life that he came to appreciate fresh samphire served with fish and other dishes, a seriously good health food.

At the end of the esplanade, south of the lagoon, the main track branched off into a number of smaller paths winding their way through the flat, marshy terrain, some grassy, some muddy and most a mixture of the two. The landscape, containing sea lavender, which had an attractive lilac colour in summer, sea aster, sea purslane and a profusion of sea couch-grass, was broken by a number of shallow creeks, which attracted gulls and a variety of ducks and small seabirds. Between this area and the sea were extensive sandhills, held together with marram grass, and then wide expanses of beach regularly washed by the tides. Inland from the mudflats was a long scrubby thicket, mainly comprising sea buckthorn bushes interspersed with elder, privet, hawthorn and a few other slightly incongruous varieties of stumpy deciduous trees. The sandy soil was pitted with rabbit holes.

Every few hundred yards or so were well-trodden narrow tracks leading to the avenues of salubrious Marshsea residences. Graham knew all of these tracks well and could easily pinpoint which avenue each led to. But what always intrigued him were the many little "unofficial" paths which disappeared into the undergrowth. On his walks with Benjy, and somewhat to the dog's surprise as he had now become used to staying on the main drag, Graham would sometimes take a short detour to explore one of these small paths. Most of them led to nowhere, just petering out after a few yards. A few led to small clearings in the thicket, perfect places for a quiet picnic or a love tryst. Morbidly, Graham also thought they would be ideal for burying a body. However, so far his swift inspections of these areas had revealed little more than empty drink cans, used contraceptives and discarded takeaway boxes.

One day when he was walking Benjy, two male heads had suddenly popped up above the buckthorn surrounding one of these clearings – and then popped down again just as quickly when they realised they had been spotted. He recognised one of the heads as belonging to a well known Sanderholme solicitor. How embarrassing!

Graham had always been intrigued by isolation and "hidden places", such as lofts, attics, derelict factories, deserted farmhouses, mountain bothies and tiny islands in the middle of remote Scottish lochs. His imagination ran riot as he contemplated their mysteries and what stories they might have to tell.

This was an example of his "split personality". When work allowed, he could be gregarious, a welcoming, if diffident, host with a wide circle of acquaintances and what many might have been considered to be an exciting social life. On the other hand he loved times when he could be totally isolated from the world, choosing solitary holidays on remote islands or just walking alone in the countryside. His best schemes were laid in these situations, or alone in bed in the wee hours of the morning.

So on his visits to the Lincolnshire salt marshes he loved to investigate the seldom visited clearings among the thickets and the remains of the abandoned World War Two pillboxes, so called because of their oval shape. These concrete structures were a type of blockhouse normally equipped with loopholes through which defenders could fire weapons whilst being protected against small arms fire and grenades.

Graham thoroughly enjoyed his daily walks with Benjy, a quiet, undemonstrative and obedient companion, not given to interrupting his thoughts and his daydreams.

On this particular pleasant day, there to be an interruption – but not from Benjy.

As Graham and the dog were about half way along their usual three mile journey they saw a woman walking towards them from the direction of the sandhills. She was tall and looked quite well built in her smart, long black overcoat. She was hatless, revealing thick light brown hair tied up in a bun. The woman had a pleasant welcoming face. Her complexion was on the florid side, but that had been accentuated by the biting wind.

As she got closer to Graham she started to smile broadly and said: "Graham. Hello Graham."

"Hi Miriam. Fancy seeing you here."

She came up close and gave him a kiss on the cheek.

Leaning forward to pat Benjy on the head, she said: "He looks like a very nice dog."

"He is. He's not my dog. He belongs to Jim Nott, the newsagent. You may remember him from school."

"I vaguely remember him at school, but I know him better from the shop. I sometimes buy a newspaper or a magazine from him."

"Poor old Jim's in hospital having a heart bypass operation."

"Oh dear. I'm sorry to hear that. Give him my best regards."

Benjy began to nuzzle into Miriam's legs in the hope of a cuddle.

What's the dog's name?" she asked.

"Benjy. He's a nice dog to walk. He's used to coming this way most days with Jim."

"You're a lovely boy, aren't you, Benjy?" said Miriam, bending down to stroke him.

When she had given the dog sufficient attention she turned back to Graham and said: "You're involved in the Beachworld development aren't you, Graham?"

"Yes, it is my project actually. I'm really quite excited about it."

"I bet you are. It will be wonderful for the town."

"I'm pleased you think that way. It should bring loads of money into the town and hundreds of jobs. I wish everyone thought like you do. We've had to fight every inch of the way to get the planning permission. Some people think I'm the devil incarnate."

"Old stuffy fuddy-duddies. It's the same with everything anyone wants to do in the town. The same stick-in-the-muds get upset about it."

"I don't so such mind about the stick-in-the-muds," said Graham. "They're just worried about change. They'd like to keep Sanderholme the way it was in their youth. The ones that really bother me are those businessmen who have done their own developments over the years but now don't want anyone else to make any money. Pure jealousy and unenlightened self-interest."

"Yes, I agree with you," said Miriam. "That's what it is. I would call it selfishness. Everyone will benefit from the extra people your development will bring into the area. We've got to move with the times. And anyway I can't wait to get into the new shops. It's about time we had some modern shops and national brands in Sanderholme."

"I can't tell you how much you're cheering me up with your positive attitude."

"Well, it's right."

"Do you still live in Lavender Avenue?" asked Graham.

"Yes, still in the same old house," said Miriam. "Still home alone."

"Oh, right."

"I believe you may live near to one of my old friends, Trevor Bincroft, and his wife, Shirley."

"Yes, of course. They're my next door neighbours.

Shirley's so lovely, a really cheerful lady, and Trevor. Well, Trevor's Trevor. He never really changes. He's got a heart of gold but he can sometimes be…"

"A bit of a Contrary Mary?"

"I didn't say that," said Miriam, laughing. "He's lovely really. His health has not been good, but he's been a lot better these last few months."

"I had heard that he'd not been well."

Graham was aware that Miriam Metcalfe had had a couple of failed marriages, but knew little else about her circumstances. He knew that she came from a wealthy family of amusement caterers and assumed that she was still involved in the various businesses. He also recalled that she had a couple of grown-up daughters. That was just about the sum total of his present knowledge of her.

Miriam had attended the same secondary school as Graham, but was a few years younger.

As a young woman she had been very attractive, tall, with a good full figure, a winning smile and a cheerful disposition, even if her stature made her look a little formidable. As a woman now in her late fifties she had retained her good looks and sunny outlook on life, in spite of trials and tribulations with a number of men who had let her down badly.

"Nice to see you again, Graham. I get home along that path," said Miriam, pointing to one of the trails through the undergrowth.

"Nice to see you too," said Graham. "I'll make sure you get an invitation to the launch of Beachworld."

"That would be lovely," she said. "When will that be?"

"We're hoping to open at Easter, but the official opening will probably be at Spring Bank Holiday."

"I'll look forward to it. See you soon."

"Yes, goodbye," said Graham.

As he continued his walk he felt contented. He had very much enjoyed this brief encounter. Meeting Miriam took him back to his school days and to his youth amid the town's social whirl. But it was more than that. He felt an animal attraction to Miriam. Although in the past she had had a reputation of being something of a "good time girl", friends had assured him that she was basically wholesome, decent and kindly natured. They had never been close, but she appeared to have been genuinely pleased to see him. He also appreciated the support she had shown for Beachworld – his overriding passion these days. He hoped he would meet Miriam again on one of his walks.

And he did. The very next day.

Some would say this was a good example of synchronicity. But they would be wrong. Graham hadn't achieved his success in life by trusting to wacky theories or superstitions. He laid carefully thought-out plans.

He figured that Miriam would have chosen to live in Lavender Avenue because she would wish to take full advantage of its proximity to the beach. He reckoned that a woman of her age, with no pressing ties, might become a creature of habit and take a stroll across the marshes and on to the beach at a certain time of day. So he planned his next outing with Benjy along exactly the same route and at precisely the same time as his walk of the previous day.

Why? Because when he had met Miriam he had instantly felt a connection. There was a chemistry between them the like of which he had seldom experienced before. This was not the sexual chemistry he had always had with Anita. It had been a brief but warm meeting between two mature people who were comfortable both in their minds and their bodies. It occurred to him – and it had occurred to Miriam too – that they had always liked each other from a distance. Since schooldays they had seldom met and when they had seen each other it was only to say a cursory "hello, how are you doing?" However, suddenly they both felt that it was a pity that they had not known each other better.

As he strode along the well-trodden path with Benjy trotting obediently behind, he kept his eyes skinned in case he saw Miriam. Little did he know that she was similarly on the lookout for him as she took her afternoon constitutional.

The routine Graham had adopted was to walk about a mile along a muddy path, the main route parallel to the beach and sea, until it reached a certain sycamore tree and then turn around to go back the way he had come. The tree was at the junction between the main path and a smaller track through the marsh which led to the beach. As Graham reached the tree he looked seaward. He saw a human figure on the crest of the sandhills which separated the marsh from the beach. At first the figure was unrecognisable, merely one of the Lowry matchstick-people. But as it got closer Graham felt his heart beating faster. It was her.

As soon as Miriam recognised Graham she raised her hand slightly to give a coy wave. Graham did likewise. Benjy was spinning round impatiently wishing to start his walk home.

"Hello, Graham," she said.

"Hello, Miriam. How are you today?"

"I'm good, thanks," said Miriam. "This is a nice surprise. We don't see each other for years and then twice in two days."

"Yes, quite a coincidence," said Graham.

They were both being arch. This was no coincidence at all nor an example of serendipity. Just two plans happily coming together.

They chattered contentedly about nothing of importance for ten minutes or so. Most of us spend years of our waking lives in just such a way. But their conversation was, predictably, rudely brought to a close by Benjy. Having abandoned his spinning effort he decided to use the ultimate doggy tactic to persuade his stand-in servant to lead him homewards – barking very loudly and continuously.

"I think we have to go," said Graham.

"Oh, I was going to ask you if you fancied coming to mine for a coffee," said Miriam.

"I would love to. But I'm afraid the dog would just be a pain. He's a brilliant dog but absolutely a creature of habit and he will play up if I don't take him home along the usual route. Perhaps another time?"

"Yes, why don't you pop round tomorrow – in the morning before you take the dog?"

"I'd like that. What time shall we say?"

"Eleven?"

"Eleven it is. What's your address by the way? I think I know the house but just to be sure."

"It's The Cedars, 9 Lavender Avenue."

"Okay, I'll be there."

Benjy jumped up, almost knocking Graham off his feet.

"I think we have to go now!" he said.

"I think you do," said Miriam, laughing. "See you tomorrow. We can have a chat about old times."

"We certainly can. Bye."

As Graham strode along home, trying to keep up with the dog, he felt a warm glow inside. He had very few close friends but he had the strong feeling that he was at the foothills of gaining a new one. And he could not help speculating that this just might be a friendship that could blossom into a romantic attachment. His wealth made him wary of the motives of new female acquaintances but in the case of Miriam he had no such qualms. He guessed that she was quite well off in her own right and past the age of having the mercenary ambitions of some of the younger women he had encountered.

****

The next morning Graham took the short walk from his own house to Miriam's. It was a dull and damp October day, a brisk east wind making it quite chilly for the time of year. Graham had taken care with his appearance. He was well groomed and wearing a smart navy blue overcoat over a powder blue pullover, a checked shirt and dark grey trousers.

Miriam's was a large 1930s-built, four-bedroomed detached house in a pleasant tree-lined avenue only a few yards from the salt marsh. It had extensive gardens front and back, bordered by mature cedars and with well maintained lawns.

As she greeted him at the front door he was struck by how much younger she looked than when he had seen her in her sensible outdoor clothes. Her light brown hair looked luxuriant as it cascaded over her shoulders and she looked slimmer in her green V-necked jumper and black trousers.

She led him into her large comfortable sitting room where the modern designer furnishings were exquisitely tasteful despite being surprisingly out of character with the traditional exterior of the house.

She showed him to an easy chair and then went to the kitchen to bring coffee.

"It's cold today," said Graham as an opening gambit on her return.

"Terribly cold," Miriam replied. "I was out this morning and I was pleased to get back in again. I would have stayed in but I was doing my daily Good Samaritan thing."

"Oh, yes. What does that involve?"

"There's a group of men living rough in the thicket at the end of the road. I feel sorry for them so I take them some soup each morning. I know I'm daft, but I can't bear to see people looking cold and hungry."

"That's very kind of you. And quite brave too. Are they okay?"

"They seem harmless enough. Down on their luck, I suppose. There's usually four of them. There's one I don't much care for and a couple who don't say very much – just sit there looking miserable. But one guy's really charming. He seems quite upper crust so I don't really know how he's come to be living rough."

"It's often drugs or drink that lead people to live like that," said Graham.

"It could be that. You don't like to ask."

"I admire what you're doing. But you should be careful."

"That's what my daughters keep telling me. But hey-ho you only live once so you might as well do someone some good."

Looking around the room it was obvious to Graham that this was not an isolated act of generosity on Miriam's behalf. He could see several photographs of her presenting what looked like charity cheques and there were posters and other paperwork lying around the room relating to the Royal British Legion and the Royal National Lifeboat Institution.

"Do you do a lot of charity work?" he asked.

"Well, I suppose I do my bit. My daughter Annette and her husband run the businesses these days and, as you know, I have no husband to look after, or bother me, so I've got to do something with my time. I enjoy helping out with these things and then I have my golf and my 'ladies who lunch' pals, so I keep pretty busy."

She said all this with a contented smile which Graham took to be an indication of a well-rounded person.

"I admire you. I wish I had the charitable impulses that you have."

"I'm not some boring do-gooder, you know. I just like helping out where I can. Anyway, I think you do a lot for the community. That business centre of yours at the school – that's a great thing to do for the town."

"I've never really looked at it as charity," said Graham. "I'm interested in business – in success. In fact I've never really thought very much about my motivation for doing it. Perhaps I just wanted the words 'The Robinson Business Studies Suite' plastered all over the place and recorded in the local history books. But seriously, though, I do want to do a bit of good for the area and its young people."

"There you are. You *are* a charitable person. I think a

lot of people are very grateful to you for what you have done. Some people have told me you're bound to get an MBE or something."

Graham smiled broadly: "Perhaps that's my real motivation then. It's just all about me."

"I'm sure that's not true. You're too modest."

"No one's ever accused me of that before – certainly not in the boardroom. But enough about me. I'm interested in what you have been up to all these years."

Miriam shrugged her shoulders.

"Nothing very much, I'm afraid. I've carried on with the businesses that my parents built up. I haven't done much to change the businesses or expand them. I've brought up two smashing daughters and I've managed to lose two useless husbands. That's about it really."

"You said you live here alone?"

"Yes, both my daughters left home years ago. Gail lives in Spain with her partner and they run a bar there. Gail has two young daughters, Lily and Lucy, from a failed marriage. Annette still lives in Sanderholme. She's married and has two lovely little boys. I see her nearly every day. So I'm not lonely at all. I keep myself busy."

"No man in your life at present then?" asked Graham.

Miriam shook her head.

"I think the last two men in my life were enough to be going on with. I've been on my own for ten years now."

"I don't want to pry, but I guess you've had some bad experiences. I did hear a few things on the grapevine."

"You will have done. Terry was a serial adulterer and eventually didn't even bother to hide the fact. God knows how many children he's fathered around the town. And Wayne? Well the least said the better. Suffice to say that I was lucky to get away with my life."

"That bad?"

"That bad. He would beat me for the smallest reason. A total control freak. It was the booze that changed him. When I met him he was a real gentleman and he still could be on occasions. But drink turned him into a wild animal, a paranoid maniac. I don't really want to say too much about it."

"I completely understand that. I'll shut up."

"But what about you?" asked Miriam. "Who do you have in your life?"

"I have a son called Austin, who heads up my businesses these days. He's married to an American girl called Phoebe and they have a son, Edward, who's 18 and heading towards university, and a daughter, Sophie, who's 15 and bright as a button. And me? I don't have a woman in my life. You know I was married to Anita Albright? The marriage lasted for four years before she went off with another fella. It was bound to happen. I don't think she was ever cut out for a long-lasting marriage. But the experience had a profound affect on me. I just haven't been able to trust anyone since she left. I've had a few brief flings but I only seem to attract money grubbers. Anita was the only person I have ever really loved. More fool me."

"You shouldn't give up," said Miriam. "You're a good looking man for your age."

"Nice of you to say so. Flattery will get you everywhere."

The pair talked for a couple of hours, about times past, times present and their hopes for times to come. Their conversation was wide ranging and incessant, both being impressed by the character of the other and yet a little puzzled.

Miriam found Graham to be amiable company, eager to listen to whatever she was saying. She had quickly discerned that he was clever, successful, highly ambitious, incredibly driven and interesting. But she guessed that he had a gaping void in his life. He needed a woman to give him company, to understand his ideas and to share in his achievements.

Graham's view of Miriam was that she was warm, kind, family-orientated and overtly satisfied with her lot. There was something, though, about the matter-of-fact and passionless way that she articulated her situation which led him to think that she too needed more in her life to make her truly fulfilled.

Graham found himself entirely at ease with Miriam but on this, their first proper meeting, he was keen not to overstay his welcome. He eventually said he ought to be getting "a spot of lunch" and then carrying out his Benjy-walking duties.

"We must do this again," said Miriam.

"We must," replied Graham. "At mine next time perhaps."

They exchanged telephone numbers and agreed to meet up again at the same time the next week.

Graham didn't go straight home for lunch. Instead he walked towards the beach. He had been intrigued by what Miriam had told him about the men living rough in the undergrowth adjoining the salt marsh.

At the end of the road was an overgrown grassy path leading towards the beach. At either side were largely impenetrable collections of sea buckthorn bushes, brambles and the odd small sycamore. But on the left hand side of the path he noticed a small gap between the bushes. He pushed his way through this, not without scratching his hand on a stray bramble stem and nettling his leg. He found a round clearing with obvious signs of human habitation.

There were a couple of bedraggled and dirt-encrusted structures which could have been described as tents, but in reality were nothing more than sheets of canvass propped up precariously by a few thin tree branches. Various items of clothing were strewn across the top of the "tents", presumably in the vain hope of their getting dried. The ground alongside was littered with empty beer cans, plates of half-eaten meals, soiled groundsheets and various piles of unrecognisable and disgusting general detritus. There were grey patches of ashes where fires had been lit and various holes dug in the corners of the site which Graham conjectured might be makeshift lavatories. He was shocked by what he took to be evidence of human degradation.

As he stood surveying the scene he could hear rustling from the bushes behind him. As he looked around a man appeared – an imposingly tall man of willowy stature, with thick, long, grey hair and a wispy beard.

Graham was startled but was soon reassured by the man's broad smile.

"Hello," said the man. "Are you having a walk?"

"Yes," replied Graham. "Just doing some exploring."

"Bit of a mess our little home, isn't it?" said the man, who had a surprisingly cultured Southern accent.

"We must have a clear-up," he laughed.

The crackling of twigs announced the appearance of another man, a short ill-shaven individual with cropped black hair and a large bald patch and fierce starey scary blue eyes.

Addressing Graham in a brusque manner, he said: "What's up, pal?"

"Nothing's *up*," said Graham. "I was just having a stroll and I happened upon this clearing."

"Okay. On yer bike then. Enjoy your walk," said the man.

"Good day to you," said Graham sharply pushing his way between the bushes to return to the path.

As he walked back home he pondered on what had just happened. He had been appalled that people would choose to live in the conditions he had seen. He was shocked that anyone could have such lack of self-respect.

Other thoughts troubled him too. The second man he had met had been quite frighteningly hostile. Graham's thoughts took him all the way back to the time of the Brighton bomb. He remembered the aggressive looking man he had passed on the promenade, whom he had always thought of as the personification of evil. The man he had just met reminded him of that man, not physically but because of the air of menace he had about him. But, ironically, it was the first man, the friendly one, who had made him feel strangely uneasy. There was something about the tone of his voice and his manner of speaking which gave him an uncanny feeling of deja vu. He had sounded eerily familiar. However, Graham very quickly dismissed this notion as just a passing fancy.

****

For the past 20 years Trevor and Shirley Bincroft had been living next door to Miriam. Their photographic and graphic design business had thrived and they had a grown-up daughter and three grandchildren.

However, in fairly recent times their fortunes had taken a turn for the worse when Trevor suffered his serious heart attack. Shirley had proved to be a very capable carer and Miriam too had stepped up to the mark and been a great help and support to her neighbours.

Trevor was now well on the road to recovery but his doctor had warned him to "take it steady" for a few months yet.

On the same day as Graham and Miriam had been enjoying their coffee morning, Trevor and Shirley were in their kitchen having an animated discussion.

"You've got to stop fretting about this and cool down. Otherwise you'll put yourself at risk of another heart attack," said Shirley. "You can't do anything about it so just leave it alone."

The subject they were discussing was what Trevor described as "the invasion" of the Lavender Avenue area by the four "men in the marsh".

He had become increasingly incensed by the presence of the group in what was one of the smartest areas of the town.

"Why can't they get proper jobs and live in proper houses like everyone else?" he asked. "They're just useless druggies and the mess they make of the beach area is disgusting."

Shirley had become worried that Trevor was becoming obsessed by the men, to the extent that he was continually taking photographs of their camp site when they were not there and then using these in a series of complaints to the police and the district council.

Shirley regularly visited Havenmarsh Academy to teach graphic design and she had told Trevor she had seen one of the men hanging around outside the school at afternoon leaving times.

"You see. Up to no good," Trevor had said. "I bet they're selling drugs to kids."

His wife said she had reported the matter to the head teacher and he had asked the school's security officer to investigate clandestinely. But since then the man had not been seen near the school again.

"I want you to promise me that you will stop going to the beach to take photos of that camp site," said Shirley to Trevor. "If these blokes are as bad as you say they are you might put yourself in danger. You're spending too much time on this and getting worked up about it. It's not healthy, love."

Trevor grudgingly agreed to his wife's demands. But he did not let the matter drop entirely. He told Shirley that he was unhappy that by keeping the men "fed and watered" Miriam was encouraging them to stay.

As what he promised would be his last act of "meddling" in the matter he suggested he went to see Miriam and express his concerns.

"Very well, if you must," said Shirley. "But don't go upsetting Miriam after all she did for us when you were ill. I'm sure she means well."

"Of course I won't upset her. I'll be as diplomatic as I can."

That evening he rang Miriam's doorbell and she scurried along the hall to open the front door.

"Oh, hello, Trevor," she said warmly.

"Hello, Mrs Metcalfe," said Trevor. "I wonder if you could spare me a few minutes to discuss something which is concerning me?"

After all the years he had spent meeting people as a photographer and businessman, Trevor remained socially awkward. Even though he had lived next door to Miriam for many years he still addressed her by her surname and would have felt uncomfortable displaying any greater familiarity.

Miriam showed him into the sitting room and asked what she could do for him.

"It's about those blokes who are camping at the end of our road. I think they're wrong'uns. I don't think we ought to encourage them. I'm sure they're into drugs and god knows what other criminal activities. One of them's even been seen hanging around outside the Academy. He might be a paedophile or selling drugs to the kids. And the mess they've made down there in the bushes. It's terrible. They're living like animals."

Miriam smiled and replied: "Shirley's told me that you're up in arms about these men and I can understand your worries. But I've seen them quite a few times now and I don't believe there's any harm in them. I think they're just drop-outs. One of them, the tall, gangly one, is actually very pleasant and really grateful for the little things I do for them. They may be on drugs – I don't know – but they pretty much keep themselves to themselves."

"Mrs Metcalfe," said Trevor. "You'll never know how grateful Shirley and I are for the help you gave us after I had my heart attack. It was far more than anyone could have expected from a neighbour. And I realise that it's the same good-heartedness that leads you to help these blokes. I've met the lanky one in the street and I agree that he's always polite. But he's only one out of four and he's not the smartest looking person in the world. He's got a strange way of speaking too. That might be down to drugs.

"I'm not the only one who's unhappy about them being here. Quite a few other people along the avenue are concerned too. And we're all worried that you might be putting yourself in danger. There's quite a few children live down the avenue and I'm sure you wouldn't want to put any of them at risk. So I would just ask you to consider ending your help to them."

"Of course I wouldn't want to put anyone in danger, Trevor. And I'll think about what you've said. But I have to say I think you're over-dramatising the situation. I'm just trying to do a bit of good for some fellow human beings."

"Well, I've said my piece, Mrs Metcalfe, and that's it. Goodnight and thank you for listening to me."

Miriam did think long and hard about what Trevor had said. He and Shirley had been very good neighbours and Shirley, in particular, had become a close friend. The last thing Miriam wanted to do was to fall out with them.

The problem she faced was a common one, and one shared by most reasonable human beings on the planet – the dilemma of holding two contradictory views at the same time. She believed that everything Trevor had said about "the men in the marsh" was correct. They were "undesirables" to be inhabiting a respectable area. On the other hand she considered what she was doing to help them was just a straightforward act of Christian charity for which she should not be condemned.

The decision that she made to continue to provide the men with sustenance was perhaps born out of some feelings of guilt, perhaps sub-conscious but nonetheless real. In material terms she had enjoyed a gilded life. She had been born into a relatively rich family and carrying on the well established family businesses had been happily stress-free.

After breaking out of her two nightmare marriages she had at first been determined to live a life of pleasure. This had involved regular visits to local pubs and night clubs, much to the embarrassment on occasions of her two loving daughters who frequented the same establishments. She spent lots of money on posh restaurants, expensive cocktails and holidays in exotic climes. But after a few years she tired of this lifestyle, finding it too superficial and unrewarding. There had always been a side to her character which had been more serious, partly evidenced by the fact that she had never ceased to be an adoring, caring and responsible mother.

Gradually, she became more of a homebird and spent more of her spare time with her family, especially with her two grandsons whom she doted on. Her other favourite activities were playing golf, tending her large garden or helping with local charities. She still enjoyed a good night out but always felt a tinge of guilt that there were more important things in life to be focussed on. Since childhood she had nominally been a Christian, of the moderate Church of England tendency. In latter years she had begun to attend church quite regularly and she sought to actively incorporate the messages she received there in her everyday life.

The story of the Good Samaritan was one which she had taken very much to heart.

****

The following week, when Miriam accepted Graham's invitation to have morning coffee at his house, the conversation turned to the makeshift camp in the clearing.

"Are you still giving food to those chaps at the end of your road?" he asked.

"Yes. I sense that you don't approve."

"It's not that. I'm just a little worried for you. When you told me about those men I was feeling inquisitive so I went to have a look at where they were living. I found their camp site but then two of them turned up. One was friendly but the other one was quite aggressive, I thought."

"I think I can guess which two you mean. The other two men are very quiet and seem to just stay in the background. But, yes there is a friendly one and a surly one."

"I hope you don't think I'm interfering," said Graham.

"No, not at all. Apart from perhaps the gruff one, I think the blokes are grateful for their soup. They look so forlorn sometimes. It's the least I can do for them."

"Some people would say that you're just encouraging them to stay longer. Have any of your neighbours said anything about what you do?"

"I'm sure that there are some that don't approve. As a matter of fact I had a bit of a lecture about it from Trevor Bincroft. But who knows what has led to those men living the way they do? We're all human beings after all. Why don't you come with me one day? Then I think you'll agree there's nothing dangerous about them."

"All right, I will do. Perhaps tomorrow? I would feel better if I came with you."

"Ten o'clock tomorrow then."

Chapter nine
Meeting the men

They set off the next morning with freshly made soup in a litre-size thermos flask and a bag full of buttered bread rolls. They were met at the entrance to the clearing by the tall friendly man Graham had met on the previous occasion.

"Hello, Matthew," said Miriam. "How are you today? This is my friend Graham. He's just come along with me for a bit of fresh air."

Matthew stopped smiling and gave Graham a sideways look.

"We've met before," he said.

"Yes, I stumbled upon your camp a week or so ago. You probably remember."

"Yes, I thought I recognised you from somewhere. You're a friend of Miriam's then?"

Graham sensed a tension in the air and a feeling that Matthew was suspicious of him.

"Yes, old school friends."

Another man pushed in front of Matthew, the same fierce looking individual Graham had encountered on his previous visit. But on seeing Graham this time he had exactly the opposite reaction to Matthew's.

"Oh, hello again. Lovely to meet you. I'm Gilbert."

He stretched out a clammy hand to greet Graham, who shook it with a firm grip.

"Good to meet you, Gilbert. I'm Graham."

"This lass here is really good to us," said Gilbert. "She's like an angel."

"No, not *like* an angel. She really is one," said Graham flirtatiously.

Miriam slapped his hand playfully. Then she walked further in to the camp where two other scruffily dressed and scarily gaunt middle-aged men were holding out mugs, ready to receive their soup. As she doled it out to them and they briefly expressed their thanks, Graham continued to talk to Gilbert, while Matthew stood close by them, hanging on to every word.

"So what brings you to Sanderholme?" asked Graham.

"We like to get around the coast and get a change of scenery. We come from down London and it's nice to see some other places. We like to commune with nature, I suppose. We're very much into the natural world. Do a bit of birdwatching and some beachcombing, you know. We all love the great outdoors."

They talked in this vein for a few minutes and Graham was struck by Gilbert's refined way of speaking which quite belied his rough exterior. He suspected something faux about the man's attitude to him – that in an inverted kind of way he was being patronised. He was also struck how quiet Matthew was in contrast to his colleague. Perhaps he was embarrassed by his friend's insincere amiability.

"I'm done now," Miriam interjected.

Addressing Matthew and Gilbert she continued: "I've put your soup in your mugs over there and left you some bread."

"An angel," said Gilbert.

"Thank you, Miriam," said Matthew.

As they walked down the road back to Miriam's, Graham said: "He's an odd one, that Gilbert. I couldn't weigh him up. Is he genuine or trying to be something he's not?"

"I don't know. What do you mean?"

"Well, he looks a real rough diamond – someone you wouldn't want to meet down a dark alley. And yet he talks in a cut glass accent. Matthew does as well. I can't weigh him up, either. He seems too good for the type of lifestyle they're leading and today he really seemed on edge."

"I must say I've never known Gilbert be so affable as he was today. He seemed to take to you. And he was nice to me. He usually almost grabs the flask of soup off me, fills his mug and grunts. I don't like him but I feel sorry for the other three. He seems to dominate them like some sort of macho man. You're right about Matthew too. He did go quiet today. He's usually the one who talks my head off, telling me about all his theories on life."

"He's another one who talks posh, but I think that's just natural," said Graham. "There's something about him. Something in the way he talks and his mannerisms. He has a slight tic as he starts to speak."

"I've noticed that. It's like he's going to stutter – and then he doesn't."

"Hm. Unusual.

"They are a strange bunch," said Miriam. "I'm sure they're all druggies. But hey-ho, they don't seem to do any harm."

"I wonder why they've chosen this lifestyle? I don't really buy the communing with nature and birdwatching stuff," said Graham.

"Neither do I. I suspect they like to keep out of the way so that they can do their drugs."

"Like I said before – I admire your humanity but I would just be a little careful."

"I will."

Miriam fully understood and largely shared Graham's

reservations about the men she was helping. But, like the great Dr Samuel Johnson, she believed "Kindness is in our power, even when fondness is not."

"I'll come with you again one day," said Graham. "I'm just a little intrigued by these guys. What makes them tick?"

"Was that T I C or T I C K?" said Miriam, grinning.

****

The weekly morning meetings between Graham and Miriam became a regular arrangement that autumn. Normally Miriam had already done the "soup run" by the time he arrived at her house. She was an independent soul and it had rather irked her that Graham always told her that she should wait for him before she visited the clearing. She knew he had good intentions but just very slightly resented the fact that he felt she needed protecting.

However, on one particular morning a long phone conversation with her daughter Annette had delayed her and she was ready to set off with her soup as Graham arrived.

"I'll come with you," he said. "See how your four boyfriends are getting on."

Miriam laughed and replied: "All right, come on then."

When they arrived at the clearing there was no one there.

"Huh," said Miriam, feeling a little put out. "They obviously couldn't wait for me. They can't be very hungry."

"What do you do now?" asked Graham.

"I'll just leave the soup here and hope it doesn't get cold before they come back. Or they could make one of their fires and heat it up."

Graham was inquisitive about the men's lifestyle and how they coped with with living rough. He went over to one of the makeshift tents and opened a flap to look inside. He saw a sleeping bag, various pots and pans, a pile of clothing and half-opened pouches of what he thought was either tobacco or cannabis. He bent down and sniffed at one of them and decided it was definitely cannabis.

Laid on top of the sleeping bag was a paperback book: "Mikhail Bakunin: The Philosophical Basis of his Theory of Anarchy".

This title would not have resonated with most people, but with Graham it immediately struck a chord. Bakunin was a Russian revolutionary anarchist and a rival of Karl Marx. From his relatively limited political studies Graham could see some superficial attractions in the ideas of Proudhon, the French politician and philosopher who was the inspiration for Anarcho-Syndicalism, but with Bakunin, with his more violent teachings, he could have absolutely no truck. He was beginning to get the measure of the camp-mates. There was obviously more to them than being a bunch of down and outers.

"I think there's more to our friends here than we would perhaps have imagined," he said to Miriam.

"There's some reading matter in that tent that suggests that at least one of them has intellectual pretensions."
"Oh, I think that would be Matthew. He's tried to talk to me about philosophy and stuff. He's an intelligent man and I can't understand why he's finished up like this."

****

The friendship between Graham and Miriam became closer as Christmas approached. They were comfortable in each other's company and there was an unsaid understanding that they were on the verge of a romantic attachment.

"What are you doing for Christmas Day?" Miriam asked.

"I haven't got anything planned. I would have spent some time with my parents, but they've taken themselves off to Valencia for three months. I usually spend Christmas with Austin and the family in Nottinghamshire but there's so much going on with the Beachworld project at the moment. We've got a deadline to meet and I'm even paying some of the blokes triple time to work on Christmas Day to get on with the building work. I feel I need to stay here over Christmas."

"Wow. That's dedication for you. Would you like to come to us for lunch on Christmas Day?"

"Well, that's a very kind offer. Actually I don't see why not. I'll have to eat somewhere and I can't think of anything better than spending time with you. You said 'us'. Who else will be there?"

"Just Annette and her husband Peter and their two boys, Robert and Arthur. We'll eat here – Annette's offered to cook the turkey this year – and then perhaps pop to the golf club for a few drinks. Nothing fancy – just a nice day with family – and hopefully a very good friend."

"Sounds wonderful," said Graham. "I'd love to come."

Christmas morning came and Graham arrived at Miriam's home at the appointed time of eleven.

He was greeted warmly by Miriam at the front door, which was decorated by a huge holly wreath. "Happy Christmas", Graham and Miriam said to each other. He kissed her on the cheek and she reciprocated.

"Come in and meet the family," she said.

A slim, platinum blonde woman wearing an apron adorned by an image of a large Christmas pudding, and holding a tea towel, bustled towards the door. She had rosy cheeks and was looking a little flustered. Graham deduced that she had just come from working in the kitchen.

She wiped her hand with the tea towel and then offered it to Graham so that he could shake it.

"Happy Christmas. I'm Annette, your cook and bottle washer for today!"

"Very pleased to meet you," said Graham to Annette. "I've heard that your Christmas dinners are a wonder to behold."

"I don't know about that," she said, laughing. "Boys, come and meet Mr Robinson."

Two tousled-haired boys, aged six and four, ran down the hall towards the front door, each carrying a plastic water pistol.

"I'm going to piss you," said the younger boy, squirting the gun in Graham's direction.

Everyone laughed.

"Oh, dear. I'm soaked now," said Graham, good-humouredly. "I've never been pissed before."

"We believe you," said Miriam.

Everyone laughed again.

"These are my terrors," said Annette, "Robert, the

sensible one, and Arthur, the pisser."

"Great to meet you, lads."

"Peter, come and meet Mr Robinson," she called out.

"Graham, please," said Graham.

"Oh, yes. Peter, come and meet Graham."

A medium-built shaven-headed man with two sleeve tattoos appeared, carrying a carving knife. He would have looked fearsome had it not been for his open, toothy smile.

"Happy Christmas, mate. Good to see you. Just bin sharpening the knife ready for carving the turkey."

The two men shook hands firmly.

"Happy Christmas. Good to meet you too."

"I've got the bits ready for your weirdos," said Peter.

"Oh, good," said Miriam. "Have we got time to take it down to them before lunch?"

"Yes," said Annette. "You've got fifteen minutes."

Graham looked quizzically at Miriam.

"Is this something for our friends in the undergrowth?" he asked.

"Yes, just a little something for them to enjoy on Christmas Day. Don't worry. It's a big enough turkey to go all round."

Graham smiled: "I'm just amazed at your generosity."

"I know you all think I'm a daft old woman. But really, it's no skin off our noses, is it?"

Peter shrugged his shoulders and declared: "Yeah. You *are* a mad old woman. No doubt about it. I don't think the neighbours will be very chuffed."

"Have there been some more comments from neighbours?" asked Graham.

"They're gunning for those blokes in the bushes. They're always complaining to the cops about them –

causing a nuisance etc," said Peter. "If mum's not careful they'll start gunning for her as well."

"I've told her to be careful," said Graham. "They're a bunch of Leftie druggies, I think. They should try working for a living. I admire your humanity, Miriam, but don't you think they're taking advantage of you?"

"Perhaps they are," said Miriam. "Let's just give them the benefit of the doubt this Christmas. Goodwill to all men and all that."

"You're mad," said Peter. "But I know how stubborn you are. We're wasting our breath aren't we?"

"Yes, Scrooge. I'm afraid you are."

"I'll come along with you," said Graham.

A few minutes later Miriam and Graham arrived at the clearing. The four inhabitants were sat in a circle on a ground sheet drinking beer out of cans. Other than that there were no signs of any Christmas cheer.

"Happy Christmas everyone. We've brought you a bit of dinner," said Miriam.

Matthew got up and shook hands with the benefactors, wishing them a Happy Holiday. Gilbert followed suit. The other two men grunted and raised their beer cans slightly.

"Are you doing anything special today?" asked Miriam, just for something to say.

"No, Christmas isn't our thing. We're not believers or anything like that. But, of course, we won't say 'no' to a bit of grub," said Matthew.

"Or mini Christmas puddings? Are they against your beliefs?" asked Miriam.

Matthew's face launched into one of his characteristic little tics – as if he might stammer but then not doing – and he replied: "I think we might manage some of those.

Perhaps we might rename them winter puddings."

"I don't care what you call them so long as you enjoy them."

"We will. Thank you so much," said Matthew.

"Have a good day," said Graham, without much enthusiasm.

Matthew replied "Same to you".

Gilbert also expressed Christmas greetings while the other two men just raised their beer cans again, as if grudging the interruption to their drinking.

On their way back to Miriam's house, Graham vented some anger about what had just happened.

"The ungrateful so-and-sos," he railed. "I really don't know why you bother with them. Those two blokes who sat there drinking. They couldn't even make the effort to say 'thank you'. They're morons if you ask me."

"I know what you mean. But Matthew. I think he's different somehow. He has a gentility about him."

"But each time I see him there's something bugging me about him. I think I know what it is. It might seem stupid but it harks back to something that happened years ago."

As they reached Miriam's front door Graham caught her arm to stop her entering the house.

"Just let me tell you about this before we go inside."

"Okay."

"Do you remember the Brighton bomb, when the IRA tried to kill Margaret Thatcher?"

"Yes, I do."

"I was there in the Grand Hotel that night when the bomb went off."

"Oh god. Were you?"

"Well, I wasn't actually inside when the explosion

took place. I'd gone to the Conservative Party Conference – as a delegate – and I was drinking in the hotel bar with some friends until about a quarter of an hour before it happened. My friends got blown around the room and the ceiling came down on them. Some people in the bar were injured – not too seriously – and some others suffered from shock."

"Wow, that was horrible. I remember it. Norman Tebbit being taken out of the building on a stretcher. He looked deathly white."

"Yes, like someone out of a horror movie.

"I'd left the bar and gone back to the guest house where I was staying. I didn't hear a thing at the time – no explosion. I don't know why I didn't hear anything because I wasn't that far away from the Grand. It was the early hours of the morning so perhaps I had gone off to sleep straightaway when I got back.

"I didn't know anything about the bomb until the next morning. When I went downstairs at the guest house everyone was sat around the telly watching the news about the bomb."

"Oh, that must have been quite a shock for you."

"Yes, it was. It all seemed a bit surreal at the time."

"But what's this got to do with the men in the bushes?"

"Before I went into the Grand Hotel bar that night I had walked along the sea front and had a few drinks in several bars. I was at a loose end really. I hadn't been to a Party Conference before and didn't know many people. In one bar I went into I met this young chap. He was a friendly guy and I think he was feeling lonely too. He started a conversation and began asking about the Conference. He seemed fascinated to have met an actual real life Tory and told me he was an extreme Left-winger. We argued about politics for an hour or so – in a friendly way. We were obviously poles apart politically but personally we got on really well. He was obviously looking for some common ground and trying to understand where I was coming from

"I'm not saying I converted him, or anything like that, but when it was time to leave the bar and I told him I was going to the Grand Hotel, he asked if I would take him there. I got the impression he wanted to have a look at some more interesting Tory specimens. But there was more than that. His name was Sebastian. He had a cultured speaking voice and said that his parents had had him privately educated. I could see him getting on well with some of the 'toffs' at the Conference.

"When we got to the door of the hotel he asked if he could go in with me. I made some excuse. I think I said that there might be security on the door and he might have to show a pass. He didn't argue with me and we parted amicably. I went inside and I imagined he had carried on walking along the sea front.

"I went into the bar and found some people I knew to talk to. Some time afterwards I looked across the room and saw Sebastian happily chatting away to some other men, including a Government minister. It seemed wrong somehow. I had this lurking suspicion about his motives and had a strong feeling that I shouldn't have brought him with me, even though I had left him at the door.

"When I learnt about the bomb the thought came to me briefly that Sebastian should not have been in the hotel that night. I even fleetingly thought that I should have told the police about him. The more I learnt about the bomb, and the fact it had been placed upstairs at the hotel some months before the explosion, the less I thought about Sebastian. Sometimes, though, when I wake up in the middle of the night, I still wonder what he was doing there."

"That's interesting," said Miriam, "But why are you telling me this now?"

"Because there's something about Matthew that reminds me of Sebastian – brings back the memory of that night. It's his way of speaking, that slight tic that we've mentioned before. And then I looked inside one of the tents the other week and there was a copy of a book there about Mikhail Bakunin. It made me think again."

"Who's Mikhail Bakunin?"

"He was a Russian anarchist. Sebastian told me he was an Anarcho-Syndicalist. Not as extreme as Bakunin but near enough to take me back to that night at Brighton."

"Interesting," said Miriam. "Perhaps you've had a feeling of deja vu."

"Yes, but not a genuine case of it, I believe. I've had such feelings in the past. When I was at primary school one day we had to make our own hobby horses. When I had finished mine I started to have a ride on it. I got this sudden, overwhelming feeling that I had done this before – in Egypt. I have never been to Egypt.

"On another occasion, as an adult, I was walking along an old street in Cheltenham and I had this strong feeling again that I had been there before. I don't think I'd ever been within 50 miles of that town previously. Since then, though, I have dreamt about that street regularly and it looks so clear to me, so real."

Miriam nodded: "I've had feelings of deja vu too. But I won't go into them now. Let's go in. Lunch will be ready."

Graham smiled and said: "Yes. I've bothered you enough with my silly stories."

They went into the house through the gaily decorated hall, and into the sitting room with its large real Christmas tree bedecked with multi-coloured lights and a plenitude of big baubles. The floor was covered with children's presents and the discarded boxes and wrapping paper. The boys themselves had already got tired of inspecting the presents and were engaged in a frantic wrestling match in one corner of the room.

From the sitting room it was into the dining room where a large oak table was resplendent with Christmas fare. This was obviously to be a good old-fashioned family celebration.

Everyone made their way to the table where Peter did the honours of serving the turkey while Annette was dispensing wine. Miriam and Graham were instructed to just sit down and enjoy themselves and the boys told to sit still, keep the noise down and stuff their faces.

When the main course and Christmas pudding had been consumed and obligatory Christmas crackers pulled, the adults grazed on the cheese and biscuits and mince pies at their leisure.

Peter was particularly interested in quizzing Graham about the Beachworld development, of which he was a keen supporter.

"I just don't understand those muppets who are complaining about it. A lot of people are just old fogies and can't stand any change. And then there's those with vested interests who don't want any competition. They're so short-sighted – haven't got the bloody brains they were born with. I reckon your centre will attract loads of people to Sanderholme. Power to your elbow, mate."

"Hear, hear", declared Miriam. "Let's drink a toast to the success of Beachworld!"

The foursome raised their glasses in unison.

"I happen to believe that most people in the town think like you do, Peter," said Graham. "But opponents of things always seem to make the loudest noise. I must say the nearer the plans get to completion the more excited I'm getting. I owe a lot to Sanderholme and I want to give it something back."

"Yeah, bugger the miserable arseholes who were trying to stop you," said Peter.

Annette interjected: "Watch your language, Peter. You're not with your mates from the arcade now."

"Sorry," said Peter. "I get annoyed at some people's attitudes."

"Anyway it's too late now for people to still be objecting. Beachworld will soon be up and running," said Annette.

"I certainly believe so," said Graham.

It was mid-afternoon now and Miriam suggested they all went for a stroll on the beach to "walk off" some of their lunch.

Annette suggested: "Shall we go to the golf club afterwards for a couple of drinks?"

"Will it be open on Christmas Day?" asked Graham.

"Yes, they're serving Christmas meals all day long, and so the bar will be open," replied Annette.

That was the plan which they followed. As they passed by the clearing they could hear very loud men's voices, sounding at least boisterous but possibly even angry.

"Sounds like they've downed enough beer," said

Graham, disapprovingly.

The group made their way across the salt marsh to the beach. It was a cold, crisp day, with the residue of an overnight frost lingering on the vegetation. Amazing cobwebs sparkled in the bright sunlight and seagulls wheeled away in the cloudless sky above, producing an ear-splitting cacophony. The golden beach, hardened by the dry weather and the frost, was firm underfoot, ideal for walking and for the "boys", including Graham and Peter, to enjoy an impromptu game of football.

The sea was flat calm and there were stunning views across The Wash to Norfolk. The tide was well out and a score or so of walkers and dogs could be seen in the hazy distance. A couple of yachts with white sails were gently bobbing around.

Refreshed by the bracing air, the rosy-cheeked party made their way to Sanderholme Golf Club. There was a hubbub of jolly looking people there, many with rosy cheeks themselves, owing more to what they had imbibed than to any venturing outside in the cold air. Some diners were still picking over the remains of their lunches while most people were standing near the bar conversing, glasses in their hands.

Graham showed his gratitude for his Christmas lunch hosts by buying everyone in his party a drink. As he stood at the bar waiting to be served he was looking around to see who he could recognise. What he saw in a far corner gave him a considerable shock. For there, looking as desirable as ever, was Anita. He was surprised to see her, but quickly concluded that she must be in town on Christmas Day to see her parents, who were now in their late nineties and living together in a local residential care home. However, as he looked at her admiringly, filled with the usual pangs of regret, he was completely taken back when he saw the company she was in. It was none other than Henry Fulford, his unlovely love rival from so many years ago. He had his arm around her waist and was talking directly into her ear.

What was this all about? Was she up to her usual games? Where was her husband Darren? Should he go over and speak to them, or try to ignore them? What would Miriam feel about the presence of his ex-wife? And how would Fulford react to *his* presence?

These were the questions that whizzed through Graham's head as he waited to be served. He was nothing but decisive so quickly resolved that he had to make contact. He bought his drinks and took them over to his group. He took Miriam to one side and explained that Anita was in the building and that he thought it would be diplomatic to go and speak to her.

"Of course. No problem," said Miriam.

He walked over and tapped Anita on the shoulder.

"Hi. Merry Christmas. What brings you here?"

Anita smiled affectionately and pecked him on the cheek. Henry Fulford turned away and started talking to another man standing behind him.

Anita explained that she was staying on Christmas Day and Boxing Day at her parents' house, which had lain empty since they went into the care home. But her explanations stopped there. She said nothing about the fact that she was with Henry and not her parents, or her husband, at this significant time.

Henry was talking loudly to his male companion and Graham had the strong impression that he was drunk. He anticipated there might be trouble if he stayed too long talking to Anita.

"I'll be back in Nottinghamshire to see in the New Year with Austin and the kids," she said. "Will you be there?"

"I'm not sure," said Graham. "There's a lot of work going on here with the development and I like to be on site every day to make sure the workmen don't slack."

"I would like to see you before I go home the day after tomorrow," said Anita, touching his cheek seductively.

"I'm not sure yet what I'm doing tomorrow. I'm with some friends today, mum and dad are away at Valencia and I ought to go and see Jim tomorrow. You know about his heart bypass. He's getting on well. I'm still looking after his dog but I don't think that will be for much longer. I'll see what I can do about tomorrow. I'll phone you.

"Do," she replied.

"Okay. I must get back to my company now. Do you know Miriam Metcalfe? I'm with her and her family. They invited me for Christmas lunch."

"I know her slightly. They have arcades and cafes and things, don't they?"

"That's right."

"Enjoy the rest of your day, Graham."

"Good to see you, Anita."

"And you."

****

Graham returned to his Sanderholme house that night, and began by presenting a doggie bag full of turkey to a delighted Benjy, who had been looked after by an elderly neighbour during the day. He had savoured his time with

Miriam and her family, especially the brief, but significant, goodnight kiss he had enjoyed with her.

He felt that a genuine romance was growing between them. Graham admired Miriam for being a stable, loving, family-orientated person, with a deep sense of compassion. He also enjoyed her positive attitude to life and her good sense of fun.

But the joy which this new relationship with Miriam gave him was tainted with apprehension. What was Anita up to? She was being her usual incorrigible, unfathomable, unreliable, infuriating siren-like self.

Sirens – "Their song, though irresistibly sweet, was no less sad than sweet, and lapped both body and soul in a fatal lethargy, the forerunner of death and corruption."

Graham knew that she liked having several men in tow at the same time. Although she was married to Darren, he thought it was quite possible that she might still have designs on him, her ex-husband. And on how many ex-boyfriends and other men too?

He had swallowed any pride he might have had because he realised that there was no malice in her infidelity. Even though she was promiscuous, she had an indefinable mental loyalty to every man she had been involved with.

In a moment of searing honesty she had once admitted to Graham: "I would rather have sex with a thousand men once than a thousand times with one man."

Despite having a totally different moral compass himself, Graham had come to tolerate and even respect her very individual view of the world. He recognised that he probably thought far more about their relationship than she did. She was like an ewe in a field waiting for whatever new tup happened to come along. He wouldn't have been much use as a tup: he would have shunned the rest of the ewes and made directly for her.

So, on Boxing Day, he phoned her.

"Thank you for ringing," she said. "Can I come round to see you, love?"

"What time?" asked Graham. "I'm going to see Jim this morning and I've been invited to lunch again at Miriam's. And then I'm popping to the site after that, to see what's going on there. So how about this evening? Say about 6.30?"

"That suits me," she said. "I'm having lunch with mum and dad at the home and then meeting Henry for a drink at the golf club. So 6.30's fine."

"I can't believe you're having anything to do with Henry again. You know what I think of him. Don't you remember he trashed my car all those years ago?"

"We're not sure it was him."

"You certainly thought it was. I don't trust the man. I would be careful if I were you."

"We're just old friends having a drink. There's nothing more to it."

Graham doubted that was the case. Had she ever been "just friends" with any man?

He heard himself warning a woman to be careful again. He had told Miriam to be careful of the men in the marsh. He was beginning to feel old.

"See you tonight then," he said.

****

That morning he visited Jim whom he found to be in good spirits, although illness had noticeably aged him. The two friends spent the morning reminiscing and gossiping before Graham went to join Miriam and her family for a roast beef lunch.

Graham noticed a change in the atmosphere following the goodnight kiss he had enjoyed with Miriam the previous night. She was very warm and attentive towards him, frequently touching his hand and smiling at him fondly. Perhaps she was a little tipsy. He felt strangely at home.

After another kiss on the doorstep as he left, Graham walked to Beachworld with a bouncy and confident gait. He sensed his life was about to change. Love was definitely in the air.

After satisfying himself that all was well at the site he made his way back home, waiting for his meeting with Anita with a mixture of anticipation and trepidation.

When he saw her alight from her taxi, looking as sexy as ever in her early sixties, his heart missed a beat. He felt the same excitement as when he had first met her. There was an inevitability that they would end up in bed together that night.

They settled down on the minimalist sofa in his large minimalist designer lounge. He poured her a glass of white wine.

"Well, this is nice," she said. "You'll have to show me round before I go."

"Of course. I know it's not very homely but it suits me. I keep it simple – less cleaning!"

After a few minutes of idle chitchat, Graham was keen to know the purpose of Anita's visit.

"Why are you here?" he asked bluntly.

"I have some news," she said. "I've left Darren."

"Oh, I see. Why?"

"I've realised he's not my type, love. He's very

controlling – and ridiculously jealous. He's extremely cut up about the whole thing – very angry and almost suicidal.

"But I couldn't go on as it was. I didn't have any space. He's not like you. You always gave me space."

"Too much, I think. I spent too long at work as usual. Left you to get up to mischief."

Anita laughed out loud and cheekily pinched his arm.

"I don't know what you're talking about. I'm pure as the driven – soot."

"I've got feelings, you know," said Graham, manfully trying to join in with the humorous way the conversation was turning."

"You've always understood me," she said. "You know how naughty I can be. But, you know, I've always loved you."

"Do you really know what love means?"

"That's cruel. You know I loved you. And you loved me too."

When he nodded in agreement he immediately knew he had given too much ground.

"Aaah," said Anita, giving *him* her most winsome smile. "So you still love me."

She touched his face.

"Will you shag me – for old time's sake?"

"Is that what you came here for?"

"Of course. What else?"

Her hand moved towards his trousers.

Anita left his bed at midnight and took a taxi back to her parents' house.

For Graham the sense of ecstasy soon passed, to be replaced by a surprise but profound feeling of guilt.

The guilt came from a sense that he had betrayed Miriam, even though physically their relationship had gone no further than a couple of brief kisses.

The truth was that he now loved two women – loved them in entirely different ways but still the guilt lay heavily.

Graham was worldly enough to understand that however differently he might feel about the women there was no fair, sensible or satisfying way of keeping close relationships with both of them. He tried to convince himself that the night's entertainment with Anita was a never-to-be-repeated experience. But how he yearned for it to be repeated! And yet he didn't want anything to spoil the warm companionship and burgeoning romance with Miriam. He decided that the best policy – that espoused by the UK's Prime Minister Stanley Baldwin in the 1920s and 1930s – was to "wait and see".

The next morning as he ate his cornflakes for breakfast, Graham received a telephone call from Anita, who sounded friendly and chipper.

"Hi Graham," she chirped. "How are you this morning, love?"

"Fine, thank you."

"I'm heading back to Nottinghamshire today, but I have something to ask you."

"Ask away."

"I am longing to have a look at Beachworld. Would you show me around? This morning perhaps?"

"Yes, of course. I'm heading that way myself as soon as I've finished breakfast. I could pick you up, or meet you there if you've got to get off quickly afterwards."

"Yes, sure. I'll meet you there. How do I get in?"

"The site's got a car park next to the main entrance. Park there and come to the reception office – you'll see a sign for it. Tell the chap in there who you are and he'll find me."

"About 10 o'clock?"

"That'll be great."

"See you there then. It'll be exciting to see what's going on."

As planned, Anita arrived at the site office where an elderly security man greeted her. Graham was alerted of her arrival by phone and was there immediately to start her tour.

He showed her the numerous shop units and catering outlets which were ready to be occupied, the exhibition and conference centre topped by an impressive glass dome and the landscaped garden centre, with its thousands of trees and shrubs, areas set aside for flowerbeds, water features and Ancient Greek-style statues. The stepped outdoor auditorium, where, as a young boy, Graham had often sat with his parents to watch the weekly firework displays, had been upgraded by the introduction of comfortable seating. It looked over to a new performance stage situated on the small grassy island in the middle of the old boating lake.

A gang of workers was busy dredging the lake and generally cleaning up the site ready for the Spring opening.

Graham and Anita were spotted by a tall, slim, good-looking man in his forties, besuited and wearing shades and with a neat moustache complementing shiny, short, curly brown hair. He walked briskly towards them.

"Ah," said Graham to Anita. "Meet Stephen Armitage.

He's my clerk of works and he's going to be the general manager here when we get open. Stephen, this is Anita, my ex-wife."

"Delighted to meet you," said Stephen, giving Anita an admiring look.

"And you," said Anita. "You're doing a great job here. I think it will be amazing when it's finished."

Stephen, who spoke with a Mid-Atlantic accent, accompanied them on the next stage of the tour, explaining to Anita some of the problems they had had to overcome, especially the fires and other acts of vandalism which had bedevilled and held up the project.

Anita hung on to his every word and nodded enthusiastically in all the right places during his discourse.

Eventually he left them when a harassed looking workman drew his attention to a problem with the amphibious excavator being used for the dredging work.

"He's a very bright chap," said Graham when he had gone. "I head-hunted him from Disney World."

"I thought he must be American," said Anita. "You've got a good bloke there. And he's dishy!"

"I thought you might notice that," said Graham, smiling somewhat ruefully. "Actually, his mother was American and his father English."

"Oh, I see. That explains his rather odd accent," said Anita. "Anyway, I've enjoyed my tour. I can see now why you've been so busy in the last few years. I really had no clue the project was as big as this. You must have pushed the boat out money-wise."

"Yes, it's cost an arm and a leg, but I've managed to get some good investors on board. Now we just need to attract some punters."

"Bloody hell. You sure do."

The visit had already taken longer than Anita had anticipated and there was no time to inspect the hotel. She had to rush away as she had arranged with Austin and his wife to meet them that afternoon.

When they returned to the car park, Anita said: "I'll see you soon then. Either here or in Nottinghamshire."

"Yes, I'll be here for most of the time until the opening. I hope to get over to see Austin and the family one day soon."

As they reached Anita's car she pulled Graham towards her and felt his crotch as she planted a large kiss on his lips.

"I hope it won't be too long," she said.

"What am I going to do with you?" asked Graham.

"A repeat of last night would be a start," she replied, licking her lips seductively.

"Maybe," said Graham, unconvincingly trying his best to sound non-committal.

As she drove away, he was metaphorically kicking himself. He was falling under her spell again.

Chapter ten
A shock for Graham

It was two days later when Graham received a phone call from Miriam, asking him what he was planning to do on New Year's Eve.

He replied that he had nothing arranged at all. He had never been an enthusiastic party-goer and found the confected excitement of New Year celebrations to be at best disappointing and at worst totally tedious. He knew that an invitation of some sort was coming.

"The golf club have a New Year's Eve fancy dress ball which is always quite fun." said Miriam. "We have booked our tickets – me, Annette and Peter and a couple of their friends, James and Rachel. We could still get you a ticket if you fancied coming."

Graham didn't especially "fancy coming" but he always looked forward to Miriam's company and thought that would compensate for any feelings of ennui he might experience at the event.

"That would be great," he said.

So the arrangements were made about times and ticket prices etc. It only left Graham to decide what costume he would choose. When previously cajoled into fancy dress he had gone as a Red Indian, an Arab sheikh and a drunken Scotsman. But current antipathy to so-called cultural appropriation appeared to rule out any such possibilities. He thought of going as the Grim Reaper, but he felt that might put a damper on the night. A Christmas elf? – probably too late for that at New Year's Eve. A pirate? – too cliched. A golfer, with stupid tartan trousers and a silly jumper? – perhaps too near the knuckle for a golf club event. A Drag Queen? - no, he might get taken for the night's entertainment.

So he eventually decided to go as one of his favourite rock musicians, Roy Wood, famed former member of The Electric Light Orchestra, The Move and Wizzard. He would find himself a suitable long multi-coloured wig, lather himself with face paint, put a star on his forehead and wear tartan trousers. People of round about his age would know exactly who he was meant to be. Younger people might just twig that he was the Brummie geezer who wrote and sang "I Wish It Could Be Christmas Everyday".

After again leaving Benjy in the care of the friendly neighbour, he arrived at the golf club for the ball and joined Miriam's party. At first they didn't recognise him. Miriam and Annette had to ask what character he had come as. Embarrassingly, he had to sing a few lines of "the Christmas song" to help them.

What struck Graham straightaway was how glamorous Miriam looked in her Wonder Woman outfit.

She had shapes he hadn't previously been aware of. Despite his initial misgivings he entered fully into the fun of the event, with sumptuous food and drink, an excellent disco and a real party atmosphere.

The one downside was when he spotted Henry Fulford, who even contrived to look miserable when dancing with a gorgeous curvy blonde. He may merely have been behaving in keeping with the character he had chosen to imitate, as *he* was dressed as the The Grim Reaper. Graham thought how lucky he had been not to choose that costume himself. It might have been "scythes at dawn" between him and his bete noire. Fortunately Henry did not recognise Graham that night.

It was 2.30am on New Year's Day when the ball finished. Miriam invited Graham back to her home for a nightcap.

He left at 11am later that day. Graham had enjoyed a Wizzard night with Wonder Woman.

****

Graham was a courageous businessman, but one who prided himself on taking decisions which kept his integrity intact. Romantically, though, he now found himself in a position where he knew he was acting in a cowardly way. He had fallen in love with Miriam but couldn't fall out of love with Anita – the age-old dilemma of the two-timer.

The problem with both of these women was that neither of them bore any malice. Miriam was the very epitome of a kind woman. If Anita only had her stunning good looks to commend her, then Graham's choice would have been easier. He could have followed the example of Hortensio in Shakespeare's "Taming of the Shrew": "Kindness in women, not their beauteous looks, shall win my love".

But Anita could also be a kind person, in a twisted sort of way. The problem was she showed kindness to all men in her singular physical fashion, not understanding that fidelity is an important trait of kindness too.

However, though fully comprehending her many flaws, Graham had become well practised in ignoring them and continued, against his better judgement, to find her annoyingly irresistible.

His cowardly tactic of "wait and see" was not working, so he had another idea – seek the help of his wise old friend Jim Nott.

Jim was convalescing after his heart operation but had decided he was well enough to welcome back Benjy after the dog's stay with Graham.

When he arrived at the newsagent's half an hour before closing time, Graham unusually found Jim alone in the shop. He looked drawn – thinner in the face and with even deeper wrinkles than Graham had noticed before. But the cheery smile which somehow always emerged from his crumpled face on seeing his old chum never diminished. He was also delighted to be reunited with his beloved labrador.

The dog was beside itself with excitement, yelping and whimpering and jumping up on to his owner's lap.

"Cuppa tea?" asked Jim. "Kettle's just boiled."

"Don't mind if I do, thanks. Would you like me to make it?

"No," said Jim, "I'm not entirely helpless now."

He indicated to Graham that he should sit on one of two wooden chairs behind the counter. Then he disappeared to the kitchen located through a door at the back of the room, re-emerging a few minutes' later with the tea.

"How's you today?" asked Jim.

"Fighting fit," said Graham, "And you?"

"Struggling on. Not letting the buggers get me down."

Graham grinned, but inwardly was feeling sad at the obvious physical deterioration of his friend.

"Jim, would you say that I'm a decisive sort of a person?"

"I don't reckon I've met anyone more decisive," replied Jim. "I think your track record in business proves that, mate."

"Well, suddenly, I'm very indecisive. Not in business you understand, but in my personal life. I'm on the horns of a dilemma."

"Women?"

"Yes, women."

"Always been your Achilles heel since you met Anita."

"I'm ashamed to say that nothing's changed. Although obviously I'm divorced from Anita, she's still in my mind every day of my life."

"Is she back on the scene then?"

"Never been off the scene. She's still Austin's mother and she still lives in Nottingham, so she will never be far away. The thing is that she seems to want to cling on even though she's officially moved on. And I seem powerless to resist. But there's an added problem. I've become quite attached to another woman recently."

"Miriam?"

"Yes, Miriam. She's a lovely person and we are so comfortable in each other's company. I do fancy her too. But Anita – she just turns me on every time I see her or even think about her. I don't know what to do."

"As you well know, I've got little or no experience when it comes to the ladies," said Jim. "Of course I know Anita quite well, both from being your wife and by reputation. I know Miriam because she comes into the shop sometimes to buy magazines and I have heard that she's a nice person. I don't know what to say, mate."

"I was hoping you might give me some objective advice," said Graham. "I feel that my life is at an important crossroads. I should be giving all my attention to Beachworld, but instead I'm fretting about women."

"Well, my advice, such as it is, is that you would be better off with Miriam. I like Anita but, let's be honest, she's a butterfly. From what I understand she'll never settle down with anyone for long. On the grapevine I had heard that she's been going about with Henry Fulford. I was going to tell you that."

"I might have guessed that you would have known about that. Your reputation as Sanderholme's leading gossip-monger would have been in question if you hadn't got wind of it."

Jim touched his nose and nodded in a conspiratorial way.

"I do pick up on little bits here and there," he said. "I know that you and Anita have split up but even so I did think it was rather disloyal of her to take up with Fulford again."

"You remember that she went with him years ago."

"Oh, yes. I remember that you thought he scratched your car once."

"Your memory is elephantine, Jim."

Jim tapped his nose again.

"What made me think it was disloyal is that I know Fulford has been one of the loudest opponents of Beachworld. Stirring up the NIMBYS.

"As you know, I'm very supportive of Beachworld – as long as the shops won't include any newsagent's or tobacconist's outlets."

Jim laughed and Graham raised his eyebrows and tutted in mock disgust.

"I take your point about Anita and loyalty. I did think it was a bit rum myself. But that's the way she is. If I'm honest she just can't resist anyone in trousers."

"And thereby lies your problem, Graham. Unless you

can get over your obsession with her you will never move forward. I know you can't completely cut ties with her, because of Austin and the grandkids, but you need to keep away from her as best you can. I've got just the solution to your woes."

"What's that, Jim?"

"Pass her on to me, of course."

Graham sniggered.

"Are you sure about that?"

Jim suddenly looked serious.

"I'm deadly serious. I could do with a bit of hot totty."

Graham was nonplussed for a moment, not knowing quite how to react to his friend's surprise suggestion. Was he being serious, or was it a wind-up?

Jim's grey countenance broke into a wreath of smiles and he slapped Graham's leg.

"Of course I'm not being serious. I'm still a confirmed old bachelor – my sad fate in life. But, being serious, mate – give her up. She's bad news – a real Miss Jobbyknickers. Mind you, I've heard Miriam's had her moments too."

"Oh, come on then. Tell me. I know you want to."

"You know she's had two husbands, don't you? Terry Paine and Wayne Consett. Terry was a right one. He passed away a couple of years ago. He was probably the male equivalent of Anita. Put it about a lot."

"Miriam's told me that."

"And Wayne Consett. Not really her type at all. He worked for her in one of the arcades. Never get involved with the hired hand, as they say. He started getting drunk and knocking her around. She's been in my shop with a black eye before now. They say he's a horrible bloke. When Miriam finally got rid of him he took up with a teenage schoolgirl. They say he knocked her about as well and her parents had to get the police involved. It never came to court or anything but he left town all of a sudden. I think the police probably scared him off. Nasty piece of work, I reckon."

"But it seems Miriam was just an innocent bystander in all this," said Graham, reassured that none of her skeletons had come out of the cupboard.

"Wait, I haven't finished yet," said Jim. "After she kicked Wayne out I think she went a bit wild for a period. She used to go up the night clubs and do a lot of dancing. I'm told she had several flings with blokes around that time."

Graham stopped Jim in his flow: "You can't really blame her, after all she had gone through."

"No, you should know that the blame game's not my thing at all."

"You seemed to cast some blame on Miriam's husbands."

"There is a limit, even given my broad view of the world," said Jim, winking. "They were bad lots. I don't think Miriam did anyone any harm – not to my knowledge anyway."

"And everyone knows that your knowledge of other people's business is extensive – universal almost."

Jim looked at his friend with an air of pride. His reputation as a disseminator of malicious gossip remained unrivalled.

"I've got some gossip for *you*," said Graham. "I'd forgotten all about it, but it's just come back into my head."

"I bet I already know it," said Jim.

"Nothing would surprise me," said Graham. "Anyway

when I was walking your Benjy one day – along the usual route in the salt marshes, I looked towards the thicket which borders on to the golf course and up popped two heads – two male heads. They looked surprised and immediately disappeared. One of them was Fred Buxton, the solicitor. They looked very embarrassed. I have heard that it's quite a meeting place for gay men. I never knew that Fred was gay."

Jim nodded knowingly and then changed the subject to some gossip of his own about the rough sleepers in the bushes near to Lavender Avenue.

"I've got him," thought Graham. "I've beaten him to some gossip. But I'll wager that the whole of his clientele will know about this before the week's out."

"I've heard a few things about your friends who are living near the beach," said Jim.

"Please don't call them my friends," interrupted Graham.

"I've been told they've been shoplifting at Tesco," Jim continued, "and that one of them's been spotted outside the Academy, supposedly offering drugs to schoolkids."

"Nothing would surprise me about them. They're just no-good dropouts," said Graham. "I've told Miriam to give them a wide berth, but she won't listen. She thinks she's being the good Christian but it's starting to make her unpopular among some of her neighbours, our mate Trevor Bincroft among them. One day when we were taking them some food I saw a book there about Mikhail Bakunin. I think they're some kind of anarchists."

"Who's Mikhail Bakunin when he's at home?" asked Jim.

"He was a Russian anarchist – around at the same time as Lenin."

"Right. A bad lot then. They won't do anything for our tourist trade, hanging about on the beach like they do. The council or the police should do something to stop it."

Graham laughed, and added: "And something about Fred Buxton and his chum while they're about it!"

Jim ignored that remark. His mood had altered and a dark cloud seem to have descended over his usual cheery disposition. He started to cough uncontrollably and suddenly looked like a very ill man again.

"You all right?" asked Graham.

"I'll live," said Jim. "I think I'll shut up shop now. I get tired quickly these days."

"Okay, I'm off then. Leave you in peace. See you soon. And thanks for your advice about you-know-who."

****

The following Saturday Anita was back in Sanderholme and having a drink with Henry Fulford in the Buckthorn Arms, when in walked Stephen Armitage, the clerk of works for Beachworld. Henry said to Anita: "I can't seem to get away from these people. If it's not Graham Robinson, the organ grinder, it's this guy, the bloody monkey."

The pub was, as usual on a Saturday night, heaving with customers. Stephen had to literally brush past Anita to get to the bar. "Hi there," she said. "We meet again."

"Oh, yes. Delighted to see you again."

"This is my friend, Henry," said Anita.

Stephen stretched out his hand which Henry took somewhat reluctantly.

"I hope you enjoyed your tour of Beachworld," said Stephen.

"I was well impressed," said Anita. "I can't wait to see it open."

Henry groaned and looked away.

"Oh, don't mind him, Stephen. It is Stephen isn't it? He's a miserable sod. He doesn't like the idea of Beachworld."

"I know," said Stephen.

Turning to Henry, he continued: "I recognised you actually. I believe you were at one of our public consultation meetings. I had hoped we might have won you round."

"No way. The bloody place will finish up as a white elephant after a year or two. But the rest of us will be pushed out of business in the meantime. I can't believe the bloody council are allowing it to happen." said Henry.

"I politely beg to differ," said Stephen. "I think everyone will benefit. It will attract thousands of people from throughout the East Midlands, and well beyond that too. Thank goodness the district council have been far-sighted enough to understand this."

"Bollocks," said Henry. "There's not enough money around these days. We'll all be scrambling for the same few pennies."

"Competition's healthy, surely," said Stephen.

"Yes, of course it is," said Anita.

"What do you know about it?" said Henry. "You always stick up for your bloody ex-husband and his crackpot scheme."

"Charming," said Anita.

Henry was on a roll now. Turning to Stephen he said: "And what would you know about it? We're not all rolling in money here like you lot are in America. If you ask me you should bugger off back there and leave us in peace."

"Don't be so rude," snapped Anita. "Stephen's come in here for a drink. He doesn't need you ranting at him."

Henry declared: "Oh, bugger. I'm off to get another drink."

He made off towards the bar in a huff, leaving Anita to try to smooth things over with Stephen.

"I'm so sorry about that. He can be a complete moron sometimes."

"No worries. I know feelings are running high in some quarters about the development. It's all water off a duck's back to me. I'm quite thick-skinned. I'll get out of your way before we have round two."

"Okay. But – but I'd like you to know that I'm 100 per cent behind Graham and his plan. And, I would welcome having another look round sometime. We whizzed round a bit quickly last time. We didn't even get to look inside the hotel."

"Any time. Arrange it through Graham. Or, failing that, here's my card. Give one of us a call when you're ready."

Anita smiled winsomely and whispered: "Believe me. I'm ready."

****

Jim Nott's recovery from his heart operation had been slow, so he had only been fit enough to take Benjy on short walks. But now, even though he tired easily, he was determined that the normal doggy walking service should be resumed.

Jim always rose at 5.30am, giving him time to have breakfast and wash before carrying out his daily chore of preparing the newspaper rounds for the delivery boys and girls. Except during a couple of recent stays in hospital his daily routine had been unchanged for some years. He worked in the shop throughout the morning, took half an hour for lunch at 1pm and then took Benjy for his hour-long afternoon walk through the salt marshes. Then it was back to manning the shop, alongside either of his two women assistants, until closing time at 8pm.

Now he felt confident enough to try out his usual walk of about a mile and a half each way. He did well, Benjy being understanding and considerate enough to his master to reduce his normal pace.

On his return journey Jim decided to pay a visit to the gents' toilets which were on the car park immediately adjacent to the start of the salt marsh path. Benjy was tied up outside and waited patiently for his master's return. When Jim reappeared and they set off again the dog picked up his pace as he knew he was homeward-bound with the promise of a tasty treat at the end of the walk to thank him for his good behaviour.

However, half way across the car park their journey home was interrupted by the arrival of a police car, with two officers inside, one male and one female. The car came to an abrupt halt alongside Jim and officers quickly left the vehicle to talk to him.

****

Darren Gibson disembarked from the Nottingham train which had arrived at Sanderholme station on a dull and cold winter afternoon.

Bearded, with long unkempt hair and a canvas rucksack on his back, he looked like someone who had just arrived from the Australian outback or from a miserable year on the hippy trail. His face displayed a grim determination, suggesting that he had a very serious mission to accomplish.

He took out his phone, studied it closely and then set off walking at a brisk pace. Ten minutes later he arrived at the front door of Anita's parents' home, a spacious detached house in a quiet leafy crescent not far from the town centre.

Anita opened the door and groaned when she saw her recently estranged husband standing there.

"I can see you're pleased to see me," said Darren with angry sarcasm.

"Oh, you'd better come in," said Anita. "Mind you, the cat's brought in better looking specimens than you are today."

"Well, whose fault is that?"

"Not mine, surely," said Anita, showing him into a breakfast room.

"I've had enough. I've had to come here on a bloody train today. The Jag's broken down again. I've got no money to get it repaired."

"Oh, dear. I'm sorry for you, love. But why did you have to come here? Train fares aren't cheap are they?"

"I'm here to beg you to come back to me. I can't cope without you."

"I'm sorry, love, but it's too late. You were a bastard to me. You hit me, you tried to control everything I did and you took my money."

"I'm sorry if I did some of those things. But I could never trust you, could I? Be honest, Neet, there was always someone else around, wasn't there?"

"I am as I am, and you knew how I was when you

168

took me on. You're no angel either, are you?"

"What do you mean by that?" he shouted.

"That bloody girl at the coffee shop – something was going on there, I know."

"That's a lie. I never touched that girl. You're just twisted, you are."

"If you're trying to win me back you're going about it in a very funny way. Anyway, I think I'll be back with Graham again soon. I was with him a couple of nights ago – all night."

Darren raised his hand and brought it down viciously on Anita's head.

"I'll kill you. I'll kill him. And I'll kill myself," he screamed.

"Not all that again. Get out, get out," said Anita, clutching the side of her head.

"Don't worry, I'm going. But I'll be back," said Darren, heading for the front door and then slamming it behind him as he left.

****

Graham is hard at work in the management suite at Beachworld when he receives a call on his mobile phone from an unknown number.

"Hello, Mr Robinson?"

"Yes, it's Graham Robinson here."

"My name's Dylan Grimes. My wife, Daisy, works at Notts' newsagents."

"Oh, yes. Hello Mr Grimes."

"I have some dreadful news for you, I'm afraid. Your friend Jim Nott was found dead this morning in his flat. He had, I'm afraid, hung himself. Daisy asked me to let you know."

"What? I can't believe it. I only saw him the other day. He was fine then. Oh, god, that's awful."

Graham's voice breaks as he fights back tears.

"I'm sorry to have to give you this news, Mr Robinson. Daisy said you were very good friends."

"We certainly were. We've been friends since school days. Is there any indication as to why he did this – any note left, or anything like that?"

"No, but Daisy knows something about it. She thinks it had something to do with the police coming round yesterday."

"The police? Jim was a law-abiding chap. I can't imagine him being in any trouble with the police. Unless of course they had brought him some bad news."

"I think you should talk to Daisy. I'm just passing the message on from her because she is so upset. She really liked Mr Nott."

"Everyone did. I'm just – sorry, I'm very upset. I'm having a job getting my words out."

"Don't worry. I understand. Daisy and Maureen, her colleague, are at the shop at the moment if you wanted to go and speak to them there."

"Thank you. I'll be right along – in a few minutes."

Graham is devastated. In spite of all that has happened in his life – the success and the numerous social and business interactions and contacts he has made – Jim had remained his only constant close friend for the past half a century. He respected and trusted him more than anyone else in the world. There are other workers in the management suite that morning and he feels quite unable to look them in the face let alone speak to them. He rushes over to the toilet, goes inside, and bursts into uncontrollable tears. Poor dear, innocent Jim, the man with the infectious smile and mischievous glint in his eye.

Graham washes the tears away in the handbasin and prepares himself to go back into the office. He takes his phone out of his pocket to send a message to Stephen Armitage to let him know he is going off site.

He notices there is a text message that he hasn't seen yet and opens it. It is from Jim. Graham's heart sinks as he reads these words:

"Dear Graham, I am so sorry, mate, to be contacting you in this way. But I owe it to you, as my best friend, to explain my actions. Yesterday I was arrested and charged with sexual activity with a man in a public lavatory. I am guilty. This will come as a surprise to you, I know. I have had these inclinations for some years but I have always kept them to myself. I cannot bear the shame. It is inevitable that there will be sad people like myself who will treat this as an excuse to spread gossip about me. I am hoisted by my own petard. I know I am a coward, but this has to be goodbye. I have remembered you in my will. Goodbye my good friend. See you in the next life, perhaps, Jim."

Graham sobs again and stays in the toilet for some minutes before he can compose himself.

He drives over to the newsagents hardly able to negotiate the roads as he tries to focus through his tears. On arrival he sees three police cars parked on the forecourt of the shop. But what really strikes him is a sight he has never encountered before on a weekday morning. The shop is shut. Of course it would be.

He knocks on the front door and is greeted by Maureen, the middle-aged shop assistant, who is red-eyed and shaky. Standing next to the counter is Daisy, a buxom elderly woman, looking equally distraught, and her husband Dylan.

"Thank you for coming," she says.

"What a sad day," exclaims Graham, conscious that no words will adequately meet the tragedy of the situation.

"We just can't believe it," says Daisy.

"Neither can I," says Graham.

"I found him," says Daisy, "In the kitchen. I'm still in a state of shock."

Dylan puts his arms around his wife to comfort her.

"What a terrible shock it must have been," says Graham. "Have the police said anything about why it happened?"

"No," says Daisy. "But they were here yesterday – the police. Jim looked ashen after they had gone. He hardly spoke for the rest of the day. You know Jim. That wasn't like him at all. What can have happened?"

"I know," says Graham. "He sent me a text."

At that point two police officers, one male and one female, enter the shop from the kitchen.

"Is it Mr Robinson?" asks the female officer.

"Yes."

"You were a good friend of Mr Nott's, we understand."

"Yes, a very good friend. I have some information you may need to see. Perhaps we could go somewhere private?"

"Come outside to the car," says the male officer.

"I'll see you before I go," says Graham to Daisy and Maureen.

Having shared the contents of the text message with the officers, Graham returned to the shop and told the shop assistants all that he knew.

Daisy and Maureen were dumbstruck at first. Then Daisy, who had worked alongside Jim for 30 years, said: "There were rumours over the years that Jim might be homosexual. But he never spoke about it and I thought that perhaps people had got the wrong end of the stick and were being malicious. It seems like they were right."

Graham said: "I have known him nearly all my life and I honestly had no idea he might be gay. I just thought he was heterosexual but wasn't all that interested. I always suspected he thought he wasn't good looking enough to find a lady. It's come as a great surprise.

"And, do you know, the officers just told me that he would probably have got away with a caution or at the very most a small fine? I guess he couldn't take the feelings of shame."

"Do we know who the other man was in the toilets?"

"No," said Graham. "I didn't ask and I don't suppose they would have told me if I had."

"In this day and age it's not all that big a deal," said Maureen.

"When you see all that goes on, it doesn't seem all that much of a crime." said Daisy.

"Apparently it's still an offence to have sex in a public toilet," said Graham. "If he'd have done it outside – on the beach, for instance – it wouldn't have been a crime, unless two people or more had seen it going on."

"Fancy that," said Daisy, welling up. "Whatever he did, I know that he was always kind to me. He was such a cheerful man. He never complained, even though some would have said he had quite a limited life. The shop was his life – and Benjy. He loved Benjy."

"I wonder what'll happen to poor Benjy?" said Maureen. "He's such a lovely dog."

"Where is he now?" asked Graham.

"He's shut up in the living room," said Daisy. "Jim must have shut him in there so he didn't see what would happen. He's got all his food and water. Jim must have left them there for him."

"I'll look after Benjy, if you like," said Graham. "He knows me well now."

"It would be great if you could," said Daisy.

"Did Jim have any relatives?" asked Maureen.

"Not that I know of," said Daisy.

"I think he had a cousin – in Birmingham, I believe. But I don't think there was much contact," said Graham.

If it crossed the mind of any of the three people present that someone was going to fall for a business, a spacious flat and perhaps some considerable savings, all were far too decent and well-mannered to mention it.

"So it doesn't look as if there'll be any competition for having Benjy," said Graham.

Both women nodded in agreement.

They all agreed to stay at the shop that day for as long as they could be of any help to the police. No one wished to venture into the kitchen to see the body.

Graham returned home, with Benjy, that evening. The first thing he did was phone Anita, who had always had a soft spot for Jim and who had never stood in the way of his close friendship with her husband. When she heard the news she was very sympathetic and offered to go over to his house to console him. However, Graham was feeling tired after a traumatic day and turned down her offer.

Next he phoned Miriam, who was totally empathetic, and who invited him to dinner the following evening.

Chapter eleven
Another shock

It is just before midnight on the same day and Graham is about to retire to bed when he receives a phone call from Stephen Armitage.

"There's another fire at Beachworld," he says. "The fire brigade are here now. The shop unit where Next will be going is well alight and the fire is spreading to the Skechers' unit now."

"Oh, God," says Graham. "I don't believe it. I'm on my way."

As he makes the three minute drive from the house to Beachworld, Graham is feeling unusually depressed. He has lost his best friend and now his dream project is under threat again. It strikes him that this has been the worst day of his life so far.

Even before he reaches the car park he can see an orange glow in the sky and black smoke billowing across the roads, blown in the direction of the town by a strong north-easterly wind.

He parks up and rushes to the retail section of the development where he sees three fire engines and members of the fire crews scurrying around. Hoses are being employed in efforts to stem the blaze.

Stephen runs to meet Graham.

"It's those bloody arsonists again," says Graham. "How do they get past security? Someone's head is going to roll over this."

"We don't know yet if it's arson. But if it is I just don't know how they manage to get in to do this," says Stephen. "We both know how we've tightened security every time we've had one of these fires."

"Are the police here?"

"Yes, they're over there."

"I'll go and talk to them."

Within an hour the spread of the fire was controlled and damage limited to the two shop units. Later that day fire officers told Graham that they had found rags doused in petrol inside one of the units. This was exactly the same method that arsonists had used in the two previous incidents at the site.

The police assured Graham that they would carry out thorough investigations. As previous assurances had led to nothing he had little confidence that the culprits would be caught. CCTV cameras had found nothing of interest so far.

Hard questions were asked at Beachworld that day. How had intruders managed to get into the complex in the first place when the main entrance to the site was manned 24 hours a day? Why had regular patrols within the site not been effective?

Graham was unimpressed by some of the answers he received from his staff. He sacked the security officer that day.

During the morning Graham's father, Ray, who had seen a Facebook post about the fire, phoned his son from Valencia to find out more about what had happened and to express his concern.

"I think someone has got it in for you, son," he said. "We all know there are some people who don't like your development. It wouldn't surprise me if some of the local businessmen are behind these fires. It's all down to jealousy, I think.

"You would think that people would be pleased to see

someone getting on in the world and putting some money into the town. There will be good spin-offs for everyone when a lot more visitors come here."

"I know, Dad. I tell people that till I'm blue in the face. But don't worry. This development is going to happen come what may. Whoever's behind this is not going to win."

Ray continued: "But you know what does worry me – that one day someone is going to get burnt alive in one of these fires. It could happen."

"I know, I know. That worries me too, believe me. Let's hope the police can get to the bottom of it this time."

"Don't hold your breath, son. Not many crimes get solved these days, do they?"

"You're right, dad. But this is a serious matter and I think they will treat it seriously."

"Well I hope so. You're going through an awful time, what with Jim dying as well. Mum sends her love. We're both thinking of you. If you can manage it, chin up, son."

"Exactly, chin up."

When he kept his dinner engagement with Miriam that evening Graham was in a sombre mood, brought on by the events of the past two days. Miriam was calm and understanding, listening intently to his accounts and occasionally taking his hand to provide comfort.

It became apparent to her that the loss of Jim was far more distressing to Graham than the fire had been.

"I wish he had spoken to me before he took that drastic step," he said. "Perhaps I could have given him some sense of perspective. I understand his sense of shame and acute embarrassment. But these days I guess he would only have received a police caution and no one would have found out about it all. When I walked Benjy along the salt marsh I sometimes saw the odd male head pop up. I always assumed that they were having sex among the bushes. Is doing the same thing in a public toilet any worse than that? We're supposed to be enlightened about these things these days, aren't we? What he did was trivial surely?"

Miriam grinned: "Just the sort of trivial thing that would have been meat and drink to Jim when he was being gossipy."

Graham saw the irony in that, but felt a need to be defensive on behalf of his friend.

"There was never any malice in what Jim said about people. It was just fun for him and never did anyone any real harm."

Miriam was sceptical on this latter point but didn't pursue this thought out of respect for Graham.

He reminisced at length about the experiences he had shared with Jim at school. He explained that although many of their fellow pupils treated Jim as a figure of fun and a target for their contempt, he could always appreciate his quirkiness, his intelligent cynicism, his wisdom and his good-natured amiability.

Graham was not normally given to nostalgia, sentimentality or introspection. He almost always concentrated on the present and the future and usually spoke in a direct manner, spare with words.

It was the first time that Miriam had seen him in this mood, and she liked him all the more for it.

He moved on to talking about the fire.

"Someone has got it in for me. I suppose it could be any one of a number of people who object to the development."

"You're right," said Miriam. "There are some very jealous people around. Some have so little confidence in their own businesses that they can't stand the thought of someone else doing better than they are.

"But committing arson. I didn't think anyone would stoop that low."

"We've had fires before, as you know. And it's been proved beyond doubt that they were started deliberately. There's no doubt that this one was arson too. The police say they're on to it. I do hope they are.

"I'm determined, though, that this isn't going to delay the opening. Even if we have to work 24/7 and pay out for loads of overtime, it's going to be done. I'll put armed guards on the site if I have to.

"Someone's been sleeping on the job so far. How did anyone get in, leave petrol-soaked rags and then get out again? The first thing I did this morning was sack Jack Toulson, our security manager. A bit hard on him, perhaps, but someone had to carry the can. Pour encourager les autres."

"You always told me the security was really tight," said Miriam. "Are you sure it isn't an inside job?"

"Of course I've thought of that. Why do you think I sacked Toulson? It'll be interesting to see if all this stops now he's gone."

"Don't you trust him then?"

"He could be a contrary so-and-so, but I always have trusted him. He was in charge of security for all of my shops. Ex-police officer with a good work record. But there's only a couple of people except me who have 24 hour access to the site.

"Apart from Toulson there's Stephen Armitage, who's

going to be my general manager. He's an American guy. Very able."

"Do you trust him?"

"I do. And anyway I didn't take him on until after the first two fires occurred. What could his motive be? He's going to have a very well paid job with me for as long as he wants it."

"A mystery then. This Toulson chap seems to be the most likely suspect."

"Perhaps. We'll see," said Graham.

****

"Stephen, Anita here. It's terrible news about the fire. I've spoken to Graham and he said it would be okay for me to have a look at what's happened. I could come this morning if you've got time to meet me. You could show me the hotel too and all the other things I haven't seen."

"Is Graham not coming in himself this morning?" said Stephen.

"He's going over to Nottingham for a board meeting. He'll be away all day. But he's quite happy for you to show me around."

"All right. I could meet you at the reception at eleven."

"That's fine. Look forward to seeing you, love."

Two hours after this phone call was made, Anita left her parents' house and walked through the town centre towards Beachworld. It was a bitterly cold day, with an east wind sending a chill through the hundreds of shoppers who had braved the weather to go to the January sales.

As she reached the reception gate of Beachworld a

man standing at the edge of the car park stared in her direction. As she disappeared from view he sat down on a sea front bench removed a rucksack from his shoulder, took out a sandwich box and began to eat.

Two hours later Anita left the site, accompanied by Stephen. They made their way across the car park and both got into a Mercedes AMG saloon. It sped away with Stephen in the driver's seat.

The man with the rucksack, Darren Gibson, observed this closely, got up from the bench and walked away in the direction of the town centre.

Later that afternoon he passed by Anita's parents' house and observed the Mercedes parked in the street outside. During the next few hours he walked past the house at least another dozen times. On the last occasion he saw Stephen getting into his car and driving away.

Chapter twelve
Goodbye, old friend

Jim Nott's funeral was an event which no one was looking forward to.

That might seem an odd thing to write. Surely, you might ask, no one looks forward to anyone's funeral? Not so. Many funerals are anticipated as a celebration of a life well lived. This is especially the case where the deceased is of advanced years and the inevitable demise is predictable, timely and in the natural course of birth, life and death. Such funerals usually begin as sad, solemn affairs. For a mourner who is not of the immediate family, there is a curiosity as to who will attend – and who will not. For such a mourner, the trick of avoiding the embarrassment of shedding tears during the funeral service itself is to avoid eye contact with any grieving widows, widowers, children, grandchildren or siblings of the deceased person. It's a little like looking the other way as the nurse approaches with the dreaded hypodermic needle or the dentist wielding the drill.

When the curtains close at the crematorium or the last handful of dust is dropped into the grave there is a palpable sense of relief.

The next ordeal for our mourner is to run the gauntlet of waiting relatives as they wait to shake hands, kiss or hug on the way out of the venue. This is much more of an ordeal for those relatives than it is for our mourner, so most will not wish to extend the process any more than is polite.

The next phase involves chatting amiably to fellow mourners, including family members, outside the crematorium or church for a decent amount of time before heading off to the wake.

The wake is where the enjoyment of the day reaches its high point. There will be a cheerful camaraderie between people who have not seen or spoken to each other for years and a resumption of relationships between some relatives and friends who used to meet at christenings and weddings but now have only funerals to look forward to. Even close kin of the deceased find themselves relaxing, sometimes against their will and their intentions.

This run of the mill sequence of events at funerals is much harder to sustain when the death is out of kilter with the expected patterns of the life/death continuum. When a child has died before its parents or a whole family has been wiped out in an accident, the normal rules of engagement are thrown into confusion. And it is the same with suicide. The very thought of it is alien to the imagination of most people and therefore casts a pall over the customs and practices of funerals.

Such was the case with Jim Nott's funeral. Those who remembered him as the affable newsagent bursting with mischievous but essentially innocent gossip, found themselves totally unable to empathise with the plight which had led to his decision to take his own life. Mentally they were unable to square the circle from the man they thought they knew to someone who would seek pleasure in a gents' toilet and who would go on to hang himself.

The bad taste left in everyone's mouth was not helped in any way by the setting and circumstances surrounding the funeral itself.

Jim's paternal grandparents, Cecil and Margaret, known to all as Cec and Peggy, had hailed from a small village called Hedgeby, a few miles inland from Sanderholme. It was set in flat, almost featureless, fenland, dissected by a network of broad dykes and prone to mists at all seasons of the year. Although shortly after Cecil and Margaret were married they had moved to Sanderholme to open their shop, on their deaths they had followed previous generations of Cecil's family and been buried in the graveyard at Hedgeby's St Oswald's Church. Jim's parents, Jim Senior and Martha, had adhered to the family tradition and had also been buried there and Jim had always expressed the wish to follow suit.

St Oswald's Church is a limestone structure originally built in the 12th century, but was restored in both the 15th and 19th centuries. Seen at close quarters it is an imposing building with an impressive tower with a Norman base later heightened in the Perpendicular style. But its location is well off the beaten track and it is cloaked in an incongruous anonymity by a cluster of tall yew trees.

Some 80 mourners arrived on a chill March morning, parking their cars along the verges of the narrow track leading to the church. As they walked towards the building there was a pervasive smell of rotting cauliflower, evidently coming from the fields surrounding the churchyard.

As people reached the front door of the church they were greeted by a very old woman with long white hair and a pronounced stoop. She cheerfully informed them that the church would be very cold as the heating bills could not be afforded.

Graham arrived accompanied by Daisy and Maureen, Jim's shop assistants, to whom he had given a lift. The rest of the congregation mainly comprised regular shop customers, together with a handful of old family friends, Jim's accountant and his solicitor, George Mounsey.

It was Mr Mounsey, who, a few days earlier, had informed Graham that he was the main beneficiary of Jim's estate. Learning of this confirmed what Graham had always suspected: that he was Jim's only close friend. There were two financial bequests, a sum of £10,000 to Daisy, his long-serving and faithful member of staff, and a £1,000 to Maureen, who was a relative newcomer to the team. Everything else went to Graham, who promised to keep the shop going and appoint Daisy as manager.

As they sat in the pews waiting for the arrival of the coffin, Graham silently contemplated what had been the essence of his friendship with Jim. It had been based on trust, each man knowing that the other would never do the other a bad turn. From the very start of their relationship Graham had been Jim's protector against the school bullies and Jim had been the calm dispenser of sage advice at any time Graham had needed it.

But the nagging feeling which Graham could not drive from his mind was that Jim had let him down at the end. Why had he not confided in him about the troubles which had led to his shocking suicide? More than that. Why had Jim never felt able to reveal to his friend that he was gay? Was the absolute trust that Graham had placed in Jim never truly reciprocated?

The more he thought about the manner of Jim's death, the more he came to doubt whether you could ever really know another human being.

Although never physically strong, Jim had always appeared to be a well grounded person, wise, utterly reliable and with a clear sense of what he wanted out of his somewhat constrained life. Now it seemed that this had all been a sham – that his seemingly indomitable amiability had always been a mask hiding a secret sadness and vulnerability.

Graham himself had an unfailingly positive attitude to life. He was seldom given to introspection or self-doubt. His view of those who opted out of life through suicide echoed that of French literary giant Chateaubriand who, writing about his own suicidal thoughts in his unforgettable masterpiece "Memoirs from Beyond the Tomb" said: "The man who tries to take his own life shows not so much the vigour of his soul as the feebleness of his nature."

It would never have occurred to Graham to criticise Jim for being gay or breaking the law in men's toilets, but he did condemn him for his "feebleness" in renouncing life.

Daisy had asked Graham to give the eulogy at the funeral service and he had, of course, agreed. He was to do the very best job he could, evoking tears from many members of the congregation. But his heart was not in it. He felt bereft and, much worse than that, betrayed.

There was a stirring at the rear of the church and everyone was up on their feet. The coffin was being processed to the music "The Lord's My Shepherd". Preceding the coffin was the hunched figure of the vicar, Father Joseph, from whose diminutive frame an inconceivably strong, deep voice boomed over the organ music: "I am the resurrection and the life, says the Lord. Those who believe in me even though they die, will live, and everyone who lives in me will never die."

Father Joseph, so titled owing to the High Anglican traditions at St Oswald's Church, was wearing a long black overcoat over his surplice, a commonsensical precaution in view of the sub-Arctic temperatures inside the church, but which did little to add to the pomp of the occasion and did nothing to advance Archbishop Laud's concept of "the beauty of holiness".

The first hymn was that old favourite "Jerusalem", an easy tune to sing and the most popular "school song" in the Anglosphere. But how many people have stopped to think about the ridiculousness of the words? Did "those feet in ancient time, Walk upon England's mountains green?" Clearly not. Others would argue differently.

The congregation sang the hymn with some gusto, so much so that the communal breath expelled in the cold air projected as much white mist as might have been produced by a score by vaping school pupils.

After a seemingly interminable address and various prayers led by Father Joseph, it was Graham's turn to give his eulogy. Despite his new nagging doubts about Jim's true character, he performed the task dutifully and with some panache. He teased the congregation that many of them would be secretly feeling a sense of relief that Jim had gone to his grave with their indiscretions yet to be imparted to the wider audience of his customer base. The manner of Jim's death was referred to only obliquely to spare any undue embarrassment.

The final prayers inside the church were accompanied by the swinging of incense around the coffin by Father Joseph. The odour emanating from this mingled interestingly with the all-persuasive smell of rotten cauliflower, thus providing the congregation with an abiding memory of this notable event.

It was with some relief that everyone filed out of the church into the fresh air to follow the coffin to the graveside. In fact there was no relief from the cauliflowers, but the freezing temperature outside the church appeared to be a few degrees higher than that inside. Father Joseph was taking no chances, though, and added a flamboyant brown fedora to his already bizarre costume, causing a few barely stifled giggles from some matriarchs among the gathering who should have known better.

The good Father conducted the commendation and committal as swiftly as decency allowed, enabling the mourners to scurry back to the warmth and comfort of their cars with minimal delay.

To complete the day's proceedings they gathered again a few minutes later at the Hedgeby Arms for liquid refreshments and sandwiches.

Everyone was satisfied that proper respects had been paid. For, as German novelist Thomas Mann reflected: "A man's dying is more the survivor's affair than his own".

Thus ended the celebration of the life and death of newsagent and tobacconist James Wilfred Nott.

Chapter thirteen
Vendetta

So what is happening in Nottinghamshire now that Graham is spending most of his time in Lincolnshire?

Austin is proving to be a dedicated and dynamic Chief Executive of the retail and property companies. His wife, Phoebe, is supportive and, as well as being a loving and caring mother to children Edward and Sophie, is a successful and lauded landscape artist.

Phoebe spent the first 30 years of her life in the United States, where she developed her painting skills in the magnificent surroundings of New England, world-famous for the magnificent colours of the trees in The Fall. Now the treescape of the nearby Sherwood Forest offers her ideal opportunities to develop her art. And inserting images of Robin Hood and his Merry Men into some of her pictures provides her with a lucrative market among the many tourists who visit the area. Nearer to home there are beautiful images to capture in the village of Papplewick and at nearby Newstead Abbey, the ancestral home of the famous poet and rake Lord Byron.

Daughter Sophie has inherited her mother's artistic flair and, at the age of 15, has already staged an exhibition of her own landscapes. What she has also inherited from her mother is stunning good looks. Phoebe is a tall, slim and leggy brunette with head-turning facial bone structure and Sophie is developing along similar lines – a real chip off the old block.

She attends Nottingham High School, an independent day school with a high reputation. At the same school is her 18-year-old brother, Edward, who is academically gifted but also a fine all-round sportsman, especially talented at rugby. He is tall and muscular and very popular with the female students at school. He is currently studying for his A' levels, aiming to go on to university, obtain a business degree and then follow his grandfather and father into the family companies.

It is a cloudy and damp winter's day and Sophie and Edward are making the short walk between school and their father's office, the headquarters of the Robinson empire in Nottingham's Waverley Street. Normally Phoebe transports them to and from school by car but on this particular day she has gone with two friends to London for a shopping trip.

Sophie and Edward both look smart in their black school uniforms, bearing the school crest with its three merles (blackbirds) and its motto lauda finem (praise to the end).

There is heavy traffic along the road that afternoon but one particular vehicle attracts the attention of the siblings. A new black Range Rover slows up as it passes them and both the driver and passenger look pointedly towards the youngsters.

The driver is a scruffy looking man with long straggly hair while the passenger is a balding slightly older looking individual.

"What was that all about?" asks Edward.

"I've no idea," said Sophie. "A bit spooky though, wasn't it?"

"I think they probably fancied you," said Edward teasingly. "Simon Atkins won't like that."

This struck a raw nerve for Sophie and she blushed. Simon Atkins was a slightly nerdy classmate of hers who had a serious crush on her. She had done nothing to encourage him – quite the reverse in fact – but he remained hopelessly infatuated.

She chided her brother, declaring: "Don't mention him, please. And as for those two blokes – they're old enough to be my grandfathers!"

****

Phoebe prided herself on being a hands-on parent. She encouraged her children to be independent while at the same time never being very far away. She was more protective of Sophie, realising that her daughter was becoming extremely attractive to boys. Although she would have hated to be thought of as a snob she believed there were boys in Papplewick who would be undesirable company for her daughter.

A few days after the walk from school with Edward, Sophie told her mother she would like to have a sleepover with a close friend and classmate, Kirsty, who was having a party to celebrate her sixteenth birthday. Phoebe, wishing to be assured that none of the "undesirables" had been invited to the party, asked her daughter for a list of the others who were likely to be there. She was happy with what she heard and gave the go-ahead to the sleepover.

So on the appointed day on the following weekend Sophie set off from home to walk to Kirsty's house. This was at the other side of the village from Robinson's family's mansion which was just outside the village envelope. It was a bright but cold day and she wearing a smart padded blue coat over a beautiful, flowery dress, very flattering but conservative enough to satisfy her mother's wishes, and carrying a small overnight bag.

Her route took her along the quiet main road through the village. She was passing the Griffins Head pub when she noticed a Range Rover passing by, with a driver and passenger aboard. In this rural area there was nothing unusual about seeing a Range Rover, very much the countryman's vehicle of choice. But this black model with two occupants took her mind back to the walk with Edward along Waverley Street. She briefly pondered this coincidence but her thoughts soon turned elsewhere as she saw none other than her admirer Simon Atkins approaching her along the footpath. She mentally flinched at the idea of meeting him so unexpectedly. He didn't even live in the village. He was a Nottingham city boy.

"Hi Sophie. Fancy meeting you here," he said nervously.

Sophie blushed but then quickly regained her composure.

"Yes. Hello, Simon. What brings you here?"

"I just fancied a walk in the country."

"It's a long way to walk," said Sophie, doubting his motives.

"I haven't walked all the way. I got a bus. I've been walking round Moor Pond Woods."

"Oh. That's a nice spot."

"Are you busy? I wondered if you fancied a drink at the Tea Rooms?" said Simon, looking flustered.

"Well, no thanks. Not today. I'm on my way to Kirsty Palmer's birthday party."

"Oh, I see. I've not been invited to that."

"Oh, that's a shame. I don't think there'll be a lot of people there. Just a few of her best girl friends from school, and one or two locals from the village."

Simon was downcast. In fact the sole reason he was in Papplewick that day was on the very unlikely off chance of meeting Sophie or even catching a glimpse of her. For the past two months he had been taking the bus to Papplewick at weekends with the very same end in view. Each time he had walked past the Robinson mansion he had peered through the wrought iron gates at the entrance to the grounds. On the one hand he was desperate to see Sophie, however fleetingly, but at the same time was fearful of her reaction if she were to catch him looking for her.

He said a doleful goodbye to Sophie and walked away crestfallen. He felt he was an abject failure. Not only was he making no progress with his prospective girlfriend but he was sorely hurt not to have been on the guest list for Kirsty's party. But he was determined not to give up. Instead he decided to redouble his efforts to woo his love.

****

Graham was cooking his dinner when there was a loud knocking on his front door. He opened it to be met by Darren Gibson, looking wild-eyed and excitable.

"Hello, Darren. Come in."

"I will. We need to speak."

Graham ushered him into the lounge and pointed him towards an armchair.

"Excuse me a second. I'm cooking my dinner. I'll just turn the oven down."

When he returned from the kitchen he sat down in a chair opposite to Darren.

"What can I do for you?" he asked.

Darren was seething with anger.

"I want to talk to you – about you shagging my wife. Don't deny it. She told me all about it."

Graham replied calmly: "It's true. We did spend one night together. She told me she had left you."

"She might have left me for a while. But we're still married."

Then he spat out these words: "Just because you're a bleedin' billionaire don't give you the right to go shagging other people's wives. She's mine. She'll always be mine. So you can keep your grubby hands off her."

"Are you sure she's still yours?" asked Graham. "She told me you had treated her badly and there was no way she would go back to you."

"She's lying. I love her to bits and would never treat her badly. Never have. You want to watch what you're saying. Why can't you find your own woman and leave mine alone?"

Graham could feel Darren's rage building up. The muscles in his neck were tense and his pupils becoming weirdly dilated. He was rubbing his hands together as if he might be preparing to spring out of his chair and land a punch.

Not at all convinced that Darren was the innocent party in his troubled marriage, Graham was not prepared to give any ground to him and therefore went on to the offensive himself.

"I think you need to go," he said. "I've got nothing more to say to you."

Darren suddenly rose from the chair, moved towards Graham and jabbed him in the chest with his finger.

"You've got nothing more to say to *me*? Well, I haven't finished with *you*. I'm telling you now, I'm going to kill you. Not tonight, but when you least expect it.

Keep watching your back fella."

Graham made no reply but merely pointed towards the door.

Darren's shoulder barge as he pushed past Graham had little effect, which was unsurprising considering his slight build.

As he reached the door he declared: "When I see you next you'll be in your coffin!"

He slammed the door behind him, leaving Graham to ponder upon what had just happened.

His first reaction was to phone Anita to warn her about her husband's state of mind.

She was alarmed by what she was told, but when Graham said he intended to tell the police about Darren's threat to kill him, she urged him not to do that. She argued that although her husband was in a poor mental state and had a furious temper she didn't believe he would ever kill anyone.

"He's a loudmouth but he's also a coward. Don't worry too much about him, love. I don't."

Graham was to some extent reassured by her words. But he went on to ask her why she had revealed to Darren that they had slept together.

"I'm sorry, love. I shouldn't have done that. We were having a row and I used that as ammunition. It was a mistake, but I needed him to know that it was all over between us. I loved him once, but I didn't expect him to turn out as such a sad bastard. You know that I don't like falling out with people. But he just won't listen to reason when he's in one of his angry moods. It's like the old red mist just comes down."

"All right, I won't take this any further, but you should be careful yourself."

"Thanks. I will."

****

Miriam and her good friend and neighbour Shirley Bincroft were in Miriam's sitting room on a wet Saturday afternoon enjoying a glass of red wine together.

Shirley, now in her late fifties, was still as effervescent as a bottle of good champagne. Her bubbly hairstyle was little changed from her schooldays and her chatter was frequently interspersed with good-natured giggles.

To all and sundry she was friendly, kind and helpful and gave the impression of being one of the happiest people alive. And essentially her outward demeanour reflected a deeper joy of being on the planet. However, it was a testimony to her good nature and resilience that she had managed to maintain her breezy disposition. For in many ways her life had not been an easy one.

It was true that she had a husband who adored her and that she also had a loving daughter and three lovely grandchildren. But she had suffered some cruel setbacks too.

Shortly after her marriage to Trevor tragedy struck when both her parents were killed in a horrific motorway pile-up. They were trapped in their overturned car and died at the scene of the accident.

Ronald and Beryl had been the sort of parents any child would have been blessed to have. Ronald, an insurance agent, idolised his daughter. A steady, sometimes taciturn, man, he had a very dry, sarcastic sense of humour and had few close friends. But he was a devoted husband and father who was kind and decent to a tee.

It was from her mother that Shirley inherited her infectiously optimistic and positive view of life. As a teenager Beryl had been a leading student of Sanderholme's premier dance and theatre school. Her performance as Eliza Doolittle in the school's production of "My Fair Lady" at the town's Pier Theatre had gained her rapturous applause. She later gained a job in the chorus line of the theatre's popular annual revue, Bert Biggins' Seaside Frolics, a mixture of comedy, magic acts, singing and dancing which delighted the town's holidaymakers for several decades. Before her retirement in her mid-forties Beryl had become the leader of the chorus line as well as a popular soubrette in her own right.

To Shirley, Beryl was the type of mother that most girls dream of – a best friend and companion who could empathise with all the stages of a young girl's growing up.

The loss of these pillars of Shirley's life was almost impossible to bear. Her grief ran deep but somehow she survived and her irrepressible smile returned. There were more traumas to come, though, in the form of three miscarriages as she and Trevor anticipated the birth of their first child. Many tears were shed on each of these tragic events and many mortals would have collapsed under the weight of sadness. But, again, Shirley managed to bounce back.

After this "winter of discontent" in her life came a period of tranquillity interspersed with some periods of unalloyed joy. The birth of her daughter, Madeleine, marked the start of one of those periods, followed years later by the arrival of the grandchildren. The business was thriving and all on God's earth now seemed to be well.

At the times when things were going badly Trevor had always been "a rock" for the wife he cherished so much. Shirley often wished, though, that he would share more of her excitement when the nice events occurred. The truth of it was that she was the epitome of a "glass half full" person while Trevor was the opposite.

In their business she was the one who charmed the clients while Trevor could be quite grumpy. Consequently in their shop he was usually banished to the back room while Shirley ran front of house. Generally that worked well for them. But as a press and wedding photographer Trevor inevitably had a good deal of interface with the public. Mostly he was able to slip back into the false bonhomie which he had employed while working for Farndales as a sea front snapper. There were exceptions, though, not least the time when a visiting Government Minister carelessly flicked ash from his cigarette on to a woman's plate of sandwiches and then on to Trevor's camera as he was taking a press picture. Trevor had used his not insignificant weight to push the Minister aside, resulting in an undignified kerfuffle between him and two security guards.

On another occasion he had been hired by a local newspaper to take photographs of the crowning ceremony of the Sanderholme Carnival Queen. The girl who had been chosen showed early signs of being a diva as she insisted on seeing all the photos before Trevor sent them to the paper. She said she wanted to make sure he had captured "her best side".

Trevor's rejoinder, overheard by an outraged Town Mayoress, had been: "I shouldn't worry, luv. I don't think you have one." This led to an ugly scene and a reprimand from the newspaper's editor.

Over the years Shirley was able to brush such incidents aside and just laugh them off as "just Trevor being Trevor".

Then came the fateful day when her husband suffered his severe heart attack. It took a few months for him to recover physically but there were some mental after-effects that remained with him. His grumpiness became much more to the fore. Shirley accepted this situation stoically but nevertheless found that working with her husband during the day and then living with him every night could often be stressful.

She eventually found some relief by taking up a job as a graphic design lecturer at the Robinson Business Studies Suite at Havenmarsh Academy and employing an assistant at the shop. She enjoyed her job enormously and Trevor seemed reasonably content while he engrossed himself in his own work.

However, his good progress stalled when he began to be agitated by the camp site set up at the end of Lavender Avenue. His anger at the mess the men were making on the beach and the threat he believed them to pose to the area's respectable residents gradually turned into an obsession.

He was constantly finding excuses to walk to the beach so that he could spy on what was going on. He showed Shirley hundreds of photographs of the camp, some taken while the men were absent, but others obtained from a hidden vantage point in the undergrowth when they were in situ. These latter pictures scared Shirley, who feared what might happen to her husband if the men caught him there.

"I don't know what to do," Shirley told Miriam as they sat sharing their bottle of wine. "He gets cross at me when I tell him to forget about those men. I have never seen him so angry. And, as you know well, he's cross with you too for helping them. After all you did for us.

"He's incorrigible!"

"That's a very good word," said Miriam.

Shirley broke into a broad smile and declared: "You see what he's done to me. I've even swallowed the dictionary now!"

Miriam laughed.

"Anyway you've heard enough about all my troubles," said Shirley. "I want to know how things are going with you."

"Oh, I'm fine. Nothing much to report really."

Shirley cocked her head to one side and pulled a funny face.

"What's all that about?" asked Miriam.

"Well, I was told that a certain handsome multi-millionaire has been seen around here quite a lot just recently."

"Where? Down Lavender Avenue?"

"Actually at The Cedars, Lavender Avenue."

"Oh, do you mean Graham Robinson? I never thought he was a multi-millionaire."

"Oh, really?" teased Shirley.

"Yes, really. I'm very disappointed to hear what you've just told me. I was given to understand he was a multi-*billionaire*."

Shirley giggled.

"You're a terrible woman. Anyway how's it going with Graham?"

"Actually, I really like him. We just seem to gel somehow. If I'm honest I quite fancy him."

"He's pretty dishy – in a mature kind of way," said

Shirley.

"We're all *mature,* dear. It's just that he's a little bit better preserved than most men of his age. And he's such a nice man."

"I've always found him very pleasant," said Shirley. "Some people have a few things to say about him, but I know Trevor thinks highly of him. I believe he was a good friend to him at school."

"What sort of 'things' do people say about him?" asked Miriam, a little sharply.

"It's about that time he was in all the papers, over being a bad landlord."

"I remember all that. I haven't said anything to him on that subject. I don't want to spoil things. One day I'll ask him all about it. All I can say is that he seems a decent chap to me. It was a long time ago now. I take people as I find them."

"I think you're right. Trevor always says there must have been two sides to the story. Do you think anything will come of it?"

"What? The bad landlord thing?"

"No, don't be silly. I mean will anything come of your friendship with Graham?"

"I like him very much. We just talk all the time. I can't tell you how good that is.

"You know, I've got a lovely family and some great friends, but when I draw the curtains every night there's just me. When I got rid of my second husband it was such relief to be on my own. No tension. No bullying. No fights. No bruises or cut lips. Sheer heaven.

"But then, after a while, you begin to feel lonely and you feel robbed of your self-esteem. I don't think I'm the sort of person who was ever meant to live alone. I just crave company. Not any old company. My two husbands never gave me proper company. The first one just wanted to use me and the second only wanted to abuse me. Sounds like a song doesn't it? Graham's always singing little songs to himself. Some people might find that annoying, but I don't mind it. It's like he's got music in his soul."

"Oh, dear. Quite smitten aren't we?" said Shirley.

Miriam grinned and nodded.

"I think you may be right. And it's not because he's a multi-millionaire!"

"I know, I know," replied Shirley. "I don't think you're that short of money that you would care about that sort of thing."

"You're right. I don't need money. I need company and contentment and to be loved. There were times when I thought that God's love was enough for anyone. But not for me, I'm afraid."

"Yeah, we don't want you taking yourself off to a nunnery!"

"No chance of that, Shirl. Matins once a week at St Crispin's is enough for me.

"You know, Graham's had a rough time of it recently. There's been these terrible fires at Beachworld and then he lost his best friend, Jim Nott. That was tragic."

"Yes, it was. Jim was a nice man." said Shirley. "Trevor and I went to the funeral. Graham gave a lovely eulogy."

"I'm sure he did. He was really cut up about the way Jim died. He just wished Jim had talked to him about his problem.

"Anyway, back to Trevor. We don't want him having another heart attack, do we? I'll tell you what I'll do.

When I get a chance I'll speak to the men at the camp and ask them if they have any idea how long they'll be here. I'm sure Matthew will tell me. Surely it's not a long term thing."

"Would you do that? Then at least I might be able to tell Trevor that those men won't be here for much longer. In the meantime don't mention anything to Trevor about what we've been saying about him."

"Of course I won't," said Miriam. "It's been great talking to you. We must do this more often. Another glass of wine?"

"Don't mind if I do."

****

Graham was working late at night in his office at Beachworld when he heard fire engine sirens. Given his recent experiences such sounds provoked a sense of foreboding. He was rational enough, though, not to dwell on it.

After catching up with his emails he decided that, at midnight, it was time for him to go home to bed. He had a routine of walking around the site when he arrived and when he left, to check on progress with the work and to make sure all security precautions were in place.

As he approached the hotel he came across a group of labourers who were working under floodlights laying a car park. Work was being carried out 24 hours a day to ensure that the development would be completed in time for the planned Easter opening.

The foreman shouted over to him: "Have you heard about the fire, Mr Robinson?"

Graham swivelled round towards the man, dreading

what he was to be told.

"No, what fire?"

"At the Academy. According to Radio Lincolnshire it's well ablaze tonight."

"Oh my god. That's terrible," said Graham.

"Do you know any more? Any casualties?"

"No, nothing else really. The fire brigade are there."

"Thanks, Larry. Goodnight."

"Goodnight, Mr Robinson."

****

Graham cuts short his walk around the site and strides purposefully to his car. He drives towards the school, his old school which means so much to him. When he reaches two blocks away he can already see flames reaching high into the sky. The whole area is enveloped in black smoke.

He parks up in the street adjacent to the Academy and walks towards the scene.

The road outside the school is lined with people curious to know what is happening. Graham can see three fire engines and a hive of activity as fire fighters scuttle around doing their job. Hoses are being directed towards the burning building.

Graham approaches a female police officer who is standing at the school gate.

"Please stay back," she calls out.

Graham stops in his tracks and joins the crowd of onlookers. Among them he recognises Alan Travis, a teacher at the school, and goes to stand beside him.

The man greets him with a woeful expression.

"Oh, Mr Robinson. This is awful isn't it?"

"Yes, it certainly is. Do you know what's happened?"

"I believe the fire started in the Business Studies Suite," says Alan.

Graham has a sharp intake of breath.

"Really?"

"I'm afraid so."

Graham remains silent and Alan too adds nothing more to the conversation. He appreciates the implication of what he has just revealed. This is not some anonymous Business Studies department. It is the Robinson Business Studies Suite. Financing it and seeing it come to fruition has been the proudest achievement of Graham's life. It means more to him than his business empire – more to him than Beachworld. It was his way of paying back what he felt he owed to the town that raised him. He has dreamt of fostering a host of wannabe Graham Robinsons to enter the world of business and make a success of their lives.

He has no more to say. He just stares at the inferno for several minutes and then, to his horror, sees a section of the school roof crumble and fall crashing to the ground.

He remains glued to the spot for a further couple of hours as the fire fighters get the blaze under control. The flames have gone and what remains is the acrid smell of burnt building materials and grey smoke which makes his eyes smart.

He is desperate to know more details about the fire, including how it started and how much damage has been caused. But he realises that now is not the time and that the authorities will only make details known when they are ready. So he heads home. As he drives along the promenade a song usually so fitting for a bright day at the seaside comes into his head: "The sun has got his hat on

And he's coming out today". He changes the words and sings out loud: "The devil has got his hat on And he's coming out tonight."

****

It was the early hours of the morning when Graham went to bed. But not to sleep. His sadness at what had happened to the Business Studies Suite was overtaken by much darker thoughts. He had begun to consider the recent chain of events, three fires at Beachworld and now a fire at a school department which bears his name.

Ever since the plans for Beachworld were first mooted he had sensed an antipathy towards him which he felt had gone further than just opposition to the scheme. The school fire had now convinced him that he was being subjected to a vendetta. But by who?

As he lay in bed tossing and turning he considered the possibilities. Could it be a local businessman who feared competition from Beachworld? Or perhaps someone jealous of his new connection with Anita? This latter option seemed unlikely as the first two fires took place before his recent dalliance with his ex-wife. Henry Fulford came into his mind as a suspect, both as an opponent of Beachworld and as someone who might well be jealous of his relationship with Anita. He thought of the scratched car all those years ago.

Did he have other enemies from the business world that he wasn't even aware of?

Then what of Darren? Graham had only just found out that he was in Sanderholme and on the warpath. But had he made previous visits to the area? And when had Anita first hinted to him that she might revive her relationship with her former husband?

Graham had always been someone who could take "the slings and arrows" in life with equanimity. Now, though, he was becoming overwhelmed with setbacks, not least the loss of his best friend, Jim.

The best thing that had happened to him recently had been his new friendship with Miriam. As the long sleepless night came to an end he decided that he needed to see her as soon as possible. This was not exactly to find a shoulder to cry on as to meet someone who would offer empathy mingled with a calm appraisal of his situation.

After he had breakfasted and taken Benjy for his morning constitutional, he phoned Miriam at 8am, the earliest he felt politeness would allow. She told him she was just about to phone him as she had heard about the fire on local radio when she rose that morning.

Graham told her he would like to see her and she invited him round for morning coffee.

At the door she greeted him with a kiss and a hug.

"Come in, my poor little soldier," she said.

Graham smiled ruefully. He was feeling better already.

For an hour or so they discussed his fears that there was a vendetta against him. Miriam was as understanding and rational as he expected she would be, but could do nothing to help unravel the mystery. He had involved the police each time there had been a fire at Beachworld but their investigations, which he had complained had been cursory so far, had led to no answers. Miriam's advice was that he should go back to them, arguing that the school fire would put a new complexion on matters.

"I'll go to the police station now," he said. "At least

I'll find out more about what's happened to the school."

At the police station he met Detective Sergeant Janet Crow, who was able to tell him that there had been extensive damage to the Robinson Business Studies Suite but that, apart from some inevitable smoke damage, there had been no appreciable effect on the rest of the school. Subject to further investigations and reports from the fire service, the police were working on the hypothesis that the cause of the fire was likely to be arson.

"It could perhaps be some disgruntled pupil," conjectured the detective.

For the first time Graham tentatively suggested the name of Henry Fulford. He also mentioned Darren Gibson and his threats to kill and his admittedly flimsy suspicions about his former security manager, Jack Toulson.

The detective noted all of this and thanked him for his information. She already knew of Fulford as he was a prominent local businessman and of Toulson, having interviewed him about the Beachworld fires. Graham was able to give her a phone number for Gibson. He came away satisfied that he had been listened to and treated seriously.

Next he was keen to visit Havenmarsh Academy to see the extent of the damage for himself. On his arrival he was greeted by the head teacher, George Campbell, a middle-aged, bald-headed rather fierce looking Scot. Those acquainted with the history of Scottish Presbyterianism might have thought of him as a modern-day John Knox without the beard and moustache.

He escorted Graham to the beleaguered Business

Suite, which presented a tragically sorry sight. The whole roof had caved in and most of the damaged materials were piled high on the floors of the four classrooms. The whole area was blackened, with floors and furniture covered with a layer of soot. The air was polluted with dust which lessened the visibility and filled the nose and ears. It got to Graham's chest and he started to cough uncontrollably. Two fire officers emerged from one of the classrooms and advised Graham and the head to leave the area before they damaged their health.

They retreated to the head's study where Mr Campbell told Graham that, although rebuilding and re-equipping the suite would take some time, the insurance would meet the costs. He had already contacted the Trust which ran the Academy and had been told that temporary portable classrooms would be provided as needed while work was being carried out.

Graham promised to help in whatever way he could but was reassured by the head's efficient "can do" attitude.

"Any idea who might have done this?" asked Graham.

"I really have no idea," said Mr Campbell. "I can't think of any particular disaffected pupil."

"I think it's someone with a grudge against me," said Graham.

"Really? I know you have had a few problems with fires at your development site. But this seems a pretty dumb way of getting at you. I certainly hope, for your sake, that it isn't the case."

"Thank you. But you can understand that I may be getting a little paranoid?"

"I do."

The two men shook hands and agreed to keep each

other in touch with any developments.

However, as Graham opened the door to leave the study he found a fire officer about to enter it.

"Ah, Station Officer Rigby. Come in," said the head in a formal manner. "Stay a moment, please, Mr Robinson. You might be interested in this."

The fire officer entered the room while Graham hovered in the doorway.

"Good morning, Mr Campbell, Mr Robinson. I believe we have found the root of the fire," said the Station Officer, "Rags doused in petrol."

"Again!" declared Graham. "The same modus operandi the arsonists used in the Beachworld fires. This is about me."

"Yes it is the same. But it's not an unusual method," said Rigby. "So I wouldn't jump to too many conclusions yet. The police are aware of what we have found. They will be coming to the site soon to carry out their investigations – forensics and the like."

****

A week went by during which time the police conducted numerous interviews both at the school and at Beachworld. Graham was at work on site there when he was telephoned by Detective Inspector Crow to keep him abreast of how the investigations were going.

She revealed that so far there had been no breakthroughs. Fulford and Toulson both had watertight alibis relating to the two recent fires but so far they had not managed to trace Darren Gibson. Anita had given them as much information as she could about his likely haunts but this had been to no avail.

"We are doing all we can to trace this man," said the detective. "Even if he has had nothing to do with the fires we take his threats to kill you and your ex-wife very seriously."

"I don't know what to think about him," said Graham. "He's certainly a very angry and jealous man. But what about the previous fires and vandalism we have had to contend with? His break with Anita has only happened quite recently, I believe. And it's only a few days ago that he found out that Anita and I had been, shall we say, intimate again."

"I take your point," said Detective Inspector Crow. "I'll be in touch again soon."

Chapter fourteen
Jealousy

Four men sat in a circle drinking tea in the thicket at the end of Lavender Avenue – Matthew, Gilbert, Harry and Gerald. No one was talking. Each man was looking around the circle nervously. There was a tangible tension between them.

Matthew was the first to speak.

"Let's forget that last conversation ever happened, shall we?"

There was some grunting and then a return to silence.

"Look, I'm with you all the way – well nearly all the way."

Gilbert threw his tea mug on to the floor into the middle of the circle.

"See, there you go again," he said. "You haven't really put your heart into revolution. I've met a few of your sort over the years and you're all the same. Your hero Proudhon was just like that. He never really believed in revolution."

"It's true he didn't want to see a violent revolution. But he did wish to overturn capitalism," replied Matthew.

"A bloody wimp!" snapped Gilbert.

"Oh, come on," shouted Matthew. "Do you never give up picking at people?"

"We can't be having any backsliding. Not now."

"Can't you two just bloody shut up?" said Harry, the scruffiest of the men. "You're getting on my tits now."

"Shut up, Harry. What do you know about anything, except where your next fix is coming from?" asked Gilbert.

"I'll shut up then. I know my place, Adolf."

Gilbert frowned angrily and threw his arms in front of him in a sign of utter frustration.

Harry turned to Gerald and nudged his shoulder.

"What do you think, eh?"

Gerald, who had been looking detached from the conversation, replied: "I don't give a fig for all your arguing. So long as I get my money, that's all I care about. It's me who is sticking his neck out here. You lot are okay."

"Armchair generals are we?" asked Matthew.

Gerald ignored the remark and returned to his previous vegetative state.

"Come on, let's get going. We have a meeting to attend," said Gilbert, jumping to attention.

Matthew rose too, but without much enthusiasm. The other two colleagues groaned, finished off their tea and reluctantly scrambled to their feet.

The foursome made their way to the main track through the salt marsh and walked in the direction of the town. It was a cool day with a gusty north-east wind which ruffled the unkempt hair of three of the party. Although the shortest in height and with something of a paunch, Gilbert presented as the most animated of the group, with his short-cropped hair and urgent stride. He marched at the front of the others, with Matthew following and the other men snail-like stragglers constantly having to be urged on by their leader.

It was late afternoon in failing light, and, as it happened, Graham was walking with Benjy along the track from the opposite direction, making his way from Beachworld to visit Miriam. As he passed the group of men he wished them a "good afternoon".

Gilbert replied with a cursory nod and Matthew raised a hand in acknowledgement. The other two men, whose heads and faces were largely covered with black balaclavas, didn't react to Graham's greeting in any way. In view of the help he had given to Miriam on several occasions when she had dispensed refreshments to the men, he found himself feeling annoyed at this low key reception.

"Miserable, ungrateful so-and-sos," he thought to himself.

There was something about this group which always made him feel uneasy. He had previously sensed some vague feeling of familiarity about Matthew. Now, as he passed the last of the four men, Gerald, there was something about his shambling gait which gave him another feeling of vague recognition.

When he reached Miriam's she had the coffee pot on the go straightaway.

"I just passed your mates from the bushes on my way here. They're a strange bunch," said Graham.

"It took them all their time to acknowledge my existence. I really don't know why you bother with them."

Miriam smiled and told him to "change the record" as she was becoming slightly weary of his moans about her charitable acts for the men.

"They are a strange bunch," she said. "But as far as I can tell they are harmless. I keep telling people that. I had Trevor here again this morning, pecking my head."

Graham shrugged his shoulders. He wanted to agree with Miriam as he could sense a tension between them on this subject.

As he thought about this he suddenly remembered something which Jim had told him. His friend had shared the rumours that the men had been been seen shoplifting at Tesco and that one of them had been spotted outside the Academy allegedly offering drugs to schoolchildren.

He had mentioned this to Miriam previously but she had dismissed it as possibly being malicious gossip.

Graham fell silent as he weighed up the implications of what Jim had said. Could there possibly be any connection between drug dealing outside the school and the fire? However, he quickly dismissed this idea on the grounds that he might be letting his prejudice against the four campmates cloud his judgement. He decided it would be judicious not to say anything more on the subject to Miriam.

He wished to lighten his mood, so he suggested that they went to the Buckthorn Arms for a bar snack that evening. Miriam agreed.

"Give me half an hour to shower and get changed and we'll go early doors," she said.

"Shall I take Benjy home and come back in half an hour?" asked Graham.

"No, don't be daft. Benjy's always welcome to stay here. Get your feet up and watch the TV or something while you wait."

When Miriam was ready they strolled down to the pub, which was only three minutes' walk away. They ordered their meals – scampi and chips for Miriam and a shepherd's pie for Graham. Miriam decided to complement her food with a glass of white wine and Graham ordered a pint of bitter.

The pub was very quiet at that time of the evening,

with just a few regulars standing near the bar. But then something happened which immediately changed the atmosphere for Graham: Anita entered the room accompanied by Stephen Armitage.

Graham was momentarily taken aback, but, true to form, he quickly gathered his composure and greeted the newcomers with a mixture of polite pleasure and undisguised surprise. He was quick to stand up and then introduce them to Miriam, whom he assumed had met neither of them previously.

Anita said: "I do think we have met before somewhere."

Miriam agreed: "Yes, probably at the golf club."

Graham was thinking of being even more polite and civilised by inviting Anita and Stephen to join Miriam and himself at their table. But Stephen, who was showing some signs of embarrassment, chipped in quickly and said: "It's been very nice to meet you, Miriam. If you'll excuse us we'll go to the bar and get ourselves a drink."

He put his arm around Anita's shoulder so that she had no option but to be shepherded away from any further awkwardness. When they were out of earshot Miriam said: "That's a bit of a turn-up. Did you know they were friends?"

"No, all I know is that Stephen showed Anita around Beachworld one day. He obvious made a good impression on her."

Graham uttered the last words in a half-joking way, but inwardly he was seething with indignation that Anita was parading yet another man before him. He tried to convince himself that there was no jealousy involved in his reaction.

Then, what should have been a relaxing meal with a

cherished and amiable companion, turned into a nightmare for Graham. For the very next person to enter through the pub door was Darren Gibson.

And, as he swayed unsteadily from side to side, he gave every impression of being under the influence of drink or drugs. As he passed by Graham he glared at him and then stopped dead. He stood there for a moment as if deciding what to say.

Then he asked: "Is this your latest conquest, Graham?"

Graham tried to ignore him, but Darren persisted: "Aren't you going to introduce me to your latest squeeze?"

"No, Darren, I'm not," said Graham, testily.

Darren walked closer to the table and turned his attention to Miriam, putting his face within a few inches of hers.

"He won't tell me your name," he slurred. "Well, will you tell me?"

"Miriam," she replied.

Darren offered his hand to her and she shyly took it.

"Could you leave us now?" said Graham.

"I'll leave you, friend. But I think your lady here should know that you're shagging your ex-wife, don't you?"

Graham took Darren by the arm in an effort to turn him away from Miriam.

"Come on, Darren. I think we've heard enough from you," he said.

"Take your hands off me!" Darren shouted.

Graham released his grip and Darren staggered away, cursing, and declaring: "You'd better watch your step. I'm going to see my wife now."

Miriam looked at Graham quizzically and asked:

"Who is that and what was that all about?"

He explained that Darren was Anita's husband and that he was clearly intoxicated.

"I could see that," said Miriam. "But what he said about you and Anita. Is it true?"

Graham replied: "I have to confess that some time ago I had a moment of madness with Anita. A big mistake never to be repeated."

"How long ago did that happen?"

Graham hesitated and his face reddened.

He knew that if he wished to avoid hurting Miriam, and quite possibly to avoid losing her, the best course of action would be to lie. He could just say that some months ago he had got together with his ex-wife. But lying was not Graham's way. Both in his personal life and in business he prided himself on his honesty.

"About three weeks ago."

Miriam just nodded and said nothing. An awkward silence prevailed for several minutes. But this was broken by a tumultuous clattering noise from the far end of the long bar. The pub's landlord, a stocky man in his late forties, rushed from behind the counter and ran over to the source of the clamour.

He returned moments later with Darren in an armlock whom he propelled towards the pub's entrance. The landlord's wife hurried from the other side of the room to open the door for him. He pushed the man outside, told him "Clear off, or I'll call the police" and closed the door after him.

Graham got up from his table and looked down the length of the bar. He saw Anita frantically dabbing Stephen's face with what appeared to be either a white handkerchief or a serviette. Concerned as to what had occurred, Graham went over to the couple. He saw that Stephen's nose was bleeding and that his formerly immaculate light grey sports jacket was stained with a mixture of blood and red wine.

"Are you okay?" he asked.

"I'll live," said Stephen, feeling humiliated and unusually dishevelled.

Anita, who was still holding her handkerchief firmly on Stephen's nose, said: "Darren's a madman. He's gone completely loco. He's threatened to kill Stephen now. He punched him on the nose and then hit him hard in the stomach. Poor Stephen finished up on the bloody floor. I know Darren's always threatening to kill people and doesn't do it, but I'm getting scared now. We're going to report him to the police this time."

"I think you're right," said Graham. "Who knows what he might be capable of in his present state of mind?"

Anita said that she ought to get Stephen home and Graham nodded in agreement. He asked if they needed a lift but Anita said her car was outside and they would travel in that.

Graham wished Stephen well and returned to Miriam, who was keen to know what had happened.

"I guess it's a case of the green-eyed monster," said Miriam.

"Yes," said Graham.

"It's a good thing that everyone doesn't suffer from that," said Miriam, looking at him pointedly and smiling.

Stephen took her hand and said: "I don't quite know how to put this, Miriam. You may have noticed that I'm not a man of many words. But... here goes. It was after I went with Anita this last time, that I realised how much I have come to appreciate you – to love you. You are a wonderful, kind and attractive lady. I'm so sorry I have let you down. Finally, though, I realise that at long last I have got Anita out of my system. I don't say that she is a worthless woman but there's no doubt that she's a faithless one. I need a woman I can trust and I believe I have found one. Can you find it in your kind heart to forgive me?"

Miriam did not reply immediately but she did let Graham continue to hold her hand.

"I will forgive you, if you promise me that I can trust you. Can I?"

Graham looked her straight in the eyes and merely replied: "Yes".

"Thank you," said Miriam. "Because I love you too."

Never normally one for public displays of affection, Graham leant over and kissed her on the cheek.

Miriam giggled girlishly and squeezed his hand tenderly.

"Well now we know where we both stand, let's celebrate," she said. "Let's have a bottle of champagne."

"What a great idea," said Graham. "It's time I packed up my troubles in the old kit bag."

He ordered a bottle of Tattinger which arrived with their meals.

After quaffing the champagne the couple were both feeling a little "tiddly" so they retired to Miriam's house where they enjoyed an episode of passion before falling sound asleep.

****

Graham felt mildly miffed at having seen Anita with Stephen in the Buckthorn Arms. Particularly after the satisfying night he had spent with Miriam he knew that there was no rational excuse for the tinge of jealously he had felt on seeing them together. It was his old Anita problem and he told himself he had to grow up and expunge her from his psyche once and for all.

He began to see a future with Miriam and feared that his obsession with his ex-wife would spoil that opportunity. He had been impressed by how forgiving Miriam had been when told of his most recent dalliance with Anita. He realised he had to show the same maturity himself.

As for Stephen, Graham had been a staunch defender of his American manager when some others among his staff had cast doubts as to whether it had been necessary to import him to take a leading role in the Beachworld project.

On seeing his star employee with Anita his first instinct had been the irrational one of feeling this was an act of disloyalty on Stephen's behalf. Feeling paranoid about the recent fires, he had even, for an instant at least, harboured the faintest of suspicions that his manager might have some malevolent intentions. In the cold light of day, though, he accepted that such thoughts were ridiculous and unworthy. Stephen had merely shown that he was a normal red-blooded male who had fallen into the clutches of a highly attractive, albeit ageing, siren. Graham had always been able to empathise with men who could see the same qualities in Anita that he appreciated himself. And, if they became involved with her, he could sympathise with them because he knew her fickleness would sooner or later break their hearts.

This sympathy even extended to Darren, who had behaved appallingly and whose personality was inimical to Graham. The poor man had been reduced to a whinging, unpleasant and possibly even dangerous individual through his relationship with Anita.

So there it was: Graham was determined to eschew any further romantic or sexual feelings towards his ex-wife. From now on any wooing would be reserved for Miriam.

On the morning following the events at the Buckthorn Arms, Graham left Miriam's home, collected his car from his own house and drove to Beachworld, with Benjy strapped into the front passenger seat. He found Stephen already sitting at his desk in the management suite. They acknowledged each other with a nod.

"Well, what a night last night," said Stephen.

"It was certainly interesting," replied Graham.

"That Darren's a madman," said Stephen. "He was hanging around outside Anita's parents' house when I left there last night. She's becoming really scared of him. He's everywhere she is. I shouted to him that I'd call the police and then went back into the house and did just that. They didn't come."

"No surprise there then," Graham interjected.

"Anyway I stayed with Anita a little longer to make sure she was okay. The police rang back to see if everything was all right. But by then Darren had disappeared. I wasn't happy leaving Anita alone because he could have just been waiting around the corner, biding his time. So I decided to stay the night – on the sofa. When I left this morning Anita promised to phone the police right away the next time she saw him loitering around."

"He's becoming a stalker – and a nasty one too," said Graham. "You did the right thing, looking after her."

"Just one thing, Graham. Anita and I have been seeing each other a little lately. Are you cool with that?"

"I'm cool. We've been divorced for years. We've stayed friends because she's the mother of our son. But I've moved on. I have a relationship with Miriam, the lady you met last night. So, yes, I'm completely cool.

"Getting back to Darren, the police already know that I have concerns about him – his threats to kill etc. Do you think he could have anything to do with the fires, here and at the Academy?"

"It had crossed my mind," said Stephen. "Anita told me that he could have grounds to be jealous of you. But he seems to have just turned up in the area and the first fires were some time ago now."

"That's precisely what I thought. But could he have been around earlier than we realised? After all, we're only a couple of hours from Nottingham where he lives."

"An interesting point. We should be on our guard against him. I'll ask Anita if she has a photo of him and then I'll circulate it to security here," said Stephen.

"Please do that, as soon as possible."

"By the way, I've had calls from a couple of national newspapers, The Times and the Daily Mail. They want to do features about Beachworld – and the fires."

"Bring it on," said Graham. "You know what they say - 'no publicity is bad publicity'. I don't know if I believe that, especially in view of what happened to me a few years ago when I suffered my tenants' revolt. But we're going to get publicity anyway whether we like it or not. What we must emphasise is that we have really tightened up on our security since the fires. We don't want the visitors staying away because they have any fears on that score."

"Understood. Will you do the interviews?"

"Yes, I'll take the lead but I'd like you to be around too – to give the Transatlantic viewpoint!"

Chapter fifteen
Crisis point

That evening Graham has come to Miriam's house again for an intimate dinner. It is something of a celebration of their newly-proclaimed love.

Miriam greets him at the door with an affectionate kiss and invites him to take an aperitif.

As they chink their gin glasses, there is a loud banging at the front door.

"Oh, damn, who can that be?" says Miriam. "Hold on a minute and I'll try to get rid of whoever it is."

A few moments later she re-enters the sitting room accompanied by Matthew, their favourite "man from the bushes". He looks ashen-faced and in a state of panic.

"I must speak to you, Mr Robinson."

"Go ahead."

"I'm going to tell you something extremely serious but I am begging you not to tell anyone ever that I'm the source of the information I will give you."

"I will do what is humanly possible," says Graham.

"My life may depend on it," says Matthew, with an imploring expression. "I am involved with some dangerous people."

"As I said, I'll do what I can depending on what it is you are going to tell me. Apart from meeting you on the beach, I don't know you from Adam."

"We met years ago," says Matthew. "In a pub along the sea front at Brighton – the night the bomb went off. My name then was Sebastian. That's my real name."

"The Anarcho-Syndicalist. I remember you. I've been thinking that there was something familiar about you, but I couldn't be absolutely certain about it."

Sebastian replied: "I didn't recognise you when I first saw you at our camp, although there was something familiar about you too. But then I was told you had a chain of corner shops based around Nottingham and it suddenly clicked into place. You told me at Brighton that that's what you did."

"Amazing," says Graham. "What a night that turned out to be..."

Sebastian interrupts: "Please stop. Listen to me. A bomb's going to be detonated on Easter Saturday at Beachworld. It's behind a bath panel in room 205. You need to act urgently or many people will be killed."

"A bomb?"

"Yes."

"How do you know that?"

"Because one of our group planted it a couple of weeks ago. It's on a timer – to go off at midday on the first day that Beachworld is opening to the public."

Graham stops him and calls over to Miriam, who has been listening to the conversation with growing alarm: "Will you ring 999 straightaway and tell them what you've just heard? Ask the police to go to the hotel at Beachworld with a bomb disposal team. Tell them the bomb's behind a bath panel in room 205."

Miriam picks up her phone from a coffee table and starts to make her call..

Simultaneously Graham uses his own mobile in an effort to contact Stephen. There is no reply so instead he speaks to the duty security man. He tells him to set off the fire alarms and evacuate the site, where men are working night shifts.

Graham turns to Sebastian: "Your group? You mean the men in the bushes down the road?"

"Yes. We're a group of anarchists. But I'm not violent – Anarcho-Syndicalists reject violent revolution. But others in the group do believe in using violence."

"But why Beachworld?"

"Because it's a scheme to enrich capitalists – and you in particular."

"Me. Why me?"

"One of our group, Dan – he introduced himself to you as Gilbert – has a grudge against you because you evicted him from his home in Nottingham some years ago."

"Oh, god."

Miriam interjects: "The police are on their way. They've told us to evacuate the site immediately."

Graham picks up his phone and scrolls down to find a contact. He passes the phone to Miriam.

"Can you please try to get hold of Stephen? Text him if he doesn't reply and tell him to get in touch with me as soon as possible. He should be there overseeing the night shift."

He turns to Sebastian "Why are you telling me all this, and why didn't you tell me before now?"

"Because I don't want to see anyone killed. I didn't agree to the fires and we fought and had rows about it at the camp. But this is a step way too far. I have nothing against you personally, or against your development for that matter. In fact you and Miriam have been very good to us.

"When we came to Sanderholme it was just to keep out of the way because of some things we had done down south. As part of our protests. But this is beyond the pale. Then Dan met a businessman who was against Beachworld and he was offered lots of money to sabotage your scheme – and your business classrooms at the Academy.

"Who is this businessman?"

"Mr Fulford – Henry Fulford."

"Christ."

Sebastian looks pleadingly at Graham: "You will keep me out of this won't you?"

Graham knows he cannot promise that.

"I'll not do anything to make it worse for you," says Graham.

Miriam interrupts again to say she has been unable to contact Stephen.

Graham's first thought is that he needs to go to Beachworld himself.

But he is keen to keep Sebastian with him as long as possible, to prise as much information from him as he can, and hopefully to see him arrested. Sebastian is twitchy and is clearly wishing to get away as soon as possible.

"So you're telling me that your group has been responsible for all the fires."

"Yes."

"And the vandalism?"

"That too."

"How did you manage to plant a bomb and petrol-soaked rags at Beachworld?"

"One of our guys, Gerald, got a job as a labourer with one of the contractors working on site. He's not much of a specimen these days – years of doing heroin have done that to him – but he's had lots of experience of this sort of thing."

"What do you mean 'this sort of thing?' " asks Graham.

"Acts of terrorism. He's a pro. He used to be paid by the IRA for doing jobs for them. Anyway, as soon as he had planted the bomb he left his labouring job. His mission had been accomplished as far as he was concerned."

"Where is he now – and the other two?"

"They were at the camp just now. The plan was to move on today, so we were many miles away when the bomb went off."

"So will you be joining them again when you leave here?"

"No, I'm too vulnerable now. They would have no compunction in killing me if they found out I had grassed on them. And anyway, now the police are aware of what's going on they will surely be here very soon."

Graham replied: "You will have noticed that I haven't said anything to the police yet about who has planted the bomb. Don't think that's because I want you to get away with anything. I wasn't sure what you might do to us if I dropped you in it."

Sebastian starts to walk towards the sitting room door but Graham grabs him by the arm to restrain him.

"You're not going anywhere until you've told me everything I need to know," says Graham.

"Okay, okay," says Sebastian. "Don't worry. As I've said, I'm not violent."

"So why have you got involved with this crew of gangsters?"

"We got to know each other at various anti-capitalist protests. Dan persuaded us that taking clandestine direct action against individual capitalist organisations and companies was more effective than taking part in street protests. He, and to a lesser extent Gerald, were always pushing us to become more extreme. Dan can be quite a scary figure and I believe Gerald just likes violence for its own sake. Harry is soft in the head and is just easily lead by Dan. But I should have stood up against him long ago. He could see that I disapproved of his methods and as time goes on he has come to mistrust me. But I've got no excuse for what I've done. I just got in too deep."

"You're a bright man," says Graham. "How could you have been such a fool? People could have died in those fires. When did you first recognise me as the man you wished to harm?"

"The first time I saw you at the camp I didn't recognise you at all, neither did Dan. But Gerald knew who you were, having worked on your site. Dan's attitude was that if he saw you again he would be nicey nicey to you so that you wouldn't guess that he had any hostile intent towards you."

"I do remember remarking that his attitude towards me had suddenly changed. What's his background? His rather posh accent belies his frightening exterior."

"He's like me, an ex-public school boy. He became radicalised at the London School of Economics, I believe under the influence of a Marxist professor. He got involved in an anarchist group and has been active in the cause ever since. He found himself a partner who had similar views to his and they had two children together. She lived in Nottingham and that's how he came to be living in one of your properties. He hated you from the time when you evicted him and when he learnt that you were planning a big development here he saw it as the chance to achieve a double whammy – to avenge himself on you and to harm a capitalist venture."

"One day I saw a book at your camp about Bakunin.

Did that belong to Dan by any chance?"

"As a matter of fact it belonged to Harry."

"Harry? He is the monosyllabic member of your group, isn't he? I think I heard him grunt a couple of times."

"You wouldn't think so to look at him, but he's actually the intellectual amongst us. He was a student at the LSE at the same time as Dan and they have been close friends ever since. Harry was once a history teacher at a London comprehensive school. But he's a victim of drugs. He took so many of them that he lost his job and his family and eventually suffered a serious heart attack. He's just a shell of the man he used to be."

"I can see that," says Graham. "What a waste of a life. Does Dan still have a family."

"No, he left them a few years ago. He doesn't believe in the institution of the family – at least that's his excuse."

"You can see through him, can't you? So why did you get taken in by him?"

"Because I'm an idiot. And he always had a plentiful supply of free drugs."

"How does he come by those?"

"I never knew. But just lately I've gained some insight into his methods."

"Explain that to me."

"He became involved with Henry Fulford, who I despise as an obnoxious individual – the very worst type of capitalist. Dan was in a pub one day and overheard Fulford ranting about Beachworld and about you.

"As Fulford was leaving the pub Dan followed him and got talking to him, He suggested that our group might be able to help him. The outcome was that Fulford paid

Dan a large sum of money to sabotage Beachworld. That money paid for our drugs. We're all hopeless addicts.

"Further money was forthcoming from Fulford when Dan suggested to him an attack on your business classrooms at the Academy."

"I was told that one of your group might be selling drugs to kids outside the Academy."

"That's right. When one of the kids got into debt with us, we used that as a lever to get him to start the fire at the school."

"You're evil."

"You will probably not believe me when I tell you that I did everything I could to stop all of this. We argued about it interminably and even came to blows a few times. I utterly failed but I believe I am weak rather than evil. I understand that you will not agree.

"I need to move on. I want to put as much distance between the police and me and between Dan and me before the shit hits the fan.

"But there's something else I ought to tell you before I go. Dan's next move involves you again. He plans to kidnap your granddaughter and demand a ransom from you."

"What? When?"

"I can't put a precise date on it. But it's imminent. He and another of his anarchist contacts have been staking out your house near Nottingham in recent months, tracking your granddaughter's movements. Dan's been borrowing one of Fulford's cars to get there."

"I can't believe this. A bomb and now a kidnapping. How do these these two things fit together?"

"They don't. Honestly, they're just the product of two diseased minds. Fulford has become totally obsessed with destroying you and your development. As for Dan, I've come to realise he's not very bright. He's so bitter and twisted that he just seems to hit out at people and things randomly. I have always realised that he was a nasty piece of work but I thought that at least we were on the same page in our political aims. I couldn't have been more mistaken. Fulford has totally corrupted him. The fires, the bomb, the kidnapping, Dan is doing them all for money and using the rest of us as stooges. Well, I'm out of here."

As soon as he finishes this sentence Sebastian pushes past Graham and rushes out of the sitting room, along the hall and out of the front door. He runs along Lavender Avenue and then turns left into a commercial street which eventually leads to the town centre. Graham gives chase and for several hundred yards can still see Sebastian in front of him. But then his quarry suddenly disappears, having taken a sharp turn to the left into an unlit service road behind a line of shops.

Graham gives up the chase and then runs back to Miriam's house.

"I've lost him," he tells Miriam. "I'm going to phone the police and tell them he's on the run. He told me something really frightening. Did you hear him? Gilbert, I mean Dan, is going to kidnap my granddaughter, Sophie, and demand money from me."

Miriam had been standing quietly in the background while the two men were talking, becoming increasingly shocked by what she was hearing.

"Whatever next? Why did you spend so much time talking to Matthew, I mean Sebastian?" she asks.

Graham says his idea was to hold on to the man as long as possible in case the police turned up in the meantime.

"I did manage to find out a lot of useful information, didn't I?"

"I suppose so."

Graham rings the police and gives them all the relevant details he has gleaned. He suggests that they need to track down Sebastian, to see if the other men are still at their camp site and to arrest Henry Fulford.

He also tells them about the threat to his granddaughter, and gives them contact details for Austin and Phoebe. Then he phones his son and warns him of the danger.

"Where's Sophie now?" asks Graham.

"She's gone for a sleepover at a friend's. I'll phone the friend's house and then go and fetch her home," says Austin.

"Now I need to get down to Beachworld and see what's going on," says Graham.

"Do be careful, darling," says Miriam.

As Graham drove towards Beachworld his head was spinning as he thought about all the information which Sebastian had just given him. As he considered the current bomb threat his thoughts turned back to the Brighton bomb in 1984 and the curious fact that Sebastian had a connection with both incidents. Was he as innocent as he was making out? He had told Graham that Gerald had worked for the IRA. Could he have been an associate of the Brighton bomber Patrick Magee? Or had he merely attempted a copycat crime by placing the bomb behind a bath panel at a hotel?

When Graham approached Beachworld a few minutes later the police had already cordoned off the car park and workers were streaming out of the main entrance and heading towards their cars. Graham parked his car in a nearby street and walked towards the police officers who were guarding the car park entrance. The officers recognised him and agreed to let him go as far as the security office where Bob, the duty security officer, was directing operations.

"Dennis is just checking the hotel rooms now," said Bob. "But no one should be in there. Then that's everyone off site."

"Where the hell's Stephen?" asked Graham. "I haven't managed to contact him."

"We don't know. He's disappeared off the face of the earth. But here's Dennis now."

Dennis, a huge security guard, entered the office followed by Stephen and none other than Anita.

"Found these two in one of the bedrooms," said Dennis, winking.

"What the hell were you doing in there?" asked Graham, angrily.

Stephen and Anita looked shamefaced.

"I was just showing Anita around the hotel," said Stephen.

Dennis smirked knowingly.

"I thought you did that a few days ago," snapped Graham.

"I found it so impressive I wanted to have another look," said Anita, not expecting to be believed.

"Incredible," said Graham. "But come on. Let's get out of here now."

As they were heading out of the building a male police officer told them that the Army Bomb Disposal Squad was on its way from Oxfordshire.

While Graham was dealing with the incident at Beachworld the doorbell rang at Miriam's house. She was reluctant to go to the door given the trauma of that evening. It could have been anyone, including someone with evil intent.

The sitting room curtains were drawn so she tentatively peeped around them to get a view of any visitor. She was relieved to see that it was Shirley Bincroft.

When she went to the front door and led her neighbour inside, she could instantly see that Shirley was distressed. The events of the evening had put Miriam on edge herself but she rallied enough to give comfort to her neighbour.

"What's the matter, Shirley?" she asked.

"It's Trevor," Shirley replied, welling up with tears. "I don't know what's happened to him. He went for a walk after lunch and he hasn't come back. I've tried his mobile several times, but there's no answer. He never does anything like this. Since his heart attack I've made him promise that he stays in touch constantly. And he has done up to now."

"Did he say where he was going?"

"Yes, he said he was just going down to the beach. He took his camera with him as usual. He's always on the lookout for a good seascape – or to take pictures of that camp he's so worried about. I've been down to the beach for ages looking for him, but there's no sign of him."

"Have you told the police?"

"Yes, I've just rung them. They say they'll come round as soon as they can, but apparently they're all dealing with a major incident in town at present."

"I'm afraid I know what that is," said Miriam. "There's a bomb threat at Beachworld. Graham's there now."

"Oh, my God. I can't believe all this," said Shirley, who dissolved into floods of tears.

"Come on, let's have a cup of tea and wait for the police," said Miriam.

At 6.45 that evening the residents of Lavender Avenue were surprised to find their road taken over by a range of police vehicles. They were shocked to see that officers who alighted from one of the vans were carrying guns. These officers hurried towards the path which led to the beach. They arrived at the camp where they hoped to find their suspects but were disappointed to find that "the birds had flown".

All that was left of the site was rubbish of the usual kind left by individuals of a careless and nomadic lifestyle. Officers put yellow tape around the area to cordon it off and placed a road block at the end of the avenue.

Several of the officers conducted a thorough torchlight search of the camp site in an effort to learn as much as they could about the men who had lived there and their activities. They were particularly keen to find any evidence of bomb-making. At the same time two other officers were questioning Miriam as to what she knew about the men. She told them she had heard only their first names, but as Sebastian and Dan had been using aliases she imagined that might have applied to the other two men too.

Shirley, who was still with Miriam, had become even more fearful of what might have happened to Trevor, having heard about Sebastian's visit. Could the men from the camp have harmed him?

Graham had now parked his car along the sea front, as near to Beachworld as the police would allow. As he sat inside he received a frantic phone call from Austin.

"Sophie's disappeared. She was meant to go to her friend Kirsty's for a party and a sleepover but she never arrived. We have no idea where she is. Perhaps those men have got her."

"Have you contacted the police?"

"Yes, they're already on their way here. We've looked all round the village. No one has seen her. It's really scary. We've tried her mobile, but it must be switched off."

"I'm coming over," said Graham. "I'll be there in a couple of hours. Keep me in touch."

"Thanks, Dad. I've got Phoebe and Edward with me at the moment. We're all going back home now to meet the police."

****

A female officer pushed her way through the undergrowth just beyond the beach camp, believing that some evidence of the men's criminality may have been hidden away from the clearing. As she prodded around, constantly unhooking herself from prickly bramble bushes which attached themselves to her uniform, she suddenly called out.

"Come over here. I've found a body."

Three male officers scrambled through the undergrowth towards her. She pointed to the body of a large man in a supine position as if he were looking towards the stars.

"Is this one of the men who lived here?" asked one of the male officers.

Another officer suggested that they bring Miriam to the scene as she would probably be able to answer this rhetorical question.

Almost immediately she was escorted to the camp and what she saw there was a devastating shock.

Shaking and fighting back tears, she declared: "I know this man. It's Trevor Bincroft, my next door neighbour. His poor wife, Shirley, is at my house now."

While this tragedy was evolving in Lavender Avenue another Sanderholme address was also being surrounded by police. This was the substantial home of Henry Fulford, situated in a salubrious road at the north end of town, overlooking the sea. The businessman was arrested without incident and taken to Sanderholme police station for questioning.

Chapter sixteen
Searching for Sophie

In Papplewick, Austin's Mercedes swept into the driveway in front of his house. Standing beside the front door was a youth, who ran towards the car as soon as it was parked.

Austin flung open the car door and said: "Who are you?"

"You need to know," said the youth. "Some men have taken Sophie."

"How? When?" said Austin.

"They bundled her into a car, near the Tea Rooms – about half an hour ago, I guess. I rang the police and they told me to meet them here."

"Do you know Sophie then?" asked Austin.

Edward, who had just got out of the car, interrupted: "Yes, he knows Sophie. It's Simon Atkins. He's at our school."

"That's right," said Simon.

"Yes, I know Simon too," said Phoebe.

At that point two police cars arrived. A male officer alighted from one of them and called out: "Are you Simon?"

"Yes," said Simon.

"Then come and sit in the car a minute," said the officer.

The family stood talking to other officers until Simon and the first officer emerged from the car.

Addressing the group he said: "It appears that Sophie was walking along Main Street when a black Range Rover pulled up. Two men got out, grabbed hold of her and pushed her into the back of their vehicle. They drove off at speed along Main Street in the direction of Moor Lane.

"This young man has given us good descriptions of the two men and of the vehicle. It appears that the kidnap plot we have been warned about may have been put into action."

A female officer who had stayed in one of the vehicles then emerged and joined the others.

"We've just had a call from Lincolnshire Police. They've been contacted by a man demanding a million pounds for the release of Sophie, with a threat to kill her if her grandfather doesn't come up with the money. Lincs Police have informed Mr Robinson and he's on his way here now. The Chief Super has been alerted and he has put the armed response unit on standby. A Mr Henry Fulford is being questioned now but so far he has denied any knowledge of the kidnap."

Austin asked if the family should continue its search of the area, but was advised this would be dangerous and that the hunt should be left to the police.

Edward got into conversation with Simon and asked him why he had been in the village that day.

"I just fancied a walk," said Simon.

Edward replied: "We know that's not true, don't we? Sophie's told me you're always following her around. I've seen you in the village two or three times myself. You're a bit of a stalker aren't you?"

"No, I just like Sophie, you know."

As he spoke Simon was brushing away tears with the back of his arm, which was noticed by Phoebe standing a few yards away.

"Edward, don't," she said. "Now's not the time for this. We should be grateful to Simon for what he told the police."

"I suppose," said Edward. "But I still think he's a creep."

"Edward!" shouted Phoebe, "Drop it."

"All right. All right."

Simon thanked Phoebe and added: "I do hope that Sophie will be okay."

"I know you do," said Phoebe, fighting back tears herself. "We all do. We'll call for a taxi to get you home."

Simon said he was reluctant to go until Sophie had been found safe.

"Do your mother and father know that you're here?" asked Phoebe.

"No, they think I've gone to see friends in Nottingham," said Simon. "I'll phone them and my dad will come and pick me up. I'll tell them that I came here hoping to meet Sophie."

****

As Graham drives towards Nottinghamshire in his Bentley he contacts Miriam on his car phone. She gives him the shocking news of Trevor's death and he is left distraught at the loss of another old friend.

When he arrives at his Papplewick home he finds that the police have descended in large numbers and are deployed throughout the village and the surrounding area. Several officers are there to meet him and to brief him on the kidnappers' demands. He has been given 24 hours to obtain a million pounds in notes and then await further instructions from an unknown source.

Graham's head is in a spin. He feels as if he is in the middle of some kind of outer body experience. His total focus is now on the fate of his granddaughter, so much so that for the time being the problems at Beachworld, normally his highest priority, are well to the back of his mind. He is jogged back into reality at 11pm by a call from Stephen to confirm that the bomb disposal team has done its job and the threat to the development has passed.

As he enters the large modern kitchen where the family have gathered he finds Austin standing with his arm around Phoebe who is visibly shaking and red-eyed with crying. Sitting at the kitchen table are Edward and a forlorn looking Simon, who is waiting to be collected by his father.

Graham tries to comfort Phoebe with some words of reassurance about the police knowing what they are doing and how he will do all he can to help them.

"If I have to come up with the million pounds then so be it," he says. "You know I'll do anything to make sure Sophie is safe. This is all down to me, you know. I'm so sorry that I've brought this upon you."

"Don't be silly, dad," says Austin. "You can't be blamed for any of this. Only the evil blokes who have done this are at fault."

Graham nods his appreciation of his son's words and then turns to his grandson and says: "Don't worry, Edward. They'll find your sister and catch these chaps."

Looking towards Simon, he adds: "I'm sorry I don't believe we've met."

"I'm a school friend of Sophie's and I saw the men put her into a car and take her away."

"Oh, yes, the police told me about that."

As he shakes Simon's hand, Edward interjects to say: "He's Sophie's stalker."

"Shut up, Edward," says his mother angrily. "I told

you to drop that."

"Well he is," Edward replies brusquely. "He's always following her around."

"Is this true?" asks Graham.

"No, it's not," says Simon. "I just love her company. I love her."

Edward snaps: "Well she doesn't love you. She's not even your friend. I've seen how she goes out of her way to avoid you."

Graham is not about to get involved in this argument. He thinks of Anita and the way he used to "stalk" her when their marriage first split up, taking detours around Nottingham in the hope of catching sight of her. He knows that frustrated love can drive the most rational being to the verge of a kind of insanity. He can see that Simon is upset by Edward's goading so he gestures to his grandson to keep quiet and says to the distraught young man: "Don't worry. These things can affect the best of us. I am sure we are all very grateful to you for the way you've helped the police today. They've told me that your descriptions of the kidnappers are really important pieces of information."

Simon whispers his thanks to Graham and Edward holds his tongue.

****

The first breakthrough in the search for the bomb plotters and kidnappers came even later that evening when a camera discovered with Trevor's body was found to contain incriminating video footage of the men as they had hurriedly left the camp site. It appeared that Trevor may have hidden in the undergrowth next to the camp to film the video before something caused his death. Shirley also provided the police with hundreds of photos which her husband had surreptitiously taken over several months.

In the early hours of the following morning at the police station, two female detectives showed the video film and some of the photographs to Stephen and Miriam and it was Stephen who was able to provide a vital piece of information.

He immediately recognised the man known as Gerald.

"I know that man," he said. "He worked at Beachworld for a few weeks for one of the contractors. I noticed him particularly because he used to shuffle around as if he had some problem with his legs."

They sent the photo to Graham who corroborated what his manager had said.

"You're right. I saw him on the beach the other day and I thought there was something familiar about him. This is the one they called Gerald. He's the bomber."

The two detectives looked at each other and smiled.

Photographs of the four wanted men and an e-fit of a fifth man produced from the description of the kidnap van driver provided by Simon were circulated to the media in time for next day's early morning news bulletins.

Details of the Range Rover were also circulated. Simon had recalled that its number plate started with the letters FY, suggesting a Lincolnshire registration. Further investigations revealed that Henry Fulford was the owner of a black Range Rover with FY on its plate.

****

The dark, dank and dreary downstairs room was hanging with huge cobwebs. The uncarpeted floor was thick with grey dust flecked with mouse droppings. Apart from two wooden chairs the only furniture was a dilapidated chest of drawers, poised at a rakish angle owing to having lost one of its round legs. The rest of the room was filled with numerous rolls of old carpet which were damp, smelly and crawling with wood lice and other assorted insects, a dozen empty paint tins and a few planks of wood. There was not a lick of paint on the walls and the plaster, black with mould in most places, was peeling away.

Two people were sitting in the chairs, a gaunt, unshaven man with large red bags under his eyes and a rumpled thatch of grey hair, and a long-legged, attractive teenage girl wearing a flowery dress. Her shiny brown hair was dishevelled. Her arms were tied behind her back and strapped to the chair and a black scarf was hanging around her neck. The man was Harry, the oldest of the four men from the marsh, and the girl was Sophie.

"Why am I here?" she pleaded.

"I can't tell you anything, my dear," Harry replied in a husky and barely audible voice.

"But I haven't done anything to anyone."

"I've told you I can't tell you anything."

"How long are you going to keep me here?"

"It's not my place to say."

The effort of replying to Sophie's questions appeared to be too much for Harry, who descended into a fit of coughing. He took a dirty handkerchief from his pocket, coughed up some phlegm and loudly blew his nose.

"You'll have to stop asking me questions. Just keep quiet and we'll get on well."

Sophie tried valiantly not to cry. She was clearly

bewildered by what had happened to her. She had heard about the problems her grandfather had suffered with the fires at Beachworld but could not imagine what that had to do with her. She had obviously been kidnapped but beyond that she had no clue as to why.

She had been treated roughly by the two men who had swept her off the street into the Range Rover. While one man drove the vehicle away the other had joined her in the back seats, tied her up, blindfolded her and gagged her with the black scarf. He then pushed her down so she was laying horizontal in the seats.

She guessed that the journey had taken about two hours. When the vehicle stopped the two men took her by the arms and marched her for a minute or so before entering a building and tying her to the chair.

Then she heard three distinctly varied voices.

The first voice, a clear and commanding one, said: "Leave her like this for now. We'll give her some food later."

A second voice, a calm and quiet one with an Irish accent, said: "Yes, we don't want her shouting and attracting attention. I doubt anyone will ever be able to hear her, but it's best to be sure. You never know who may be lurking around outside."

A third voice entered a hesitant note of dissension: "I don't think there's any need to leave the poor girl like this. There's no one about."

Sophie was later to realise that this was Harry's voice.

She spent hours in a state of terror, wondering if she was to be killed or abused in some horrific way. Eventually, after midnight, the blindfold and the gag were removed. She saw that she was encircled by four men. She felt certain that two of them, a fierce looking balding man, and a tall man with long straggly hair had been the driver and passenger in the Range Rover. She did not recognise the other two scruffy individuals in the room.

A frisson of fear overtook her as she looked at her surroundings in what appeared to her to be a semi-derelict building. The room was extremely cold and she began to shiver.

"Has she got a coat, Dan?" rasped Harry.

"Yeah, it's over there on the floor," said the fierce man. "And mind what you bloody well say, you old duffer. No names!"

"Sorry," whispered Harry, who appeared in fear of the fitter looking man.

Harry picked up Sophie's coat from the floor and wrapped it around her legs.

"Can she have some food now?" he asked.

"There's a couple of sandwiches here," said another scruffy looking man, reaching into a backpack. "Corned beef. Would you like them?"

"Yes, please," said Sophie reaching out with a trembling hand.

"Why am I here?" she asked.

"Shut up," said Dan. "That's got nothing to do with you. Eat your food and keep quiet. Otherwise the gag and the blindfold go back on."

Sophie acquiesced and slowly chewed the sandwiches.

"I'm leaving you in charge of her," Dan said to Harry.

"Don't tell her anything. Anything. Do you understand?"

"Yes, I understand."

The other three men left the room, leaving just Sophie and Harry. She heard a key being turned in a lock.

Her later efforts to engage Harry in conversation were

unsuccessful. She decided to try to sleep in the hope of becoming oblivious to the horror of her situation and her surroundings. For an hour or so she could not manage to do this as she turned over in her mind the possible reasons for her being there. That what had happened to her was a kidnapping she had no doubt. She could only assume that this was because she belonged to a rich family. It gave her some little solace to appreciate that her family were loving, caring people who would never let her down. But she was also sufficiently worldly to realise that there was always a reluctance by the authorities to give way to ransom demands. Eventually sheer exhaustion following her night's experience induced the sleep she craved.

****

There had been no sleep, however, for any of the Robinson family in their Papplewick home. They stayed up all night waiting for news of Sophie and endlessly discussing the plight they found themselves in.

Graham kept blaming himself for his obsession with Beachworld while Austin, Phoebe and Edward were constantly assuring him that he was not in any way at fault. They knew that he loved them all and stressed how grateful they were for the wonderful life he had given them. The police remained outside the property to provide security and assurance for the family.

It was 11am the next day when at last the family learnt there had been a further breakthrough in the hunt for Sophie. A woman from the very small and relatively isolated village of Panton, more than 50 miles away from Papplewick near the town of Wragby in Lincolnshire, had reported seeing a black Range Rover in the village. She had seen two men in the vehicle, the driver and a passenger, who, quite unusually, appeared to be sitting in a back seat alone.

The police immediately swooped on Panton.

A patrol car travelling along the village lanes was waved down by a young man walking along the road. He had been watching breakfast television that morning and had seen the appeals for help relating to the kidnapping. He told the officers he had just seen a Range Rover parked along a narrow track leading to the ruins of Panton Hall.

When the police found the car they were able to confirm that its owner was Henry Fulford. The question which then arose was whether the kidnappers had dumped the vehicle at Panton and moved on, or if they were still close at hand.

****

Five police cars gather on the lane outside a pair of isolated semi-detached former farmworkers' cottages just a few yards from where the Range Rover is parked.

A dozen officers alight from the vehicles, including six armed officers, and stealthily make their way through long grass to one of the red brick cottages. This is the cottage which looks the more likely to be inhabited. There are some dirty white net curtains at some of the windows and a couple of wheelie bins just outside the door. The adjoining cottage appears to be disused. It has no curtains, the wooden window sills are rotting away and there are plants growing out of its bowed roof which is missing an alarming number of tiles.

The police knock on the door of the first house, and, receiving no reply, then open the door, which they find unlocked. The armed officers, with their Heckler & Koch G36C rifles and stab vests, file in and then spread out to search each room in the small dwelling, which comprises a living room, kitchen and utility room containing a chemiloo on the ground floor and two bedrooms on the first floor.

No one is at home, but there are numerous signs of very recent occupation. There are full ashtrays and examples of drug-taking paraphernalia, empty beer bottles and half-empty glasses, plates of half-eaten food and, perhaps, most significantly, a recent edition of the Communist-backing daily newspaper The Morning Star.

"This is it. This is where they've been," declares the towering and bulky male sergeant in charge of the operation.

"Look at this," shouts another officer, picking up a mug from the living room. "There's coffee in here – and it's still warm."

"So they're close by," says the sergeant. "Next door, quick!"

The officers file out again and make for the door of the semi-derelict adjoining cottage. This door is locked so they force it open with a battering ram. Then they storm in, loudly shouting "Police! Nobody move!". They find no one on the ground floor. However, lying on the dust-laden floor next to a basic wooden chair is a woman's blue coat.

"She's been here," calls out a female officer, pointing to the coat.

"Upstairs!" orders the sergeant.

A crocodile of officers dashes up the wooden stairs to

the bedrooms, which are dominated by the handiwork of spiders, both ancient and modern. But still there is no one to be seen.

"Look!" says the sergeant.

He points to a metal ladder laid on the floor of one of the bedrooms. He looks up and shouts: "The loft!" and then bellows "Police – come down!"

A shuffling sound is heard from above. The loft door slowly opens and a hand carrying a pistol can be seen pointing towards the sergeant.

A voice from above screams: "Leave the house now, or I'll shoot."

One of the officers aims his rifle at the hand carrying the pistol and fires. There is a blood-curdling yell followed by a dramatic fall of plaster and a man comes crashing through the ceiling and lands on the bedroom floor in front of the officers. One of them leaps on to him and grapples a pistol from his bleeding hand. Other officers pile in and restrain the individual. It is Dan.

Rafters in the loft have become dislodged and the officers see the face of a second man peering down at them. Another officer points his rifle at the man while the sergeant picks up the ladder and places it near the loft door, which is now hanging down at a precarious angle.

"Come down or we shoot," he shouts.

The man, who is covered with dust, descends the ladder and is immediately handcuffed. It is Gerald – the bomber. He is followed down by the man with straggly long hair – the Range Rover driver, Dan's anarchist accomplice who has helped him plan the kidnap. Then comes Harry who is also quickly cuffed.

"The young lady is still up there," says Harry. "She's tied up, so she'll need some help getting down."

"Is there anyone else up there?" asks the sergeant.

As soon as he has uttered these words there is an almighty crash and the remainder of the bedroom ceiling comes tumbling down on the heads of the officers and their prisoners.

Sophie, whose arms and legs are tied together, screams as her body hits the wooden floor with a frightening thud.

She appears to be lifeless and Harry, who is being held firmly by two officers begins to weep.

"The poor girl," he wheezes."It was never meant to turn out like this. We're meant to be socialists, not barbarians."

Nodding in the direction of Dan, he says: "It's his fault. He's no socialist. He's a criminal. He's just interested in the money. What have we done?"

He then bursts into another coughing fit.

The four prisoners are bundled into the police vehicles while the sergeant and two female officers remain with Sophie. They untie her hands and legs but she remains unconscious.

"She's taken a nasty bang to the head," says one of the women.

"I've called for an ambulance," says the sergeant.

Later that day Sophie regains consciousness and finds herself in a bed at Lincoln's County Hospital. In the waiting room and eagerly hoping for this moment are all members of her close family – Austin and Phoebe, Edward and Graham.

She has suffered concussion and a broken ankle and has to stay in hospital under observation for two more days. She eventually walks out of the hospital building on crutches to get into her father's car. Austin is carrying a large bouquet of red roses. The label attached to it reads: "Get well soon, Sophie, Love from Simon."

****

While the drama was unfolding in Lincolnshire, Sebastian was arrested at a squat in north London.

In the hours that followed Sophie's rescue and the arrests, police conducted a thorough search of the two cottages at Panton. In the loft of the habitable cottage they found a large stash of cocaine. Further investigations revealed that the cottage was being rented from a local farmer by Henry Fulford.

All four men captured at Panton, together with Sebastian and Fulford, appeared at Sanderholme Magistrates Court. They faced numerous charges, including intent to cause an explosion likely to endanger life or cause serious injury to property and kidnap. Fulford was also charged with possession of drugs with intent to supply. They were remanded in custody. If they were eventually convicted there was a chance all could be given life sentences.

A post mortem on Trevor Bincroft revealed that he had died from a heart attack. The "men in the marsh" all denied having seen Trevor on the day when he died and they had disappeared. But there would always remain a question-mark over how he met his end. Shirley would never cease to believe that he had been frightened to death having been confronted by the men.

Beachworld had become the centre of a media storm, with Graham and Stephen giving many interviews. Both of them had conflicted views as to whether the publicity would be detrimental to the project or whether it was really true that "no publicity is bad publicity".

Work on the development was suspended for a few days while the police pursued their investigations and bomb disposal experts carried out thorough checks to make sure no more devices had been planted. Now there was even greater urgency to complete the project in time for the planned Easter opening little more than a month away.

The traumas of the winter brought Graham and Miriam much closer together. Graham as usual worked extremely long hours but spent most of his limited leisure time with his new love. Anita was seemingly infatuated with Stephen and so no longer posed any threat to the relationship between her ex-husband and Miriam. Darren had not been seen since the altercation in the Buckthorn Arms. The fact that he had come to the police's attention may have persuaded him to return to Nottingham out of the way.

****

Easter Sunday arrived and Beachworld opened to the public for the first time – again provoking a torrent of attention from national television and newspapers. The shops in the complex did a roaring trade and the hotel, much to Graham's relief in view of the bomb incident, was fully booked.

That evening Graham and Miriam celebrated the opening with a meal at Beachworld's restaurant. It was there that Graham got down on his knees and proposed marriage.

"Yes," said Miriam. "On one condition."

"What's that?" asked Graham.

"No more bombs."

As he drove home with Miriam along the sea front that night Graham had only one song on his mind and he sang it with gusto: "The sun has got his hat on and he's coming out today."

The Epilogue

A few weeks after the public opening of Beachworld, Graham experienced a frighteningly vivid nightmare.

His marriage to Miriam was still three months away and they had decided to take the traditional route of not moving in together until after the nuptials. He was therefore sleeping alone at his house in Sanderholme, with only Benjy for company.

The dream he had was so traumatic that he was able to recount it in horrifying detail for the rest of his days. Although still a relatively young man in the dream he was being forced into committing an act of euthanasia upon himself. All the people he knew best were cajoling him into this course of action. He was screaming and crying uncontrollably at this unnecessary prospect and when he awoke he felt a strange numb terror.

As he lay in bed, his teeshirt and boxers drenched in a cold sweat, he began to think about his mortality. If he died that night what would be his legacy? Then it struck him like a bullet through the heart – "Is This The Worst Landlord in Britain?"

Beachworld, the Academy's Business Studies Suite, his successful companies, his care for his family, friends and employees would all be forgotten. It was that newspaper headline that everyone would remember. His Devil's mark.

That dark period of his life had scarred him with feelings of injustice and shame in equal measure:

the injustice of his being found guilty in the court of public opinion when he had honestly tried to be a good landlord in spite of having some vile and devious tenants; the shame of having to admit to himself that on a few occasions he had been thoughtless – callous even – in the treatment of some other tenants.

In his nightmare, like Scrooge in "A Christmas Carol", he had imagined himself looking at his own gravestone, which bears the epitaph "Britain's Worst Landlord". He saw former tenants, including Dan, aka Gilbert, lining up to spit on his grave. His own father was looking on in horror and shame.

"Pull yourself together," Graham told himself. "You've just had a meaningless dream."

As he gradually regained full wakefulness and the early morning light began to stream through his window, he returned to his habitual state of rationality. He comforted himself with the thought that on his death the people he really cared about would consider his character as a whole, not just a cliched headline dreamt up by some lazy sub-editor.

He would no doubt be remembered, as all people are, as a flawed human being, with some good points and some bad. His funeral service and gravestone epitaph would accentuate the positive aspects of his life and character. If newspapers still were still writing obituaries – increasingly unlikely in this age of the internet – then they would inevitably dredge up the negatives too. His alleged shortcomings as a landlord were already recorded for posterity in his Wikipedia entry, but so also were his imaginative efforts to fully involve his workforce in the success of his businesses. A score draw perhaps?

His thoughts turned to his beloved family members and to some of the other significant people in his life and their own fallibilities.

Jim Nott: loyal, kind and witty, and yet not trusting enough to confide in his friend about his sexuality or about the event which led to his death. Graham still believed his suicide was a selfish act. And was his gossip always as victimless as was commonly thought? Jim had left to Graham the lion's share of his estate, including his business. This surely had proved the depth of affection he had for his old school friend.

Anita: promiscuous, faithless and self-centred, often crude in her thoughts and vocabulary, and yet, lacking in malice, and, at heart, strangely loyal to everyone she had closely encountered.

Miriam: in many ways saintly, but sometimes ridiculously naive and trusting and, according to Jim, the gossip, had had a "wild" period following her marriages.

His thoughts then turned to the dark side, and first and foremost, to Sebastian aka Matthew. A rebel, now serving time in prison for his crimes and yet someone Graham had found to be pleasant and polite.

Then the even darker side. What of Dan, aka Gilbert, a thoroughly nasty piece of work with no redeeming features that Graham was aware of - willing to see people killed to fulfil his twisted political and mercenary aims?

Graham pondered whether, in these times of moral relativism, there was anyone who could be classed as fundamentally evil?

The usual suspects raised their ugly heads: mass murderers such as Hitler, Stalin and Mao Tse Tung; serial killers such as Peter Sutcliffe and Dr Harold Shipman. Graham, though, had a candidate more personal to himself – Patrick Magee, the Brighton bomber.

He is evil personified.

****

Dan (aka Gilbert), his accomplices, Gerald and Harry, and Henry Fulford were all given life sentences for the bomb plot (although, as we all know, "life" in the United Kingdom rarely means life) with concurrent sentences for arson at Beachworld and Havenmarsh Academy. Dan was given a concurrent life sentence for kidnap and a 15-year concurrent sentence for drug dealing. His straggly-haired accomplice in the kidnap was given ten years' jail.

However, Sebastian somehow managed to convince the jury that he had been ignorant of the bomb plot until the day he had revealed what he knew to Graham. He was given a nine and a half years' sentence for the arsons.

****

On the morning when Graham had the nightmare about his own euthanasia he was unwilling to go back to sleep so he rose early and went straight to work. He completed a 12-hour stint in his office at Beachworld, where he mainly based himself these days, returning home at 6.30pm.

A letter was waiting for him on his doormat. The address on the envelope was handwritten. This was fairly rare these days and it provoked Graham's curiosity. He opened it immediately and was taken aback when he read that it was from Sebastian.

Dear Mr Robinson,

I am writing to profusely apologise for my disgraceful behaviour. Having had time to reflect, I feel that my nine-and-a-half year sentence is totally inadequate considering the bad things I have done. The fact that the bomb and the fires were not instigated by me by no means excuses me in any way for not disassociating myself from the group earlier. I always knew what was happening was wrong but I was too weak to stand up to Dan.

The last few weeks have made me rethink my whole outlook on life – a life which has been utterly wasted. I contrast my own gross stupidity and mindless crimes with your own achievements.

Since being in jail I have had the opportunity to read widely. Much of that reading has been on politics, an area which you may think I should studiously avoid in view of where it has lead me in the past.

You may be heartened to learn, though, that what I have read has resulted in my total rejection of Anarcho-Syndicalism! I now consider it to be a muddled and unworkable ideology, which puts much too great a faith in the ability of workers to control the economy. There needs to be an element of elitism. As Dagny Taggart says in Ayn Rand's 'Atlas Shrugged': "Nothing can make it moral to destroy the best". (You will no doubt be surprised by my choice of reading matter).

Keep up the good work, Mr Robinson. You are "the best".

May I repeat that I feel abject shame for everything I have done and beg your forgiveness, which I am unworthy to receive,

Yours sincerely,

Sebastian Fawcett-Jones.

Graham was astonished by the contents of this letter and not a little moved by it. He had met Sebastian less than of handful of times in his life and had thought him a naive fool who needed to get a proper job. And yet there was something about the man which he liked. He had a style which shouted out a respectable middle class background and a private education and this was in no way inimical to Graham's outlook on life. But there was a gentle kindliness about Sebastian too, which belied the rebellious and no doubt sometimes criminal and aggressive behaviour which had permeated his life.

Graham could be tunnel-visioned, always ruthlessly ambitious and, in his business dealings, sometimes dismissive of the concerns of others. But hatred was no part of his makeup. His anger towards Sebastian for being so heavily involved in the plots against him was tempered by the fact that ultimately this man had been the whistleblower.

Delaying dinner, Graham set about composing a reply to the letter.

Dear Mr Fawcett-Jones,

Thank you for your letter, which came as a great surprise to me. I have noted your apologies, which I am sure are sincere. I cannot condone or forgive any of your crimes, but I wish you well for the future when you have completed your sentence.

I was delighted to learn that you no longer adhere to the excesses of Anarcho-Syndicalism. However, I am sure you will be pleased to know that in my own companies I do everything I can to ensure that the workers are treated decently and have a full share in the benefits resulting from well-run, profitable businesses.

I was particularly interested to learn that you were reading the work of Ayn Rand. She has a lot of good ideas, but I cannot accept her view that capitalism and altruism are completely incompatible.

From our talk all those years ago at Brighton I believe

you may be interested, as I am, in wider share ownership and profit-sharing schemes in companies which will narrow the gulf between business owners and their workers.

Here is a quote from Sam Walton, the American Walmart stores boss, which I think you may find interesting:

"Share your profits with all your associates, and treat them as partners. In turn, they will treat you as a partner, and together you will all perform beyond your wildest expectations."

From time to time over the years I have attempted to compile a dossier of material in support of wider share ownership and profit sharing with a view to eventually proposing a plan of action which I can pass to Government.

As I imagine that you currently have some spare time, I wondered if you would be interested in doing some research into this area, which you might then share with me. I would be happy to credit you for any worthwhile material you might be able to unearth.

Please let me know if this idea appeals to you.

In the meantime, thank you again for your letter.

Yours sincerely,

Graham Robinson.

Sebastian received this letter with good grace and some excitement. He believed that Graham was giving him a point to his prison existence and he replied immediately accepting the proposal to carry out the research.

Over the succeeding months he provided Graham with reams of useful material. When he left prison having served half of his sentence, Graham allowed him to rent one of his properties, a one-bedroomed cottage in a village a few miles from Sanderholme. Occasionally the two men would meet each other to further their project. To say they became friends would be an exaggeration, as Graham could never bring himself to forgive Sebastian entirely for his part in the attacks on Beachworld and the Academy. But what did emerge over the years was something akin to a meeting of minds.

****

The official opening of Beachworld on Spring Bank Holiday Monday by "a Celebrity" had been a resounding success, attracting a great deal of national and local publicity. All of Graham's family and close friends were there for the celebration, together, of course, with the ever popular Benjy. One special guest was John Hampden, now in his early eighties and, in recognition of decades of work for the Conservative Party at all levels, ennobled as Lord Hampden of Sherwood. And also present were the General Manager of Beachworld, Stephen Armitage, and his soon-to-be-wife, Anita.

The progress of the development had been far from smooth, with hostile opposition to the plans, vandalism, fires and the bomb threat. And its trials and its tribulations were not over yet.

The first eleven months following the public opening were highly successful, but then in March 2020 Beachworld had to close owing to the introduction of Covid restrictions.

This was a body blow to the enterprise and Graham had to draw on all the goodwill he could muster from investors and plough in additional funds from his own companies. The furlough scheme, through which the Government met 80 per cent of employees' wages, saved him the embarrassment of having to sack the many local people he had taken on, including apprentices recruited straight from his beloved Havenmarsh Academy. Through its hotel restaurant the complex was also able to participate in the Eat Out to Help Out Scheme, which was popular with Sanderholme people but small beer compared with the colossal loss of revenue overall.

The setback caused by Covid might have driven lesser men into a state of depression. The fact that Graham remained buoyant was partly due to the success of his marriage to Miriam. She was a loving, sensible and supportive companion, but her greatest attribute was her kindness and this was a quality which Graham valued more than any other.

Their wedding had been celebrated at the Beachworld Hotel in the autumn of 2019, with Lord Hampden as best man. The bridesmaids were Sophie, Miriam's granddaughters, Lily and Lucy, the page boys were her grandsons, Robert and Arthur, and Edward Robinson was the usher.

In his best man's speech Lord Hampden reminisced about the time when he and Graham had taken on the job of clearing out Miss Norma Whitehouse's extraordinary house.

"And we never did solve the mystery of the bus ticket in the wardrobe!" he quipped.

The happy wedding celebrations were followed by a honeymoon in The Seychelles.

The slight lull in Graham's business activities, enforced by Covid, gave him a smidgeon of extra free time. Miriam persuaded him that he needed something which he had never really had in his life previously – a hobby. The result was that he took up golf, an interest which his new wife shared. And he found he was quite good at it.

One morning Graham opened his post and found an invitation to be knighted in the Queen's New Year's Honours List in recognition of his service to business and charity.

Sir Graham Robinson was as happy as he had been since the very early days of his marriage to Anita. His stock had risen and even he began to believe that some people might forget that he was "The Worst Landlord in Britain".

THE END

Also by John Pendleton...

"Hector's Revenge" - a touching romantic story with strong elements of mystery. It follows one man's love for a woman from being a teenager in the Swinging Sixties right through to the time of the Covid-19 pandemic.

Hector Ratcliffe, a shy and bookish Grammar School boy with an obsession for Greek Mythology, has a crush on Penelope, the prettiest and cleverest girl in school. It becomes a passion which dominates his life.

The relationship is thwarted by Penelope's indifference, by a love rival from school days, and, more surprisingly, by mysterious family opposition. With its dramatic twists and some violent turns the story has readers gripped to the end.

"Hector's Revenge" is available from Amazon as a paperback and as an e-book on Kindle.

About The Author

John Pendleton is the pen name of John Cowpe, a former newspaper editor who had a 39-year career in journalism and public relations. Born in the English holiday resort of Skegness in Lincolnshire, John edited a series of local newspapers, most recently for Johnston Press.

His third novel, "Hector's Revenge," is a romantic tale set in an east coast seaside resort and the surrounding rural area. He has published two previous novels, "Ill Winds" and "All For Blood," and "Skegness Past," a mainly photographic record of his home town.

Now running a property rental business, John is married to Wendy and has two grown-up children, Colin and Trudi, and four grandchildren. His interests include politics, reading, angling, tennis and going to the gym.

www.blossomspringpublishing.com

Printed in Great Britain
by Amazon